SWEET POISON

SWEET POISON

by

Rupert Penny

RAMBLE HOUSE

ISBN 13: 978-1-60543-190-1

ISBN 10: 1-60543-190-7

Cover Art: Gavin L. O'Keefe
Preparation: Fender Tucker

SWEET POISON

PART I

THE VICTIM ALIVE

I

HERBERT WEEKES banged the table smartly with his left hand, making half a dozen cups and saucers rattle.

"Less noise," he said, in a distinct deep voice. "Otherwise I shall have to put you on silence."

The chatter died immediately, there came a moment's appropriate hush, and then a self-assured but modulated schoolboy treble broke the spell.

"Pass the bread," it requested, and the headmaster's eyebrows lifted irritably.

"Pass the bread, *please,"* he corrected. "Your table-manners are simply appalling, Dorland. Do you behave like that at home? Do you say 'Pass the bread' to your mother? Or 'Pass the cake', if you're too refined for mere necessities?"

"No sir," was the prompt reply.

"Very well, then kindly don't do it here."

"No sir," agreed the culprit, unabashed, and the general hum resumed.

Carmichael, one of the bigger boys, thin-lipped and studious, turned to his neighbour.

"Jumbo's got the rats," he whispered. "Wonder why?"

But there was no answer, for every child in the room could have told him that the complaint might be due to any of a hundred reasons. The rats were no strangers to Herbert Weekes.

The dining-hall was long and narrow, and contained four tables. At either end of each sat a grown-up: the head and his sister, Miss Charlotte Weekes; Miss Wood the matron and Mr. Lloyd Gregory, the senior master; Miss Chew the housekeeper and Mr. Elkington the day-master; Miss Tilling the governess and Mr. Birkett the junior master. Separating the various pairs were boys, forty-one of them, and a stranger observing carelessly might have supposed them all variants of the same boy, because all were dressed alike in green jerseys and brown corduroy shorts. Some were larger than others, and some had conspicuously red or black or flaxen hair; a few wore spectacles, and one had a bandaged eye, the result of contact with a cricket ball; but the main effect was of similarity.

Collectively the boys and staff constituted Anstey Court Preparatory School, near Hindhead, Surrey, or that part of it which lived and breathed. For the rest the buildings were well-designed and spacious, standing in a dozen acres some distance back from the Portsmouth Road and a few miles from the Sussex border. 'There are bigger preparatory schools, and more expensive ones,' Herbert Weekes was fond of declaring, 'but I think I may safely say there are few so well adapted to meet the requirements expected of them.'

He spoke like that, a good deal of the time: rather vaguely and windily, with a kind of verbose pomposity which impressed some of the parents and profoundly annoyed his assistant masters. Occasionally, though, he could be concise and direct, and also, when he chose, sarcastic. In this it was suspected that he took after his sister, who bit almost whenever she opened her mouth. Most of the boys respected him, but without affection, many feared him, and he was relied upon by none. What was right today might easily be wrong tomorrow: a way of setting out a quadratic equation, a closed window, a forward stroke to a short off ball. His charges knew this, accepted it as an inevitable part of his character, and grumbled only when he was more than usually trying; but the staff were less philosophical. Lloyd Gregory alone seemed genuinely not to mind a direct reprimand; but he had grown so cynical after nine years at Anstey Court that he could tolerate a complete *volte-face* with no more than a sneer to himself.

"I don't know how you can stand it—I simply don't!" Birkett was always protesting in the safety of the masters'-room. "The man's an utter sweep—he positively makes my blood boil."

Gregory, who was thirty-five and beginning to go bald, would curl his lips a little and contemptuously survey the younger man—twenty-four and only a year down from Cambridge.

"You'll learn," was his usual weary answer. "By the time you're my age you won't have any blood left—only school ink and school tea; and a leavening of beer if it takes you that way."

And he would smile to himself even more contemptuously, for it was a poor week when he failed to drink his twenty pints.

Towards the end of the meal—high-tea for the boys, supper for the adults, and taking place between 5.45 and 6.15—the headmaster banged on the table again, as he did so rubbing his adam's-apple against the rim of his stiff collar. It was a gesture so familiar to all that no one noticed it, himself least of all.

"Silence please," he said, and glanced coldly round. "I shall be glad to see everyone in the schoolroom immediately after grace," he announced. "Including the staff, if you please," he added, without looking at any of them. "Thank you."

Again there was a hush, and again there grew into noticeable existence the confused hum of voices, a steady background for the sharper click of knives on plates and spoons in saucers.

"What's up?" asked several of the boys at once, stealthily, and suggestions were put forward to explain this breach with custom.

"Something about tomorrow," said Jacoby, who had the makings of a stylish batsman and lived only for the half-term match against the Fathers' XI the following afternoon. "First time out don't count," he added, with a grin.

"He's going to let us off prep," hazarded Askew, a freckled slogger who was also an optimist.

"Bet you he don't!" was the instant challenge from Maurice Weekes, the elder of the head's nephews.

"All right—how much?"

"Bet you a lend of my batting-gloves he don't, and you give me a packet of stamp-mounts if I win."

"Coo, you old Shylock! No fear—I've only got one left."

"There you are—you're wrong!"

"No I'm not!"

"All right then, half a packet."

"All right, if you lend me your bat as well for practice—just in case I bust mine."

"All right, only you be careful."

"All right. Slap in the middle every time—that's me!"—and Askew laughed cheerfully.

The staff too were curious, Pat Tilling raising her pretty brows interrogatively at Lloyd Gregory when she managed to catch his eye. All she received in exchange was a shrug and an expressive twist of the mouth which indicated that she had better be prepared for anything from bankruptcy to a bomb explosion. She smiled, not disappointed because it was something to have got so friendly a reception for her glance. Lloyd had an uncomfortable way of not seeing her sometimes; of looking straight through her and then elsewhere, as if she were invisible. Unaccountably it made her feel thoroughly miserable when he did that, but now she was suddenly elated. Only for a second or two, however; then she became aware of Miss Charlotte's calculating stare, and shivered inwardly.

The wretched woman always saw everything, trust her, and always gave the impression of a vulture waiting to pounce, with her beaked nose and her drooping eyelids, her black dress and her air of patient malevolence.

A few seconds later still she noticed that Mr. Birkett was gazing at her too from the opposite end of the table, and frowned. There he was again, she thought, trying to trap her into some intimate interchange of looks which would give him the excuse to seek her out afterwards and inflict himself upon her. It was ridiculous, really; he ought to know well enough by now that as far as she was concerned he scarcely existed, and that the less she had to do with him out of school hours the better she would be pleased. Not, of course, that he was bad-looking or a lout; simply that he seemed too utterly pink-faced and juvenile to be taken seriously. Twenty-four he said he was, the same age as herself, but she would have been readier to believe him nineteen and fresh from the Upper VI instead of from Cambridge. He had no poise about him; he wasn't a man yet.

She was roused from her reverie by the voice of Edwin Weekes, the headmaster's younger nephew.

"Please Miss Tilling, when will you have the half-term marks ready?"

"Tomorrow morning and not a minute sooner," she answered shortly. "And I'm not going to tell you the placings now, so please don't ask."

"Oh, but I wasn't going to!" he assured her, his round face smugly virtuous.

"Splendid—then you won't be disappointed," she said.

'Beastly child!' she thought. 'Horrible slimy child—knows he's top in practically everything and wants to see it written down. Wish I could cook the dam' marks somehow so that he came out bottom, or in the middle even—anywhere but first. Still, better not after that other business, else I probably would get the sack. Darling Edwin, Uncle's joy; in the winter he sniffs, in the summer he sweats, and still he comes out top, rot him! I must settle down to those cursed marks, though, or Jumbo'll start trumpeting like he did last term. Oh lord, who'd be a governess? With tomorrow ahead, too; thousands of stuck-up parents grinning and jabbering and saying 'Oh how *are* you, Miss Billing?' Or Drilling or Milling. 'And how's dear Peter getting on? And who dear Peter is heaven only knows unless I remember her painted face. And I haven't a dress fit to bury a beggar in except the blue, and he said he hated blue. Not that it'd make any difference, I dare say.'

For the third time Herbert Weekes banged on the table.

"Grace!" he called, and everyone rose with a scuffling of feet and scraping of chairs and forms on the wooden floor.

"Benedicto benedicatur per Jesum Christum dominum nostrum," mumbled Lillywhite, the captain of the XI, in response to a nod. Herbert frowned at him.

"Again, please," he requested, "and endeavour not to make it sound like one word. Articulate, and remember you're giving thanks to God for favours received."

'*And* paid for!' thought Lloyd Gregory sourly. 'Hell, the old fool's on the scratch tonight.'

Lillywhite repeated the grace very slowly and clearly, and rather obstinately, and a minute later the dining-hall was deserted except for Miss Charlotte and the housekeeper. Miss Chew was small and bustling, the exact opposite of the head's sister; perhaps that was why they disliked one another so much, the matron sometimes thought. They had scarcely passed a friendly word in twelve years.

"Pike has left his crusts again," observed Miss Charlotte, somehow implying that it was the housekeeper's fault.

"Why, so he has—and the times I've told him about it," was the airy answer. "I wouldn't be surprised if he didn't want his teeth attending to."

"Really? Then you'd better tell Miss Wood."

"Ah!" murmured Miss Chew darkly, regarding a tea-stain on the cloth where Lloyd Gregory had been sitting. "Matron wouldn't thank me to be teaching her her job, I don't suppose. Has your parcel turned up yet, Miss Weekes?" she added.

"Not yet," was the reply. "You questioned the servants?"

"Yes—they know nothing."

"Oh, quite—that was always my impression."

And, with one mocking look from under her drooping eyelids, Miss Charlotte was gone, moving slowly out of the door and up the stairs to the private part of the school. She was lame in her left leg, but refused to use a stick more than was absolutely necessary; yet she contrived to get about with surprising stealth at times.

Meanwhile, in the big schoolroom, the boys sat down at their desks while the staff leant awkwardly against the wall. It was characteristic of Herbert Weekes that he let them stand, men and women alike; and equally significant that neither the matron nor the governess expected a seat. Over the door a large clock ticked onwards from 6.13; above the mantelpiece was a tear-off calendar registering that the date was Friday June 16th; out of the windows could be seen the cricket-nets, where presently the XI would practise in the cool of the evening. For the present the headmaster held everyone's attention as he stood at the masters'-desk rubbing his neck on the edge of his collar, and the gravity of his features troubled many of those who watched him. He was a tall ungainly man with grey hair, hazel eyes, and a cropped moustache; his tweed suit was well cut but ancient, and his fingers were stained with nicotine. Yet despite his surface shabbiness he had for the moment an air of authority which seemed to belong not only to his position but also to his person.

"I must ask you all to pay particular heed to what I have to say," he began. "It's a mysterious and possibly unpleasant matter, and I shall be thankful to dispose of it quickly. It concerns a parcel, an oblong parcel about the size of a dozen French grammars, belonging to my sister Miss Charlotte. As usual, I put the afternoon post on the hall table just after half past four, and inadvertently included this parcel. In fact, to make things quite plain, I was careless; yet that doesn't explain why the thing has completely disappeared. Completely and utterly disappeared, let me repeat,"—and he stared hard at two or three random faces.

No one spoke. The boys stared back at him, dully expressionless. The staff lounged idly by the wall. A breeze from an open window at the far end of the room caused a canvas map of the world to swing first a few inches one way, and then a few inches the other.

"If any of you knows anything concerning the whereabouts of the missing object," continued the headmaster deliberately—"remembers picking it up by mistake, let us say—perhaps he will hold up his hand."

There was no response.

"At the moment no question of punishment arises," he went on, his voice a trifle more informal. "At present I shall be prepared to accept a genuine mistake as the explanation. After all,"—with a not very successful smile, "it would hardly be fair to make an example when I have set a bad one myself."

'Which means what?' Lloyd Gregory asked himself dreamily. 'Something wrong with his syntax—syllepsis?'

There was still no sign of a hand upraised, and the five grown-ups standing under the honours-board seemed wholly mystified.

"Needless to say, none of the staff can help me?" queried the head perfunctorily.

"No sir," said Gregory, knowing a verbal answer was expected, and the others murmured in agreement.

"Except that I believe I saw the parcel in question, Mr. Weekes," put in the matron in her flat tired voice. She was a tall anemic-looking woman of forty, and she rarely smiled.

"About a quarter to five, that would be," she added. "It had some foreign stamps on, had it not?"

"Yes, Matron—I was coming to that. Then possibly you saw the address as well?"

Miss Wood frowned.

"Really, I don't remember," she said vaguely. "I don't somehow think I noticed any writing."

"I see—thank you. Yes, Burnaby?"—as a small spectacled boy in the front row of battered single desks lifted his hand.

"Oh sir, I saw it too!" exclaimed the child, getting to his feet. "When I went to be excused in Geography, sir. And it hadn't any writing on the side the stamps were on, sir, 'cos I looked, 'cos they were French ones, sir—25-centimes."

"Now take it quietly," advised the head with manifest patience. Burnaby always gabbled. "You passed the hall table, and you glanced at the letters to see if there was one for you, I suppose?"

"Yes sir."

"And was there?"

"No sir. Then I saw the stamps—"

"Ah, of course—you collect, don't you? They attracted your attention, and that makes you recall the parcel."

"Yes sir."

'Ass!' thought Lloyd Gregory. 'Why the devil doesn't he let the brat say for himself what he did? Talk about shoving words into somebody's mouth—no wonder they're always failing their exams.'

"And was there any address visible?" pursued Herbert Weekes, regarding Burnaby so intently that the boy squirmed.

"No sir—yes sir."

"Well, which is it?"

"Not the stamp side—only I turned it over."

"Indeed? To see if it was yours?"

"Oh no sir—to see whose it was, 'cos if it was somebody's who didn't collect then I could do a swop—I mean I could ask him to let me have 'em, sir."

"In return for a suitable consideration, presumably? I believe 'swop' carries that meaning."

"Yes sir,"—amid faint and dutiful laughter from the others.

"Well, Burnaby, what was on the other side of the parcel?"

The reply came promptly. "Miss Charlotte, sir."

Then, after a pause during which someone found time to stifle a spontaneous giggle, the boy corrected himself.

"I mean her name, sir. In a funny sort of writing, all up and down and thin."

"In short, a typically continental hand,"—and the headmaster nodded and chuckled, with a glance at the staff to see if his superior knowledge were appreciated. Then in a moment his face became stern again. He put his hands on the desk and leant forward.

"And when you had finished your slightly irregular examination of the other side?" he suggested.

"Oh sir, I went to be excused."

"I see. And when you returned, was the parcel still there?"

"Yes sir."

"And can you tell me what time that was? Within a few minutes?"

"Sir, it was just after you'd put the post there—I saw you going through the swing-door. I thought you saw me too," he added amiably.

"No, Burnaby, I fear my mind must have been occupied with other and possibly more important subjects."

His mouth began to smile again, and then stopped. "I hope our proximity was accidental?" he asked pointedly.

"Sir?"

"I mean, you had not been listening for me to put the post in the hall instead of attending to your lessons?"

"Oh, no sir!"

"Mr. Weekes," interrupted George Elkington timidly, "do you require me any longer? I'm afraid I may miss my bus."

The head turned towards him impatiently, never dreaming what an effort it had cost the chinless little man to be so bold. Birkett had said once that the day-master reminded him of an orphaned dormouse stranded in a jungle.

"Very well, Mr. Elkington," agreed Herbert Weekes distantly. "I regret delaying you—good-night, good-night."

"Thank you sir—good-night. Good-night, everybody,"—and he trotted out, bound for a lonely bed-sitting-room where he would conscientiously prepare next week's history lessons and perhaps treat himself to half an hour of Bach on the gramophone before retiring.

"All right, Burnaby, sit down," said the head. "Now,"—to the room at large, "one boy has been good enough to speak up and say what he knows. Has anyone else any information to offer? Who else saw the parcel?"

But apparently nobody had. Further question and answer revealed that when the various classes were dismissed at 5.30, and the usual concerted rush to the hall table for letters took place, the parcel was no longer there. Beyond that, nothing was definite.

"I see," growled Herbert Weekes, and pulled at his moustache.

"Mr. Gregory, may I have a word with you?" he requested presently, and the two of them walked to the corner of the room furthest from the boys.

"What d'you think?" he asked in a low voice. "Could it have been taken for the stamps?"

The senior master shrugged, as if to imply that any of the forty-one boys might have stolen the thing for sheer devilry. Yet his answer contradicted his manner.

"I shouldn't think so, sir—though it'll have to be considered if all else fails. But it doesn't strike me as likely."

"Then what does?" demanded his superior bluntly. "The servants?"

"They assure the housekeeper they know nothing. Nor does she. Nor does my sister."

"Of course not, sir," agreed the other gently. No sense in getting on the wrong side of the man, especially with half-term so near. He might find himself being imposed upon in the matter of extra work.

The headmaster grunted, and was about to turn away, but Gregory stopped him.

"Have you any idea what was in the parcel, sir?" he asked.

"As it happens, yes. To the best of my knowledge it contained chocolate liqueurs—or perhaps one should say liqueur chocolates."

The senior master repressed a smile; Miss Charlotte's liking for such confections was notorious.

"And one more thing, sir; have you mentioned the matter to Lady Weekes?"

The head stared at him.

"Lady Weekes?" he echoed. "But she's gone to Farnham for the evening."

"Yes sir—but I saw her in the hall myself at about ten minutes to five."

"Really? That's strange. Did she speak to you?"

Lloyd Gregory shook his head.

"She was talking to Maurice—I don't suppose she noticed me. I only just looked out to see who it was."

Herbert Weekes rubbed his neck thoughtfully against his collar.

"Maurice!" he called, and his elder nephew came forward; a tall dark-haired boy with a pleasant smile. "Yes sir?"

"You spoke to your mother in the hall this afternoon?"

"Yes—she was saying good-night to me because she wouldn't be back before I'd gone to bed."

"Oh, of course—I'm sorry. I remember her asking me about it in the drawing-room now. You didn't see the parcel?"

"No sir."

"Very well, that's all. I shall have to mention it to her," he added, as if he found the prospect distasteful. "Thank you, Mr. Gregory."

Thus dismissed, the senior master rejoined the others by the wall, this time ignoring Patricia Tilling's smile. For some seconds the headmaster stayed where he was, his back to everyone. Then he turned.

"It appears that I have overlooked a possible source of information," he observed. "Not that I expect much from it, however. I will ask you all once again; can anyone tell me anything concerning the present whereabouts of Miss Charlotte's parcel, or say what happened to it after I put it on the table with the letters?"

Nobody spoke, and he nodded a little grimly.

"Then for the time being I shall leave the matter where it is," he informed the school. "Perhaps I need hardly point out that the sooner it's cleared up the better? There's probably some extremely simple explanation, and I only hope it will be forthcoming soon. Otherwise there may be cause for regret."

He paused significantly, his aspect suddenly threatening.

"Otherwise I may be forced to think the worst," he finished, "and that would be a pity, with half-term tomorrow."

He glanced up at the clock, and saw that it was after 6.30.

"You ought to be settling down to prep now," he said, "but in view of the circumstances I think it would be as well if you had ten minutes' break, to talk things over among yourselves. There's no objection, Mr. Gregory?"

"Of course not, sir," was the polite reply, but to himself Gregory fumed. 'As though it would matter if I screamed my head off!' he thought. 'You old hypocrite!'

"Thank you. I shall take the XI in the nets after prayers as usual."

"He did let us off some of the prep," asserted Askew.

"Ah, but you bet he wouldn't let us off it all!" declared Maurice Weekes, his blue eyes twinkling. "No, I never!"

"Oh you did!"

"Well, let's ask Taffy!"

"All right."

Lloyd Gregory delivered his verdict with his most solemn expression.

"Askew received 25% damages, Weekes major 75%," he said. "In other words, three-eighths of a packet of mounts in exchange for the loan of one batting-glove."

"Coo, sir! What on earth's the good of one glove?" demanded Askew.

"My dear boy, I haven't the slightest idea. Judges seldom trouble themselves about what good then-decisions will be. Perhaps one glove might convey the impression that you're at least partly civilized—who knows?"

II

THERE are four Assistant-Commissioners in the Metropolitan Police Force. The one known as "C", in charge of the Criminal Investigation Department, leant forward and tapped Chief-Inspector Edward Beale on the knee as their train drew slowly out of Waterloo Station. The day was Saturday June 17th, and the time 1.45 p.m. They had the first-class compartment to themselves, and a clear run to Woking, the first stop on their journey to Haslemere.

"I've a lot to tell you," said Sir Francis Barton, "so you'd better listen carefully. Then, if you're very clever, maybe you'll manage to prevent a murder, and that's something that doesn't often happen."

"No sir," agreed Beale unenthusiastically. He was still a little resentful at having to spoil his own week-end plans in order to share the Assistant-Commissioner's, and reflected that at the moment he felt more like committing a murder than forestalling one. Anyway, the wretched man had said there was no question of work attached to their outing.

Sir Francis was tall and lean, with a refined face and well-kept hands of which he always seemed not wholly unconscious. Someone had once likened him to Hollywood's idea of a Cabinet minister, and he had not objected. He was just over fifty, and probably aware of his distinguished bearing and good looks, whereas Chief-Inspector Beale had little to worry about in that respect. He was not an ugly man, merely a plain one; only his clear grey eyes, when looked at carefully, suggested that he might not in fact be quite so ordinary as he appeared at first glance. For the most part he considered his lack of facial elegance an advantage and not a handicap. He was old-fashioned enough to believe that a detective-officer did well to avoid public notice.

Sir Francis leant forward again, extending a cigar case.

"You can't smoke that pipe here," he said, nodding at it, "this is a holiday. Have one of these things, and do for heaven's sake stop looking so miserable. I dare say you'd rather be in a thousand other places, but there simply wasn't anyone else to take, and I'm not such a fool that I fancy my own powers of detection overmuch."

"Detection?" repeated Beale distinctly, and contrived a smile. "You *said* it was nothing to do with business, sir," he added.

"Who, me? Well, perhaps it isn't—I don't know yet. In any case, you'll have to give up calling me 'sir'. The last thing anyone's to suspect is that you're connected with the Yard."

"Then what am I?"

"A friend of mine; possibly a prospective parent."

"I don't think so—I hadn't heard about it."

"I meant with regard to Anstey Court—as you knew perfectly well. Now, sit back and let me talk, or you'll get there knowing nothing about anyone or anything. To begin with, I suppose you've heard of Sir Robert Weekes?"

"The politician?"

"Well, call it statesman for the next day or two. You see the chap we're visiting—the head of this school where you may be sending little Alfred if you like the look of it—is his brother. Sir Robert's, not little Alfred's—I'm not telling this too well."

He paused, pulled thoughtfully at his cigar, and appeared to set his mind in order. Then he continued.

"Robert and Herbert are brothers," he said again, "Herbert being the schoolmaster and about six years the younger. There's also a sister, Charlotte, who comes between them, but they all look much alike; nearer sixty than fifty, and tough. They're solemn, and sarcastic, and all a bit too fond of themselves for my taste.

"Herbert's had Anstey Court since 1921; built it out of a legacy, I fancy. Before the war he was Classics master at some fifth-rate public school—a mere nobody. Now I suppose you could call him a success, if preparatory schoolmasters are ever successful. Anyway, his fees are a hundred and sixty-five guineas *per annum,* which bears the same relation to whatever that represents in hard cash—I can't count, you know—as statesman does to politician; it sounds better. Every item that could conceivably be an extra is one, too, even laundry and exercise books, though you get the ink for nothing, and he makes no reduction for anybody or anything. Some schools do, you know; the youngest of triplets and sons of minor clergy and orphans of rowing blues. But not Herbert; we all pay the same, even me and Sir Robert."

"A hundred and sixty-five guineas!" repeated Beale in awed tones. "Good lord, I thought you could go to Eton for that."

"Well, part of the way," conceded his companion. "But it isn't extortionate as prep school fees go—there's one at least at a hundred and eighty, and a rotten bad place at that—boys mayn't even talk without written permission. All but, anyway. Anstey Court's not like that, though, and I suppose you get good value. The food's eatable, which doesn't always happen, and the teaching seems quite adequate. All the same, the fees are a big item. I know; you see, my own brat goes there."

"What, where we're going?"

"Exactly—mind?"

Beale laughed, and settled himself more comfortably. Sir Francis was certainly doing his best to create a holiday impression.

"Not a bit, sir—though to be quite truthful I didn't even know you had one. But I begin to see a glimmer of sense. A little something's gone wrong somewhere—somebody's pinched somebody else's fountain-pen or pet rabbit, and the frantic headmaster remembers his distinguished patron, and the patron remembers me, and here we are. Unless you were serious when you mentioned murder?"—and he regarded the Assistant-Commissioner very hard.

"Yes, I'm afraid I was; at least, Herbert was. Now perhaps you realize why I picked you?"

"Well, it could be clearer. Why not one of the younger brigade—somebody who remembers what a prep school's like?"

Sir Francis sighed.

"In the first place, I want a man who can behave tactfully," he explained. "In the second place, I don't want a young smartie who's going to spend all his time behaving prettily to all the pretty sisters. Finally, if there is a job to do then it'll be serious—right up your street."

Beale nodded, displaying more interest.

"Perhaps you'd better tell me, sir—especially about the sisters. Is this one of those co-educational shows?"

"Don't call me 'sir'," his superior reminded him, "and don't be purposely dense. Didn't I say it was half-term? If not, I meant to, and everybody knows that half-terms and pretty sisters are synonymous. But let's get back to the Weekes family. Sir Robert's the eldest, and the biggest pot; Under-secretary for something or other just after the war, and been dodging about on the outskirts of the Cabinet ever since. Until he resigned last year because of ill-health, that is—there's something quite wrong with his heart, I believe."

"Still, that doesn't matter to us, nor his political activities. What's more likely to be important are his matrimonial activities. Late in 1924, when he was about forty-five or so, he married a beautiful Irish girl very much his junior. In 1926 they had a son, Maurice—you'll be seeing him presently. In 1927 Sir Robert divorced his wife."

Again Beale nodded.

"I seem to recall hearing about it," he put in. "She was a bit upset, wasn't she?"

"Extremely upset. She swore—and probably still swears—that she was entirely innocent. What the truth of things was I can't say, but Sir Robert's as stiff and strict as they're made. He'd think the worst on any given occasion, and he's blown-out with self-esteem. He said she'd misbehaved herself with a cousin of hers, and there seems no doubt he honestly believed as much. The court took the same view, and divorced they were. The child stayed with him, though she was to be allowed access to it now and again.

"Well, the subsequent history of the woman is just a trifle obscure, but she hasn't got married again, and she still goes on calling herself Lady Weekes. She's quite entitled to, of course, but I expect she does it out of spite. You see, Sir Robert had a second go in 1929. This time he played safe and chose his secretary, but again he had bad luck. She died in childbirth in the following year, and since then he's had about as much use for women as you have for sneak-thieves. The child survived, however, another boy; you'll be seeing him too. In fact, Lady Weekes will be there as well, so you'll meet most of the family."

"But presumably not Sir Robert?"

"No fear. Actually he's abroad—just had another heart attack in the south of France; but he wouldn't be going our way if he hadn't. As I said, the first wife was allowed to see Maurice every so often, and the present arrangement is that she goes to Anstey Court one half-term and he goes the next. They split the holidays up too, but we're not concerned with them. Now, any questions so far?"

"Well, sir—I mean, just plain well. You'd better tell me what to call you—then I shan't make a hash of things. How friendly are we? Same school, next-door neighbours, or what? And anyway, who am I? It's all most confusing."

Sir Francis smiled.

"I think we'd better be club acquaintances," he said. "We met a couple of years ago at the *Omega*—it's quite respectable, so you needn't worry. As for what you are, I don't suppose anybody will ask questions, but you can always say you paint or play the trombone or collect bugs."

"I could, but I'd rather not. I think I'll be a novelist—I understand from some of my friends that it needs no technical skill or special knowledge."

"Please yourself—but don't be too definite in case the kids start asking for your autograph on spec. Commercial-minded little beasts nowadays, boys. Now, any questions?"

"Only one: how do Herbert and Charlotte get on with the divorced Lady Weekes?"

The Assistant-Commissioner stared at him in surprise.

"Now, what the devil makes you ask that?" he demanded.

"Oh, I don't know—it seems fairly sensible. You wouldn't be telling me all about her if she weren't mixed up in whatever it is we're going to prevent."

"And you say it with a straight face! I'm sorry I can't tell you the answer—I haven't the slightest notion. You'll have to judge for yourself, and it won't hurt if you watch Lady Weekes as if she was your favourite film-star. You may see why in a minute.

"Now, I don't pretend to be particularly intimate with Herbert Weekes; I've met him about a dozen times, I suppose. He's never struck me as at all imaginative, though, and I dare say his evidence is pretty reliable. What he tells me in effect—I had a long talk with him last night over the telephone—is that to the best of his belief there have been two separate 'accidents' to the younger Weekes boy in the last six months, and in view of a rather odd occurrence which took place yesterday, and another which he can't date with any certainty, he wants my advice. I'll leave him to tell you about the 'accidents' himself, though if he isn't a bit more specific than he was last night it won't help much. I'll confine my information to the other business.

"As you suspected, something's been pinched, or at any rate something's missing. In fact, two things are, though whether the losses are connected isn't yet known. The first lacuna is due to a box of liqueur chocolates sent to Miss Charlotte—that's what they all call her—from France."

"Sent by whom?" interrupted Beale.

"Sorry, don't know precisely—some firm or other. It seems the old wretch has a sweet tooth, and I must say she's always been sucking toffee or something whenever I've seen her, which is about half a dozen times too often. She's a horror—tongue like a whip unless she likes you, and that's improbable. Anyway, she saw an advertisement in some French magazine, doubtless the respectable kind, for these chocolates, and ordered a box to see if they were any good. The parcel duly arrived yesterday afternoon, and promptly vanished, and nobody knows how or when or where. Or nobody admits to knowing, which mayn't be quite the same thing, of course. You'll get all the circumstantial details down there, so I won't bother with them now. What's more startling is the other loss. Herbert says he's been relieved of roughly a hundred and twenty grains of potassium cyanide."

With an anticipatory smile Sir Francis watched his companion sit up abruptly at that, for potassium cyanide is one of the deadliest poisons known.

"Has he now!" exclaimed Beale softly. "Five grains make a pretty certain lethal dose for an adult, I believe, and I don't expect it takes as much to kill a child. There'd be enough there to polish off twenty or thirty of them."

"And there's only forty-one, so it might just go round."

"But what in the world was the man doing with stuff like that? How did he get it?"

"He says he's had it for about fifteen years—that it was a relic from the days when he was a keen photographer. Apparently it can be used for reducing a heavy print, though I don't know much about that sort of thing myself; I send all my snaps to Boots'. From what I could understand it's been in a small bottle in a cupboard in his study, thick with dust and all the rest of it. The disappearance of the chocolates made him think to look, and he found that had gone too; whereupon he telephoned."

"Just a minute please, Sir Francis. Is he naturally a suspicious man, or had he any reason for connecting the chocolates with the poison?"

"Ah, that's what we must find out—that's where the two 'accidents' to young Edwin Weekes come in. It's Herbert's theory that there may just possibly be a plot on hand to get rid of the boy. Yes, thinking it over I suppose you could call him suspicious. Unless he reads detective stories, of course; then it would be the obvious notion."

Beale admitted the truth of the suggestion.

"Anyway, I hope you told him what you thought of him?" he remarked.

"More or less. It *was* pretty careless to leave sudden death about like that. What we've got to do is to locate it, if possible, and the chocolates."

"And how does he propose we do that, tactfully or otherwise?"

"I can't imagine. As usual, we're expected to be miracle-men."

"Or perhaps he expects you to be, and you expect me to be. The more I hear about this week-end the less I think I'm going to like it. I can see myself slinking about corridors when everybody else is having supper, and prying into desks and popping into dormitories and poking under mattresses looking for a dusty bottle."

Sir Francis laughed cheerfully.

"I'll come with you to keep *cave,"* he promised. "But does anything strike you about the situation so far?"

"I fancy I'm being gently led to suspect Lady Weekes, but whether by you or by Herbert I don't know."

"Well, say by reason of your naturally suspicious mind. If there's anything in the idea of a plot against the younger boy, then she'd come under the heading of possibles, wouldn't she? In view of her known attitude to the father?"

"She might—in a detective story. What does Herbert say?"

"Nothing. I threw out several delicate hints, but he either couldn't or wouldn't understand. He professed to be completely in the dark about why anybody could possibly want to hurt the child. All I learnt definitely was that Lady Weekes arrived at Anstey Court for half-term on Thursday evening, and is known to have been on the premises when the parcel of chocolates was mistakenly put with the boys' mail on a table in the hall. That was where it vanished from, but how she could know it was coming, or that it had chocolates in it, short of second sight, is a mystery."

Again Beale interrupted.

"And whose mistake was that?" he asked. "Putting the parcel in the wrong place?"

"Herbert's again, I'm afraid."

"Really? He doesn't sound very reliable."

"Oh, well, don't be too harsh on the man. One was an error of commission and the other of omission, and anyway he wasn't expecting anybody to collar the thing."

"It's reasonably certain the parcel was stolen?"

"There seems to be no other explanation. At first he thought perhaps one of the boys might be responsible, because a lot of them collect foreign stamps furiously and it was a foreign parcel; but now the cyanide's gone he can't decide what to believe. The fact that he hasn't any clear idea of how long the bottle's been missing doesn't help, either. He says he hadn't been near the cupboard in a month. In any event—and this is worth noting—he assured me solemnly and at great length that his sister was the only other person bar himself in the place who knew there'd ever been cyanide within reach. The bottle wasn't labelled."

"Yes, that's something," agreed Beale doubtfully. "He wouldn't be trying to blame her, would he?"

"I shouldn't think so; it would need a moral Hercules."

"Ah well, we shall see. But it looks like a sticky time ahead, and I'm quite sure I wouldn't send little Alfred to Anstey Court even if he existed and the fees were quartered."

III

YET WHEN HE GOT out of the car which had met them at the station, and stood for a moment looking at the red-brick school buildings, the close-mown lawns, the flower-beds bright with candytuft and pinks and pansies, he admitted to himself that Anstey Court seemed a pleasant enough place. Away to the left were tennis courts, and near them a deserted practice-ground, the cricket nets still up and the turf worn at block and bowling-crease alike. It was a blazingly hot day, and the grass seemed brown rather than green. When he heard from the distance the click of bat and ball, and the sound of discreet clapping, he wished for a moment that he were younger, and playing.

The time was just after half past three, and they were informed by a maid that the match against the Fathers had already started.

"Right, then we'll walk across," said Sir Francis. "I know the way."

"Oughtn't you to be performing?" asked Beale, as they strolled towards the playing-fields. He remembered that the Assistant-Commissioner had represented his county in earlier years.

"What, at my age? I did last year, though, and nearly got double figures. You wait till you see these boys—they're good. Herbert Weekes does know something about cricket, whatever his faults. Not that he was ever much of a hand at it himself, but he gets good results as a coach."

The field seemed to Beale enormous. He had been expecting something perhaps a little smaller than Trafalgar Square instead of something at least three times as big. On either side of the part being used for the match were vast lonely expanses, and beyond a hedge at the back was another field. To the right a dozen tall beeches provided shade, and under these were groups of people in deck-chairs. Nearer was the pavilion, resplendently white in the full glare of the sun, and by this also were people; fashionably dressed women, men in flannel suits, small boys in green blazers edged with yellow, little girls in patterned frocks and floppy straw hats. Nearer still were cars, dozens of them drawn up in line, some empty and some tenanted, but almost all sleek and shiny and expensive. As he walked by he noticed four Rolls-Royces and the biggest Daimler he had ever seen, its sole occupant a supercilious borzoi intently sneering at the cricket.

"No, I don't think I shall be sending my infant here," he murmured. "Not on a chief-inspector's pay. If you could make me a chief-constable, now—"

"Wait till you get little Alfred," advised Sir Francis. "They certainly look a swank lot, though. Stop here for a moment, and I'll point a few people out. See the man in whites and a pinky blazer—the one going bald? That's Lloyd Gregory, the senior master. Been here about ten years—a queer chap, pours beer down his throat quicker than you can watch. And that woman in black sitting over there holding court is Miss Charlotte, the head's sister. She's an absolute tartar, but I think I said that before. I'll introduce you presently—there's just a chance she might like you, I s'pose. Anyway, she don't like me, though I can't imagine why.

"Now, who else is there? The fellow with the monocle is a general, but I forget his name. His wife's exactly like a llama if she's still alive. Oh, and there's Lady Weekes, just walking across from the tress. The brat with her is Edwin, the one who's going to be murdered. So they say," he added hastily, as Beale stared. "Anyway, take a look at her; she's something after my idea of Lady Macbeth when young."

Beale obeyed the instruction. The boy struck him as much like any other, except for a vaguely porcine expression; the woman was between thirty and forty, and wore a dove-grey dress which admirably set off her raven hair and slim figure. As she approached he saw that she had deep brown eyes, and was ready to believe that as a girl she must have been strikingly beautiful. Now, though, there were lines round her mouth which she was either unable to banish, or thought not worth bothering about. They gave her face an unmistakable touch of severity in repose; yet a moment later, when she smiled at something Edwin said, and then laughed, the lines and their effect were wholly forgotten.

"Not a nobody," he remarked rather obscurely, but knowing quite well what he meant. Lady Weekes would never go into a restaurant unnoticed, nor be overlooked by her friends in the street, nor—he felt—do for very long precisely what was expected of her. She had sat down by the pavilion now, and as he watched took from her handbag something which unrolled into a hat. He had no idea what it was made of, but as soon as she had put it on, and given it one adjusting tug, it looked as neat as if she had spent an hour over it.

"Money?" he enquired softly, and his companion shrugged.

"She did have, though not always, and I don't know how much there is left. She won about £25,000 in one of the Irish sweepstakes a few years ago."

"Lucky woman! And how does the divorce go down with the other parents?"

"Yes, Herbert's a snob all right," agreed Sir Francis obliquely. "Still, twelve years is a long time—most people have forgotten. And he probably reckons that for those who haven't, the title will counterbalance the notoriety. If she were Mrs. Grey or Mrs. Jones I don't suppose he'd have her near the place. Ah, pull yourself together—he's spotted us! Yes, he's coming over."

Again Beale watched, as unobtrusively as possible, and was not altogether impressed by the big man who walked towards them with a heavy step. He had a pale square face, a short moustache, and was rather carelessly clad in grey flannels, a Free-Forester blazer, and a panama hat by no means new. He looked neither particularly intellectual nor particularly athletic; in some subtle manner he seemed more ordinary than a headmaster should. But perhaps that was less the fault of the man than of the setting. These women and little girls and cars were clearly outside the scope of normal school life; it would give a better idea of his quality, thought Beale, to see him in three days' time, when the last of the intruders had departed and he was back again teaching or taking prayers or coaching at the nets.

For some moments they talked about nothing much. Then Herbert Weekes assumed a conspiratorial air.

"There will be little opportunity to discuss matters until later," he whispered ponderously. "I'm sure you understand. One has other responsibilities, you know,"—and he indicated the parents of his charges with a comprehensive gesture.

"Of course," assented the Assistant-Commissioner. "Meanwhile, has anything further occurred?"

"Nothing, I'm thankful to say, nothing. The parcel is still missing, and the bottle too, I fear. I have told no one about that, naturally—no one but my sister, that is. I will put myself at your disposal at the earliest possible moment, but I can't promise it will be before dinner. Perhaps that won't matter, though, since you're both staying at the school. And now you must excuse me. Malcolm is waiting to go in soon, Sir Francis—I'm sure he'd like a word of encouragement. Will you come across?"

Beale suffered himself to be included in the invitation, chiefly because he could think of no way to avoid it, and was presently involved in a series of rapid and inaudible introductions. Then he was given a deck-chair, assured that he might smoke his pipe without fear of offending delicate nostrils, and for the first time was able to turn his attention to the match.

As he had gathered from the headmaster's remark, the boys were batting, and the score-board showed that so far they had obtained forty runs for the loss of two wickets. A fat man with a very red face had just begun bowling, tossing up slow and grossly inaccurate leg-breaks. The first two were treated with respect, in case they might constitute some unknown form of trap; the third and fourth were sent skimming to the boundary by strokes which seemed to him eminently disciplined. Then Herbert Weekes loomed over his chair for a second.

"That's my nephew batting," he said, "the elder one. He's very severe on the leg side—he responds to tuition."

Having thus contrived to take the credit for the two boundaries, the headmaster disappeared, and very shortly a new voice addressed Beale.

"Please sir, are you Mr. Parker-Smythe?" asked a tall thin boy in a pessimistic tone.

"No—I'm sorry."

"Then please do you know who is?"

"What's the matter, Abel?" enquired Patricia Tilling briskly. "Mr. Parker-Smythe? Why, he's playing—you can't possibly speak to him now."

"No, Miss Tilling," agreed the boy listlessly, and turned to go.

"What do you want him for?" she asked, stopping him. "Is it important?"

"Well, Miss Tilling, Piggy's nose is bleeding—that's all."

"What, again? Tell him to lie down till it stops, and then go indoors to Matron."

Then she faced Beale with a smile, and he saw that she was both young and pretty. She had fair hair which glinted attractively in the sunlight, and wore a blue frock. He thought it suited her.

"I'm sorry if he was bothering you," she said.

"Of course not. But do tell me, who is Piggy?"

"Peter Parker-Smythe."

"And he doesn't even know his own father is playing in the match?"

The girl laughed gently, almost significantly, as if she found satisfaction in showing him that he was wrong.

"Not his father, his uncle," she explained. "And Piggy doesn't know anything except about things to eat. Besides, he's very short-sighted."

"I see—thanks. He sounds decidedly interesting. Oh, I'm sorry—will you have my chair?"

She laughed again, shaking her head.

"I'm the governess, in case you hadn't guessed," she told him. "If anybody saw me sitting down I'd probably be sacked. There's roughly fifty parents here, not to mention uncles, and I've only done about half. 'Oh, how do you *do,* dear Mrs. Cluck? Archibald is simply marvellous at long division.' Now I must go and do some more—good-bye."

He was left with a slight feeling of bewilderment, but quite what it was which puzzled him he could not be sure.

For the next twenty minutes he was free to watch the cricket, and soon saw that the Assistant-Commissioner's opinion was justified. The two batsmen in, whose names he ascertained to be Lillywhite and Askew, put on forty-five runs in three overs, the former by stylish drives and cuts, the latter by stupendous swipes which always somehow managed to send the ball over a fielder's head or wide of his hand. As far as he could tell the bowling was good enough to deserve kinder treatment, but he was not surprised when a change came. A dark burly man in extremely short trousers—possibly borrowed for the occasion, thought Beale—rolled up his sleeves, handed his crested blue cap to the umpire, measured out a run of about fifteen yards, and proceeded to hurl himself back again towards the wicket. His first two balls were unplayable because they went soaring high above the batsman's head. His third, in contrast, hit the pitch less than half way down and almost decapitated Lillywhite. The fourth was equally fast but perfectly controlled, and sent the middle stump tumbling madly towards first slip; and the two succeeding batsmen, the first of whom was young Barton, were similarly treated.

"A hat-trick! A hat-trick!" exclaimed an excited boy, and began rushing away towards the cars. Beale smiled, suspecting that the bowler was his father. 'Or his uncle' he added to himself, remembering his previous error. A moment later Herbert Weekes appeared from nowhere.

"That's Captain Hewston," the headmaster informed him. "His game is really rugger—he's the international, of course—but he seems to be quite effective with the smaller sphere"—and he laughed rather loudly at what seemed a poor enough joke. "A pity Maurice didn't play back to the ball that got him," he went on, and Beale agreed unblushingly. He had completely forgotten he had not noticed the head's nephew lose his wicket.

Again there was an interval of peace. The sun was so hot that he closed his eyes to its brightness, and listened instead of looking; by degrees he began to doze. Then, for the third time, Herbert Weekes returned. His hazel eyes were now serious, and he leant over until his moustache was all but touching his visitor's ear.

"A development has occurred!" he breathed fiercely. "Sir Francis would appreciate your advice."

The Assistant-Commissioner was standing under one of the towering beech trees talking to a young man in a dazzling striped blazer; yellow seemed to be the only colour missing.

"My junior master, Mr. Birkett," observed Herbert briefly, and without much warmth. "He's just found one of the chocolates in his pocket."

"And I'm certain it couldn't have been there ten minutes ago," declared the victim, obviously in a bad temper and as obviously trying to conceal the fact.

"What makes you so sure?" asked Sir Francis.

"Because I was looking for a pencil to lend Miss Tilling, sir, and it was the only thing in there. I don't understand it at all."

"And where is the—the discovery?" queried Beale. "May I see?"

For answer the young man held out his right-hand blazer pocket, presenting a sticky mess of silver-paper and dusty melted chocolate, and what smelt like *creme de menthe.*

"Better get it out, hadn't I?" he suggested.

"Yes, as quickly as possible," agreed Sir Francis. "Would you care to go with him, and take charge of the remains?"

He addressed Beale, and as he spoke indicated with a slight twist of the head that he wanted a word in private. They moved apart from the other two, and the Assistant-Commissioner kept his voice very low.

"The old fool's told all his staff you're a cop!" he said. "God knows why—he just says he 'thought it best'. He swears the parents don't know, but I wouldn't be too sure. Anyway, you needn't trouble to pretend with Birkett. If you can, find out who he's been talking to recently, and get back soon, just in case."

"In case of what?"

"Well,"—with a smile, "the presumption is that the chocolates were stolen, and it seems only common sense to suppose they were stolen for some definite purpose. To ruin the most hideous blazer that ever came out of Cambridge? I doubt it, and I don't believe there can be two lots of liqueurs going the rounds. I shan't be surprised if the things start turning up in all the oddest places, because it couldn't very well have got into that pocket by accident. See what I mean?"

"I think so. Somebody will try to give the impression the whole business is a practical joke? Then surely we ought to find out how many there were in the parcel to begin with, oughtn't we?"

"It's being done—sorry if I forgot to tell you."

As Beale walked after Birkett he was thinking that he understood now what had struck him as queer about the governess' behaviour towards him. She had acted just as if she knew he was no parent but a detective; not making the least attempt to 'do' him, and appearing glad to trip up his false assumption about Mr. Parker-Smythe. He also wondered why the headmaster had considered it necessary to inform the staff of his occupation. The disclosure seemed unlikely to make his uncertain task any harder, provided they kept their knowledge to themselves; but if one of them gave it away to the boys, purposely or by accident, then as far as secrecy went he might just as well dress up in uniform at once. He was still musing, and a dozen yards behind the dawdling master, when he heard a shout from behind. He turned to see his superior wildly beckoning him to return.

"I say, they want me back there again," he called to Birkett. "Will you take your blazer off and put it somewhere safe?"

The young man halted, and then came towards him frowning. He had green eyes, a pink smooth face, and a somewhat petulant mouth; he looked as if he would not be even-tempered many days together.

"Safe?" he queried in a superior tone, as if he believed he were addressing a servant. "Safe from what, pray?"

"I've no idea," replied Beale, ignoring his manner. "Someone put a chocolate in your pocket, and the same person may equally well feel like taking it out again for all we know. Just see that he doesn't have the opportunity, please; and do nothing yourself."

"Right oh!" agreed Birkett, with unexpected mildness. "And perhaps I'd better keep quiet?"

"It might be as well. And one other thing, if possible; will you jot down a list of everyone you can remember speaking to between the time you lent Miss Tilling your pencil and the time you found the mess? It may help indirectly. Ah, they're calling again—I'll see you presently."

"I told you!" said Sir Francis, looking pleased. "The avalanche is just beginning, and it may be funny. One of the XI has just sat on one of the things, and it didn't improve his prospects. To make it worse he was next man in, and almost in tears a moment ago."

"Sat on it where?" asked Beale. "A chair?"

"He doesn't know—somebody spotted it when he was walking about. It was *maraschino* this time, for a change. Now I'm waiting for one of the more fashionable mothers to follow suit."

But he was disappointed; the next three chocolates which turned up did no material damage. A Mrs. Wainwright found one in her handbag, still secure in its wrapping, and was tactfully relieved of it. Major Drummond's had lodged in the brim of his pork-pie hat. One fell off Miss Charlotte's lap when she leant forward to discourage an inquisitive fox terrier. The three were, in order, a *curacao,* a *benedictine,* and a *cognac.*

Sir Francis took the opportunity to introduce Beale, but the headmaster's sister merely nodded absently, scarcely looking at him. Then there was a period of inaction; to the Assistant-Commissioner's patent surprise, no discoveries were made during the tea interval, taken when the boys' innings closed for a hundred and twenty-one. He remarked that he would have expected the occasion to furnish the unknown distributor with a chance for excellent sport.

"Unless he's too busy elsewhere?" suggested Beale. "Or unless she is—I suppose it might just as well be a woman as a man?"

He began to stare about him watchfully, but soon desisted. For one thing there were too many people moving. No sooner had he located Miss Tilling, for instance, than she was hidden by two small boys in green blazers and grey felt hats and a tall girl in white, and when they had passed on the governess was gone. The same thing happened when he attempted to follow Lloyd Gregory. By and by he found himself, not quite acquiescent, standing with a cup of tea in one hand and a ridiculously fragile cucumber sandwich in the other, listening to an unknown paunchy man telling just how Hammond had scored a century the week before; almost stroke by stroke. The teller was accompanied by a solemn snub-nosed schoolgirl of fifteen or so, who seemed in trouble with her stockings. Every two minutes she would fumble dreamily under her blue serge skirt, oblivious of the unattended youth staring nearby.

From the corner of his eye he presently saw that Birkett was back, now resplendent in pale green and old gold, busily talking to a dark-haired gipsy-looking girl. Then he noticed Sir Francis again, bending over Miss Charlotte's chair and apparently cracking a joke with her.

("Nobody else plays that stroke quite like that these days . . ." asserted the bore. Down went his daughter's hands, fumbling. He could cheerfully have smacked them both.)

The elderly woman nodded, almost smiled, seemed to protrude her beaked nose, opened her mouth, and to judge from her listener's expression delivered one of her sharper verbal thrusts. At any rate, she was alone the next moment; surprisingly so, considering that she was the hostess of the afternoon. "Not popular?' he wondered, and fleetingly transferred his attention to the voice droning earnestly in his ear.

". . . just stepped back and drove it off his right foot a yard past cover's left hand . . ."

Up went the edge of the blue serge skirt once more, and this time a shade too far. Beale saw the reason for the incessant fidgeting, and almost forgave the girl. The tops of her black stockings were upheld not with the normal appliances but by string, tightly tied and biting into her thighs. Then the skirt fell, till the next time. Five yards away the youth still stared, apparently no wiser.

'And I might be a hundred miles away playing golf!' he thought. 'Curse chocolates and cyanide and half-terms. Especially half-terms.'

IV

NO MORE LIQUEUR CHOCOLATES were found until the match was over. It ended at twenty minutes past six, after an exciting attempt by the Fathers' last two batsmen to knock off the runs. From 54 for 9 the score rose steadily to the hundred, and the Anstey-Court fielding began to get just the least bit ragged. Then Maurice Weekes at point took a fast slash from Mr. Parker-Smythe off the end of his nose, and the game was won.

Scarcely had the congratulatory clapping died away when Beale was called over to one of the Rolls-Royces. There the Assistant-Commissioner showed him a slowly melting *chartreuse* on the glittering aluminium bonnet, while an indignant chauffeur hovered nearby. They questioned the man, but he was unhelpful. It must have happened between 5.30 and 6.00 when he was having tea with the other chauffeurs, he said; and anyway, what the devil did it mean?

Five minutes later they were examining another *cognac* which had been inserted into the crack between the pavilion window and the surrounding woodwork. Then Herbert Weekes lumbered across to say that there was a *kummel* neatly impaled upon a knitting-needle belonging to Hewston's grandmother. She was making a scarf; she had just put down her handiwork for a moment to clap the winning catch; that was all she knew.

Sir Francis turned frowningly to his companion.

"How many does that make—eight? It begins to look to me as if there may be more than one person playing tricks."

"Perhaps, but I rather doubt it," said Beale. "I don't think they're coming quickly enough for that. Still, we've no idea how many there are to dispose of yet."

"But we soon shall have. They'll telephone me from the Yard the minute they've got in touch with the firm the parcel was sent by."

The *kummel* was removed from the knitting-needle and transferred as unobtrusively as possible to a clean envelope; the headmaster had sent indoors for a packet. Nevertheless, there were one or two interested spectators: small boys who sidled by staring, a stout elderly woman in black who seemed to have bathed recently in scent, Lloyd Gregory smoking a pipe and carrying a shooting-stick. The chocolates were the size of walnuts, covered with heavy silver-paper, and each labelled with an appropriately coloured band bearing the name of the liqueur inside and the words *Boucard, Paris* in very small print.

"Any chance of fingerprints?" asked Sir Francis, observing how careful Beale was not to handle the tinfoil directly.

"If he was careless; but I wouldn't expect him to be. In any case, fingerprints won't be much good while we're being tactful."

"Well, how would you like us to tackle it?" enquired the other jocularly. "Line everybody up and take their impressions?"

"It would be a start, certainly, and it wouldn't hurt to search them all, either. At present we're just looking on and doing nothing."

"I know; but what is there to do?"

"Exactly. Nothing in the circumstances. Yet the fact remains that someone on this field is carrying these things about and dumping them—unless the supply's exhausted or he's gone. What happens to the parents now the cricket's over?"

"Most of them clear off and come back tomorrow to take their kids out for the day. One or two will stay to dinner, I expect. But we needn't worry much about parents, need we?"

"Not as agents, but I shall be glad to see the back of them. They get in the way, and they provide the joker with victims; and one of 'em's a most colossal bore."

"Ah, the personal touch!"

"Not entirely," said Beale, and paused thoughtfully for a moment.

"Do you feel it's safe to count the boys out as well, for the time being?" he asked. "It would make things a great deal simpler. Discover what adults were on the field today who could possibly have stolen the parcel, and there you are."

"Yes, that *sounds* all right, but—"

"I know, Sir Francis—there's about a dozen buts. To my mind the biggest one is, how could a potential thief conceivably know what was in the parcel before opening it? Well, there may be answers to that. Miss Charlotte was one person who could have told him, and Herbert may very well have been another. Can they either of them swear positively they didn't mention the ordering of the chocolates to a soul? That doesn't attempt to explain the missing cyanide, of course, but what will? All we can do so far is guess, and the best seems to be that it was taken *after* the chocolates—assuming the same person to be responsible. Otherwise—otherwise—"

He broke off, frowning.

"Unless somebody's being a lot cleverer than we suspect," he said after some seconds. "Suppose the chocolates are a blind? Suppose we're meant to find them all, and go away satisfied; and then little Thingummy swallows a poisoned doughnut and dies that way? You must admit they've all turned up in pretty conspicuous places."

The Assistant-Commissioner nodded.

"But it still limits the suspects," he pointed out. "And how was anybody bar Herbert and his sister to know about the dusty bottle in the cupboard? Unless you're making the same suggestion; they told someone about that as well. The same two; why not accuse them and have done with it?"

Beale grinned.

"Hardly the woman," he said. "She's been stuck in a chair all the time. And you wouldn't really expect Herbert to be the one to drag us down here, would you? And anyway, I should hate to have to accuse him tactfully. As a matter of interest, though, I've just the vaguest idea about the poison. Herbert said he's had the stuff about fifteen years, didn't he? That would date it back to 1924, when he was a keen photographer, and when also, presumably, Lady Weekes had just been married and was in favour. Would it be so impossible for her to know about it? Then perhaps last time she was down here she noticed the bottle in the cupboard, recognized it, and began to plot. After all," he added apologetically, "you told me to suspect her, Sir Francis. And while I remember; does it matter if Herbert realizes she's under consideration? I don't see how I can question him properly and still keep him in the dark, unless he's exceptionally dense."

His companion shrugged elegantly, then smiled and raised his hat as someone he knew went by.

"I don't suppose it matters," he answered, "so long as he doesn't talk. Only I don't feel inclined to trust his discretion too far, after that business with the staff. I really don't understand why he need have told them who you were, but perhaps he'll be able to offer some excuse." He sighed, staring unseeingly at the deserted pitch. "It isn't going to be easy," he prophesied, "and for all we know, there may be absolutely nothing in it. The bottle may merely have been mislaid, and the chocolates taken by some practical joker with a grudge against the Weekes. Still, even at that it isn't nice to be done in the eye so blatantly—I don't like people being funny at my expense. After all, practically everybody here this afternoon knows who I am, confound it!"

Now it was Beale's turn to sigh.

"If you're going to take the thing as a personal affront!" he murmured pessimistically.

By half past nine that evening they were in possession of further information, of which he made careful notes. They knew that the parcel, when despatched from Paris the previous Tuesday, contained exactly four dozen liqueur chocolates: six each of *kummel, curacao, cognac, benedictine, chartreuse, creme de menthe, kirschwasser,* and *maraschino.* Of these, twelve had so far been recovered. Four more were found in the school buildings between 7.30 and 9.00; one in the senior changing-room on the ground floor, one in a washbasin in a dormitory, one pinned to the map of the world in the schoolroom, and one lying under the hand-bell used for notifying meal-times and breaks between lessons. This bell was always kept in the same place, said Herbert Weekes bad-temperedly; on the bottom stair of the half-dozen which led from the dining-hall to the headmaster's part of the house, where no boy ventured unless summoned. At the top of this small flight was a glass door; then on the left came the study and the morning-room, and opposite the drawing-room and a staircase to the first floor.

As well, Beale had succeeded in getting from Lloyd Gregory a list of the adults who had been both in the school on Friday afternoon and on the field that day for the match. It contained seven names: Gregory's own; and those of the headmaster and his sister, Thomas Birkett, Patricia Tilling, Lady Weekes, and George Elkington, the non-resident master. The latter had spent the afternoon umpiring, however, and so seemed beyond suspicion. The housekeeper and the matron had not visited the playing-fields, being too busy indoors.

Finally, the boys were all interrogated again before they went to bed, and all positively asserted complete ignorance about the parcel's fate, *qua* parcel. They were told its contents, though in view of the afternoon's events Beale suspected that the information was unnecessary, instructed to look out for chocolates, forbidden to do anything with those they might find but deliver them immediately to one of the staff, and warned on no account to breathe a word of the matter to their parents. It was hinted fairly openly that their collective denial of relevant knowledge was not quite believed in, and more plainly that at the slightest provocation one and all might face a fortnight's extra prep.

"An hour every morning from 6.30 to 7.30, perhaps," Herbert Weekes suggested frigidly, glaring at sullen eyes. On the whole it seemed probable that the pupils of Anstey Court would soon hate the idea of chocolates in a parcel.

V

AT QUARTER TO TEN, in the headmaster's study, a conference took place. Miss Charlotte was present, free from any possible duties as hostess because Lady Weekes had gone out with Major Drummond and his wife. She sat very upright in an ancient leather armchair, and directed her clear blue eyes unwaveringly upon Beale's face. The intensity of her gaze disturbed him until he grew used to it; yet indefinably he felt that in spite of what Sir Francis had said, she was not hostile towards him.

The study struck him as gloomy. Two sides of the room were lined with books, unopened apparently from one year's end to another; from some of the titles he guessed that this might be because they were unreadably dull. *Notes on Speech-Making, Graver Thoughts of a Country Parson, The Six Systems of Indian Philosophy, The Fly-Fisher's Entomology*—he almost fancied for a moment that he was in Charing-Cross Road. On the back of the door hung a tattered black gown; the faded curtains shut out the gathering dusk; the air smelt faintly of stale tobacco. The only objects of interest seemed to be a dozen record-albums of Beethoven and Schubert, and a rusty spear suspended over the fireplace.

Herbert Weekes began by relating laboriously the circumstances connected with the parcel's arrival and disappearance. His voice was solemn; he spoke as if he expected his listeners to pay close attention, and be ready to answer a short examination-paper when he had finished. Later, and even more portentously, he passed to the missing cyanide of potassium.

"To my certain knowledge the bottle had lain undisturbed in that cupboard for a full year," he said, glancing over his shoulder at a door by the window. "It must be quite that long ago since this room was turned out, Charlotte?"

His sister nodded without speaking.

"I thought as much. I remember seeing the bottle this term, but not for some weeks. It was approximately half full, and the amount of potassium cyanide it contained I should estimate as being in the region of a hundred and twenty grains."

"In crystal form?" enquired Sir Francis, and Herbert inclined his head.

"In crystal form," he agreed. "I was led to look for it because of two somewhat peculiar occurrences at Easter, when I was staying with my brother in Hertfordshire."

Without ceasing to regard Beale, Miss Charlotte interrupted.

"Wouldn't it be slightly more accurate to say that you were led to look for it because I suggested that you should do so?" she asked bluntly. "That's my recollection of what took place. You were wondering for what possible purpose anyone could have taken the parcel of chocolates, unless one of the boys did it for the sake of the French stamps. My answer was poison, because almost the same thing happened in the last book I had from the library. I remarked that it might be as well to find out if Matron's medicine-chest contained any poisons. Then I remembered that some years ago you expressly told me on no account to handle something or other you used for your photography, and I asked if you still had it."

Her brother conceded the point rather curtly.

"You certainly helped to put the idea into my head. At all events, I immediately came in here to see for myself. That was late yesterday evening, and as you know I found the bottle to be missing. By and by I will show you where it used to be, Mr. Beale, but first I think I had better deal with the two 'accidents' about which I told you on the telephone, Sir Francis."

He became a degree more solemn still, though it had not seemed possible. At great length he described his Easter-holiday plans, the size and nature of his brother's estate in Hertfordshire, and gave other details of no apparent importance. As Beale reflected afterwards, the whole matter could have been imparted in half a dozen sentences.

What was alleged to have happened was, first, that on the night of April 27th some person unknown had fired a pellet from an air-gun or air-pistol through Edwin Weekes's bedroom window as he was undressing; and, second, that the following day the brakes on the boy's bicycle were found to have been removed. It had never been learnt who was responsible for either misdeed. Little in the way of investigation had been done at the time by anybody except Herbert himself, and in fact no one else had seemed to treat the matter seriously.

"Did *you* ever have any suspicions about the culprit?" asked Sir Francis, and the headmaster frowned.

"No," he answered, after a moment's hesitation, and then repeated his denial more firmly. "No, none whatever. It remained a complete mystery."

Beale, looking at Miss Charlotte, thought he saw her sneer disbelievingly, but could not be sure.

"Was the boy frightened?" continued his questioner.

"A little, naturally, but he behaved very well—very well indeed, on the whole."

"And Sir Robert wasn't inclined to call in the police?"

"Oh no, nothing like that. He put it down to some of the rougher elements in the village. There had been a prosecution for poaching a short time previously, with the usual misdirection of sympathy."

The Assistant-Commissioner turned to Beale.

"Any points you care to raise?" he enquired, in a tone which made it clear that he wished the other would say something, and not go on sitting unproductively silent.

"I don't think so, not about the Easter business," was the quiet answer. "I should like to know more about the missing bottle, though. Can you tell us when you acquired it, Mr. Weekes?"

"Several years ago; I can't be sure of the exact date."

"Early in 1924," said his sister firmly. "Towards the end of the Christmas holidays."

"Thank you. And what colour was it?"

"Black, or very dark blue," was Herbert's verdict.

"Dark green," contradicted Miss Charlotte. "It had a round base, and the outside was corrugated. I dare say it stood some four inches high."

Again he thanked her.

"It helps to know what one's supposed to be looking for," he observed, with a slight smile, "especially anything which contains an extremely deadly poison."

Herbert Weekes nodded glumly at the implied rebuke.

"I looked up the nature of the substance in the encyclopaedia," he remarked. "I confess I had never realized how deadly it actually is. Everyone knows it's capable of killing people, of course, but I had no idea so little was required. This is a serious matter."

"Most serious," agreed Beale readily. "In spite of what happened this afternoon, we mustn't let ourselves be side-tracked, you know. The chocolates are important only as possible receptacles for the poison; the missing bottle must be the first concern."

He purposely spoke with an approach to the head's own pompousness of manner, feeling that the man was more likely to be impressed by wordiness than brevity.

"Now I should like to see the inside of the cupboard," he continued. "Incidentally, how many persons resident here—grown-ups, I mean—would cause no comment if they were seen entering or leaving this room when you were known to be elsewhere, Mr. Weekes?"

"I can tell you that," said Miss Charlotte, before her brother could reply. "Two only: myself and one of the maids, a girl by the name of Perkins. And I may add that it would be most unusual for her to come in here during the daytime in summer, since there is no fire to look after. She does the cleaning before breakfast, of course. It would also be unusual for me to come in here alone at any time, unless I wanted a book."

Her tone implied that that would be never.

"Thank you," said Beale, and rose to join the headmaster by the cupboard. It was built-in, stretching from the floor to about seven feet up the wall, and was a yard in width. On top, between it and the ceiling, were two limp footballs and a bicycle pump, very dusty. The four shelves inside were mostly in the same state, and all loaded with objects of astonishing diversity. It seemed that anything no longer wanted was at once tossed inside, and left there indefinitely. In the first few seconds after the door was opened he saw a broken desk-lamp, several old pipes, a dozen exercise-books, a cane, a glue-pot, a mortar-board, a lidless box of dominoes, a magic-lantern lens, a shrivelled orange, a cup with a broken handle, and a water-pistol. Even Herbert Weekes appeared surprised by the condition of the crowded shelves, for he cleared his throat unhappily and murmured that it was really time he had a clear-out.

"High time!" assented his sister sharply. "It shall be done next week without fail."

The place where the bottle had stood was marked by a significant circle, clearly defined by the surrounding grime, in the far left-hand corner of the second shelf down. Beale realized at a glance that he would get little help in the way of fingerprints: too many things had been moved, in particular a loose pack of playing-cards, smudged and dirty. Nevertheless he obtained permission to take some of them away, explaining his reason for asking. Then he leant forward to examine the neighbourhood of the circle.

Most of the articles near were also connected with photography. There was a pile of developing dishes, a tin marked 'Hypo', a couple of printing-frames, a packet of lantern slides, and a plate-carrier. He noted also a camera lens and old-fashioned hood, black lined with red. Everything looked as if it had remained undisturbed for years.

"I understand you used the cyanide for some kind of reducing," he said, addressing the head.

"Yes—it has certain advantages over other methods. A good photographer rarely needs to reduce at all, of course, but I was an absolute beginner in those days."

"When did you give up the hobby?"

"About 1930, I should think."

"And may I ask why?"

"Oh, I don't know; chiefly because an incredibly clumsy boy I had here then managed to smash my best camera to atoms, I think."

He turned to where his sister was still sitting in the leather armchair.

"Do you remember Burroughs minor, Charlotte?" he enquired, and then went scarlet. "Oh—I beg your pardon!" he exclaimed. "I forgot."

But she betrayed no emotion, replying as if he had merely asked a casual question.

"I'm scarcely like to forget Burroughs minor." she told him. "He was responsible for my limp, which I don't doubt you've noticed," she added, to Beale. "He ran into me on his bicycle."

"Ah, rotten luck!" said Sir Francis, but she pointedly ignored the comment, and for some moments there was an awkward silence. Herbert Weekes stood by the cupboard, clearly regretting his *faux pas;* the Assistant-Commissioner was humming softly to himself under his breath, a sure sign that he was annoyed; the elderly woman continued to sit upright, her eyes now gazing at the carpet.

Beale was aware of the silence, but not perturbed by it; he was still busily staring at the crowded shelves. More precisely, he was staring at the bottom one, at a folded newspaper.

"When did you say you last looked in here, sir?" he asked Herbert.

"I couldn't tell you exactly. It must have been a month or so ago."

"And who else would be likely to open this door?"

"Nobody."

"The maid you mentioned?"—to Miss Charlotte.

"Perkins? Improbable," she replied at once. "Perkins does the minimum of housework, and in any case my brother dislikes having his personal possessions touched. Hence the deplorable state of that cupboard."

"So I may take it that no one has put anything in here for the last month, sir?"

"Yes, yes," agreed the headmaster shortly. "I thought I had made that plain."

Beale faced him gravely, and once more felt that in some obscure way the man fell short of expectations. Perhaps he needed his cap and gown to make him a figure of authority, or perhaps he was at his best only with boys. At the moment he seemed ineffectual and shambling; a tall nonentity with an irritating habit of rubbing his neck against the rim of his stiff collar.

"Then I feel entitled to ask how you account for that," he said briskly, pointing to the newspaper. It was a *Telegraph*; part only of the outer page was showing, but that part included the top of the *Personal* column, and Beale had a good memory.

"Unless I'm greatly mistaken, that paper came out early last week," he explained. "I remember the first advertisement—*P.O.H.H. Do please send address to write* . . . Perhaps you'd better verify the date."

Without speaking Herbert Weekes did so.

"Tuesday, June 6th," he read. "I appreciate your point. Charlotte, can you offer any solution?"

His tone held something of accusation, and that of the answer confirmed a suspicion which Beale had already formed: that this brother and sister were not over-friendly towards each other.

"Why should *I* know anything about it?" she demanded. "The *Telegraph* is your paper—I never touch it."

Then, as if recalling that they were not alone, she considered his request for help.

"Tuesday, June 6th," she repeated, looking down her curved nose. "Wasn't that the day that appalling man came round performing? Yes, of course it was; the whole thing's obvious."

She glanced at Beale again, and smiled fleetingly.

"My brother invariably reads for half an hour after lunch," she told him. "After that the paper goes into the library for the boys. Last Tuesday week this person called, however—an entertainer of some kind. We always hold a concert on the last night of term, and in some mysterious way he had learnt about it. He came hoping for an engagement, and insisted on performing conjuring-tricks in the morning-room with coloured handkerchiefs and rubber balls and lengths of string. Consequently I have no doubt the paper was put in the cupboard because it had not yet been looked at—the man arrived before lunch was over, and stayed the best part of an hour; and there it remained. Herbert's inclined to be absent-minded at times," she finished, as impersonally as if he were a mile away. The headmaster grunted.

"So you've remarked before," he said doubtingly. "Still, we can easily find out tomorrow. If the boys had no *Telegraph* on June 6th, that must have been what happened, though I've certainly no recollection of opening the cupboard recently."

"But wouldn't the boys have made a fuss?" enquired Sir Francis innocently; at which Miss Charlotte stared at him icily before sharpening her tongue.

"Oh, we teach them manners as well as the more ordinary accomplishments, you know," she informed him.

"Oh, quite!" muttered the Assistant-Commissioner, colouring. "I'm sure you look after that part of their education admirably."

He then started to hum again, and Beale spoke in order to relieve the tension.

"And now may I ask you some questions, Mr. Weekes?" he said, moving away from the cupboard and sitting down.

"By all means," agreed the headmaster, after glaring crossly at his sister. "I shall be glad to tell you anything I can."

"Thank you. Then, first, have you the smallest doubt that if the cyanide was taken for criminal purposes, the intended victim is your younger nephew?"

"*I* have none, but I naturally don't expect you to take that as certain. I mean, I should prefer not to limit your point of view, just in case I should be wrong."

"I don't think you need be afraid of hindering us, sir. Now, assuming that you're right, what in your opinion would be the motive for an attempt on your nephew's life?"

Herbert shuffled uncomfortably.

"Ah, well—that's not at all easy to answer."

"Then let me put it more simply. Is it likely that anyone wishes to harm the boy because of personal dislike or hatred?"

"Oh no, certainly not."

"Good—that's one thing clear. Again, does anybody stand to benefit by Edwin's death?"

"Financially, do you mean?"

"Or in any other way, though I admit I can't suggest one."

"Nor I. No, to the best of my belief his death would do nobody the least service. His mother had little property of her own, so nothing like that arises."

"But—presumably—his half-brother would inherit a larger share of Sir Robert's estate when the time comes?"

Herbert stared, his square face solemn.

"You know, I had never thought of that," he observed, as if the statement were a great compliment. "Yes, I imagine that to be a fair comment, though I'm not familiar with the terms of any will my brother may have made."

"Very well, sir, one possibility emerges. Until we're proved wrong we'll suppose that someone with the elder boy's interests very much at heart may be seeking to improve his future."

"Ha!" exclaimed Miss Charlotte, peering up at him from under her drooping lids. "You've learnt how to phrase things nice, Mr. Beale."

He smiled at that, but made no direct answer; he was not yet sure if her attitude towards him was reliably friendly or not.

"Now, Mr. Weekes," he continued, "I propose to leave that suggestion in the air for a moment, but I shall return to it later. Meanwhile, can you think of any other *personal* motive for killing Edwin?"

"None. I had not even thought of that one."

"Then let us now suppose that the chief sufferer is designed to be someone else. If the boy were harmed, whose feelings would be primarily affected? In other words, to whom is Edwin particularly dear?"

Miss Charlotte muttered under her breath, while her brother furrowed his brow at the question, stretching his neck and jerking his head up and down rather like a chicken walking, thought Beale.

"His father, plainly," he said at last.

"Then the next step is obvious. Has Sir Robert any serious enemies, and if so, who are they?"

He rather expected that Herbert Weekes would refuse to commit himself, but to his relief the question was treated seriously.

"If Robert were the sort of person one could ask, I should suggest your doing so," was the reply. "Unfortunately he isn't. In general I think it would be fair to say that he's abnormally detached from human intercourse. He has but few friends, and I don't honestly believe that he would know whether anyone was his enemy or not; he would never have noticed. You agree, Charlotte?"

"Yes, Robert is quite superior; nowadays he looks over everybody's head. That doesn't mean no one dislikes him, though."

"Of course not," assented her brother readily. "But Mr. Beale was looking for something stronger than mere dislike, I fancy?"

"Decidedly stronger. Can you help?"

"Well, I don't know—I don't know at all."

He paused, and surveyed the others unsmilingly.

"No," he decided, "I think not. I'm sorry, but I fear I shall be of little use to you. It's all such a delicate matter,"—and he waved his hands vaguely, as if that explained everything. But Miss Charlotte snorted, positively and without embarrassment. Her blue eyes opened very wide, and her nose seemed to jut further out in scornful disapprobation.

"Herbert!" she said sharply. "I suggest that you take Sir Francis into the drawing-room and leave *me* to talk to Mr. Beale. I think we shall get on a lot better alone—luckily I'm not so distressed by indelicacy."

The Assistant-Commissioner seized his opportunity without hesitation.

"I believe you're right, Miss Weekes!" he declared warmly, and got up smiling with the air of one who has scored. The headmaster rose too, apparently little less enthusiastic; yet he seemed to feel that a word of apology was due.

"My sister's a better hand at this sort of thing than I am," he murmured. "You don't mind?"

"Of course not, sir," said Beale, and a moment later settled down to confront the woman he felt was undoubtedly the real authority at Anstey Court.

VI

MISS CHARLOTTE WEEKES struck him as having twice her brother's force of personality, and he hoped he was not mistaken in supposing that she found him tolerable. It was very evident that she had small use for his travelling-companion. If she were informative he might perhaps get somewhere at last; yet at his most optimistic he would never have looked for the directness of speech which he was to encounter.

"And now we can talk properly!" she remarked, opening a large black handbag which had been lying on her lap. "We can also eat chocolates," she added, producing a box with satisfaction. "Have one? You needn't worry—they're perfectly all right. There, I'll put them on the table. Help yourself when you like, and don't wait for any more invitations. And mind you tell me if you get a hard one, because I gave special instructions that they were all to be soft. When I want nuts and toffee, I told the girl, I'll ask for nuts and toffee—until then, oblige me by their absence. And don't start asking questions until I've had my say, because it'll save time and breath."

She nodded emphatically, straightened her greying hair, dipped into the box, and began to speak again with her mouth full and her eyes steadily staring at him.

"I shan't try to put things in order," she warned. "I expect you'll be clever enough to sort it all out, and if you aren't, then it won't help you anyway. To start with, my brother's not only absent-minded but also disgustingly erratic. Things are right one day and wrong the next; he's not dependable. He has habits, of course, the same as everyone. He doesn't forget to shave or dress properly, and as I told you he always sits down with the paper for half an hour after lunch. Perhaps erratic was the wrong word—call him careless. You've seen the state of that cupboard, and you heard him admit it was time he cleared it out. Yet by next week it's certain he'll have changed his mind. Dear me, that's going back to being erratic. Still, it doesn't much matter—I dare say you'll follow."

In point of fact Beale was already doubtful about that, but endeavoured to look as if every word his companion uttered was crystal clear. He helped himself to another chocolate, an action which was regarded with approval, and waited patiently for Miss Charlotte to continue. When she did so, it was at a tangent.

"What he told you about Robert would just as well apply in his own case," she declared. "They're both cold-blooded; in fact, all the Weekes are. It's a sort of family taint. I'm no exception, either. I don't suppose I like one person in a hundred I meet, and for all I mind most of them could die on the spot. At any rate, Herbert doesn't care about people in general. So far as I know there's only one he'd go much out of his way to do anything for, and that one isn't me. I wonder,"—looking at him speculatively; "would you be able to make a guess, Mr. Beale?"

He felt that her question constituted a kind of test. If he refused, or failed, she might lose interest and not bother to help him. Fortunately, he had a shrewd idea of the correct answer.

"At a guess, then, Miss Charlotte, I should expect it to be the boy Edwin," he said, and knew by her sudden twinkling nod that he had satisfied her.

"Good for you!" she exclaimed indistinctly, munching. "And heaven only knows why, because I can tell you outright and without any sort of quibble that Edwin is one of the most repulsive children we've ever had here. You mustn't think I lack experience, either, for some of them have been unbelievable; boys who sniffed, boys who went about with jam on their ears, boys who cheated and stole and broke windows and rarely washed.

"However, it isn't Edwin's actions which count against him so much as his manner and character. He's sly, mentally dishonest, and incredibly greedy. If you want to know what he's really like, watch him watching someone else eating a bun or a toffee; you can almost see his mouth water. You needn't take my word about him, though. Ask any of the staff, and if you can persuade them you're not spying for Herbert I expect they'll tell you just the same thing."

Again she paused, reflectively.

"On second thoughts, perhaps you'd better not ask Miss Tilling, the governess," she advised. "It's likely to be a sore point with her. You see, Edwin is in her class—she takes all the small fry for everything. A fortnight ago she caught him looking at her markbook; quite naturally—and I say that although I don't greatly care for the girl—she smacked his head, since it wasn't by any means his first offence. Naturally but unwisely, because at that very moment in walked my brother and saw her. He was extremely cross, and earlier this evening he gave her notice. No,"—as Beale was about to speak, "don't start your questions yet. There'll be plenty of time later—I'm not particular when I go to bed. Come along, have another chocolate—you're not eating your share, you know.

"Now, a little while ago you were asking why anybody should wish to kill Edwin. It seems to me that there are three possible answers; because he's objectionable, because Maurice would inherit more money, or because someone supposes that his death would grieve the boy's father. The first answer gives you almost anybody as a suspect—I believe that's the correct term? Anybody but Herbert, that is. The second and third are quite a different pair of shoes, however. If you were to ask me who would do a murder to benefit Maurice, or who dislikes Sir Robert to the point of hatred, I should make the same reply in each case. Again, can you guess?"

"Yes, I think so," he said, glad that she was becoming more to the point. "I imagine your choice would be Lady Weekes."

"And you'd be right—have another chocolate. I suppose you're heard all about the divorce? Very well, let's consider if Lady Weekes could possibly be the person you're looking for. I need scarcely mention that I dislike the woman? In fact, you may take it that there's hardly anyone who might be connected with this affair that I do like. The point is, *could* Lady W. either have known about the bottle of cyanide, or, knowing, have taken it? She could certainly have removed the parcel, because I'm assured she was in the house at the time. Lloyd Gregory—that's the senior master—tells me that he saw her talking to Maurice in the boys' hall twenty minutes or so after my brother put the post on the table, and Gregory's quite reliable. He drinks, admittedly, but he doesn't drink in school hours."

Beale's patience was almost exhausted.

"Do please let me ask one question!" he begged. "Otherwise I may go and forget."

"Very well, just one."

"Thank you. Then, as well as being in a position to steal the parcel, was Lady Weekes also in a position to know the contents beforehand?"

"Oh, come!" said Miss Charlotte, a trifle tartly. "You surely don't suppose I credit her with second sight? What possible use would she have for the thing unless she did know what was in it? For instance, I don't imagine you can put poison in butterscotch, and I quite often have packets sent to me. Edinburgh Rock, too, for which I have a great liking. It's all a matter of discovering where the best supplies come from and getting the people to send direct. Stale confectionery is an abomination.

"Of course Lady W. knew the contents. I told her myself the same morning, Friday, that I was expecting some chocolate liqueurs from Paris, and hoped they'd arrive in good condition. We were talking about the post-office at the time, or Herbert was, and how careless they are with things. Either careless or deliberately destructive—I've never been able to decide which. At all events, intentional or not, you may take it as absolutely certain that she was well aware what would be inside any parcel addressed to me with French stamps on it."

"I see. And does your brother realize that?"

"He should do—he was in the room at the time, as I said. What you really mean is, if he knows, why hasn't he told you? I can only suppose he's too timid."

"Timid?"

"Exactly. You see, you might go to Lady W. and say 'Oh, I understand you knew a parcel of chocolates was expected—anyway, so Mr. Weekes tells me,' and that would place him in an awkward position, and Herbert tends to avoid awkward positions. The point is this, Mr. Beale,"—and she prodded the air with her forefinger. "In my opinion Herbert already suspects Lady W. on the facts, but can't wholly credit the possibility—or rather, doesn't want to credit it. Consider the scandal. Consider how Sir Robert would receive the information that his divorced wife may have been planning to poison his son by a second wife. Why, the two boys would be whisked away in no time, and what sort of a school is it from which the headmaster's own nephews have to be removed?"

"But consider the greater scandal if one of them were permanently removed by poison," suggested Beale quietly.

"Oh, I know; but that's your way of looking at it, not Herbert's. Still, I don't wish to wrong him. If you were to demand point-blank if Lady W. could have known, I don't doubt he'd tell you. Then he could truthfully say it was your idea and not his, and that would satisfy his conscience. He pays it great attention, you know."

"I understand. But what makes you think he suspects Lady Weekes? And do you mean only about the parcel, or about the cyanide as well? And where do the two 'accidents' come in?"

"I allowed you *one* question," Miss Charlotte reminded him good-humouredly. "However, once you begin perhaps you find it difficult to stop—habit again, I dare say. At any rate, I'll deal with the last one first. I know nothing of the accidents myself, because I was abroad at the time, but I gather from Robert that the culprit was probably a boot-boy whom he'd just dismissed. Herbert said something earlier about ill feeling in the village, and in that he was perfectly sincere because he doesn't know any better. You see, Robert isn't particularly fond of Edwin himself but knows that Herbert is, and on that account refrained from hurting his feelings. Unusually considerate of him, I thought.

"The truth of the matter was that Edwin saw the boot-boy kissing one of the maids, and promptly told the housekeeper. Did I say he was also a sneak? If not, I meant to. The housekeeper tackled the boy, who was impudent, so of course he had to go, and I understand he did so with no very pleasant feelings towards Edwin. After all, nobody likes a sneak, which was why Robert said nothing to Herbert. It all sounds most involved and quite trivial. If I were you I should disregard the whole thing."

"So your brother couldn't have suspected Lady Weekes then?"

"Oh good heavens no! Of course you haven't met her yet, but I can assure you she isn't the sort of woman to creep about in the dark with an air-gun. The idea's ridiculous."

"The boot-boy was never questioned?"

"No, for the very good reason that he wasn't available. He lived in Northumberland or somewhere remote, and presumably returned there after doing his best to get his own back. And now, why do I think Herbert suspects Lady W.? I'll tell you; because he dismissed Patricia Tilling today. There—does that leave you any wiser?"

He had to admit that it did not, and she chuckled.

"I thought it wouldn't," she remarked. "Still, I oughtn't to flummox you deliberately—this affair must be quite complicated enough without that. The explanation is that Miss Tilling happens to be a friend of Lady W.—was recommended by her for the post here, as a matter of fact."

"But I thought you said your brother gave her notice because she smacked Edwin's head?"

"So he did, so he did—ostensibly. But I don't believe that's the real reason myself, fond of the little toad as he is. In my opinion he intends the dismissal as a gesture to Lady W. 'Be careful what you're up to—I am alert.' "

Beale frowned, and from what he had seen of Herbert Weekes felt little inclined to agree with her.

"Is he capable of such subtlety?" he asked bluntly. "And is Lady Weekes the sort of woman to appreciate it?"

Miss Charlotte nodded and smiled, as if to say that the points were well raised.

"She is, but I'm not absolutely sure about him," she admitted. "All the same, I can't imagine what else it can be. You see, Herbert was furious with Miss Tilling after the face-smacking, and wanted to get rid of her on the spot. I told him not to be stupid, because she's very good at her job, and it would have meant engaging a stop-gap till the end of term, and all the stop-gaps I've ever met were simply deplorable. They know they aren't staying, and so they don't care how they behave. We had one woman who regularly combed her hair during prayers. In the end he worked round, and wrote her a short note to the effect that he was prepared to excuse the matter provided that nothing resembling it occurred again."

Beale looked, and felt, more puzzled than ever. He began to wonder if Miss Charlotte found some obscure delight in mystifying him.

"But how can he possibly forgive the offence at the time, and yet dismiss her for it a fortnight afterwards?" he demanded, and again his companion chuckled.

"Oh, there's nothing very extraordinary about that!" she assured him. " 'Dear Miss Tilling, after due consideration I have come to the regretful conclusion that after all it will be better if I make a change at the end of the term.' Something like that, very polite but equally definite."

"And if she produced her earlier note and began to argue?"

"It wouldn't help her. She's got two choices: to go quietly, with a good reference, or to go vowing vengeance and babbling of law-courts without a reference at all. And what chance has a penniless governess who's dependent on her job for existence against a headmaster? Why, even if she brought a case against him and won, it wouldn't do her the least good apart from any damages she might be awarded. Nobody would dream of engaging a possible litigant.

"Yes, I can see what you're thinking. It's a kind of moral blackmail—or immoral, if you prefer it. But that's how things stand, only I'm still convinced that Herbert has some other reason at the back of his mind besides the smacking. A hint to Lady W. is all I can think of, so I suppose that must be it. Needless to say I've asked him, but to no result. He declares the letter dismissing her expresses his whole feelings on the matter. He intends to keep his suspicions of Lady W. secret—I'm sure of that."

"And are you just as sure he doesn't suspect Miss Tilling in any way?" he asked.

"Of acting as Lady W.'s agent? I don't know—it's possible. Not that I do myself—I don't think she'd have let four terms go by without doing anything if that was what she came here for. Mind you, I'm not sticking up for the girl—she's no favourite of mine. Her skirts are too short, especially for cycling, and she turns down the pages of books. But there's a difference between not much liking people and being ready to believe they have criminal intentions."

"Of course," agreed Beale politely. "Then who has, Miss Weekes, in your opinion?"

"My dear man, haven't I told you? Lady W."

"Yes, you said she might have taken the chocolates, but what about the cyanide?"

"I haven't had a chance to deal with that yet," she retorted. "I can't talk and answer questions at the same time—I've only the one tongue."

He thought for a moment that he might have offended her, but a second or two later she was amiably unwrapping another chocolate and examining it attentively before putting it into her mouth.

"Have you any ideas on the subject yourself?" she asked presently; almost, he felt, as if she were able to read his mind.

"As it happens, yes," he answered. "Lady Weekes's married life occurred between the time your brother bought the poison fifteen years ago and the time he gave up photography, didn't it?"

"Good—good!" exclaimed Miss Charlotte. "You sound like a real detective, and it was extremely clever of you to remember that advertisement, by the way. Yes, the marriage took place during that period all right—'occurred' expresses it beautifully. What's more, she knew all about it—Herbert's photography, I mean. As a matter of fact, Mr. Beale, and this may surprise you, she even used to help him develop and print, or whatever it is people do. The two of them came here in the holidays now and again. We were more friendly with Robert in those days—he was younger, and less unpleasant than he is now. The divorce changed him a lot, and then the death of his second wife just about finished him as far as humanity went. Today he's a retired party spokesman with a very weak heart—no more, no less; a superannuated cog of the political machinery which misgoverns us all. Still, we'd better not start on *that* subject!

"Lady W. doubtless knew then that Herbert had some cyanide, and what sort of a bottle he kept it in; but of course I can't say if she would remember, or for how long."

But her tone showed that she had fully made up her own mind on the matter, and Beale smiled.

"Given the mental stimulus, I think we can assume the possibility," he observed, rather afraid that he was talking nonsense.

"She'd remember if she had any reason for wanting poison later? I consider it more than probable."

"Then it comes down to the question of opportunity. Since that cupboard was last cleared out, how many times has she been in a position to notice the bottle? And more particularly, how many times since she arrived here on Thursday has she had a chance to steal it?"

Miss Charlotte made a comical gesture of helplessness.

"How on earth do you expect me to know?" she demanded. "Until last night I'd no occasion to bother my head about when she was in this room and when she wasn't. She may easily have seen the thing when she was down here last tune—that would be at the Michaelmas half-term. Anyway, I know we had a lantern-lecture then, and the book of words got lost, and she helped Herbert make one up; all about the history of printing, incredibly dull. I dare say she was alone in here quite a lot, and if she wanted to nose round there was nobody to stop her. She could be pretty sure he wouldn't have thrown it away, too, because he keeps everything, and she might guess that the cupboard would be the best place to look."

"And this time? Presuming there's no question of the bottle's having been lost since last year?"

"No, I think not. The ring of dust seems recent, and in any case Herbert says he remembers seeing it within the last month or two. Well, Mr. Beale, frankly I'm afraid I can't help there. So far as I know, Lady W. hasn't been in this room at all since she came. Nevertheless, that doesn't settle the matter beyond dispute. Do you agree that if the same person took both chocolates and cyanide, then they were probably taken in that order?"

"Yes, that's how I've been working it out."

"Good, I'm glad you think the same. Myself, I should never be surprised to learn that it was the possibility of stealing the chocolates which started the whole thing. Liqueurs would make such an admirable disguise—cyanide tastes quite strongly of almonds, doesn't it? Then in that event she'd obviously take the greatest care *not* to be in here alone when anyone could catch her. She'd do the sensible thing; tiptoe downstairs in the middle of the night and take the bottle that way. Assuming she was already aware of its presence, of course. At least, that's what I should have done."

It was then, belatedly, that an idea struck Beale which he thought might materially alter the whole aspect of things; but he decided not to mention it for the moment.

"And now you'd better start asking your questions in earnest," Miss Charlotte remarked, after she had selected the largest of the few remaining chocolates. "I've told you everything that occurs to me."

"You've certainly given me a great deal of information," he responded warmly.

"Which you wouldn't have got elsewhere," she emphasized, and nodded several times as if pleased with herself.

('But why tell me?' he wondered. 'Spite? Nosiness? Genuine desire to help? And how reliable is it all? But I can worry about that afterwards.')

"First, something rather off the point," he continued, having obtained permission to smoke his pipe; his tongue was tired of the taste of chocolate.

"Why did your brother find it necessary to tell the staff I'm a policeman?"

Instantly Miss Charlotte sat bolt upright again.

"Did what?" she exclaimed. "Told the staff about you? My dear man, that's news to me, indeed it is! What in the world can he have been thinking of? I understood it was to be a deadly secret."

"So did I."

"How did you find out?"

"He informed Sir Francis this afternoon that he had thought it best."

"Ha! That's one of his stock phrases. There, the very first question you ask stumps me, and I'm sorry. I'll find out if I can, though, trust me."

"Thank you—I should rather like to know. And now something which has been bothering me quite a bit, Miss Weekes. Whoever took the chocolates must have known very well that there'd be a fuss about their disappearance. Then what chance is there likely to be of persuading Edwin to eat one?"

"Persuading? The difficulty would be to persuade him not to, if he got near one. He's quite the greediest boy in the school—probably in any school."

"Really? Even greedier than Piggy?"—and he explained what the governess had told him on the cricket field.

"Well, there isn't a lot to choose between them," admitted Miss Charlotte, "but I think Edwin just has it. Parker-Smythe—queer how people think two common things become quite exclusive when you join them, isn't it?—Parker-Smythe is only interested in food when he's hungry, but my nephew's capable of thinking ahead. He might be full to bursting-point—it has happened—but that wouldn't stop him laying in provisions for next time. I don't imagine it would be very hard to make him accept a chocolate, poisoned or otherwise."

"In spite of your brother's instructions?"

"Yes, in his particular case. You see, Herbert's inclined to favour him, as I may have hinted, and the little beast knows it. He'd think he probably wouldn't be found out, and that even if he were nothing much would happen to him, being Edwin. Of course, not one word has been breathed about poison."

"Of course not. Would it be possible to hide a chocolate where he'd be reasonable certain to find it sooner or later, and everyone else reasonably certain not to?"

"I can't say definitely, but I don't see why not. If it were put in his locker, for example—all the boys have separate ones where they keep their toys and stamps and letters and things. For anyone to be seen going to a locker which doesn't belong to him, with or without the owner's permission, is equivalent to imploring Herbert for a thrashing."

"Even in Edwin's case?"

"Well, let's hope so. Favouritism of any kind leaves a nasty taste, and the more so when it's nepotism of the most literal sort. My brother really is strict about the locker business, though; he calls it inculcating respect for other people's property. Or one could be put under Edwin's pillow, or in a pocket, but that wouldn't be so safe—Matron might find it. Or what would there be to stop Lady Weekes from handing him one, and assuring him it had nothing to do with the stolen parcel? Except that I suppose she wouldn't be able to get far enough away before he dropped down dead. Cyanide is very rapid in its effects, I believe?"

"Extremely rapid," agreed Beale with a smile. "Most people don't live more than a couple of minutes after an adequate dose—

five grains, say. Now, Miss Weekes, do you consider that the boys can be ignored as far as the theft of the chocolates goes?"

"Yes, emphatically, and of the poison too. You know my opinion."

"And that covers all the staff?"

"Yes, unless Miss Tilling did it on Lady W.'s behalf, which I don't believe. I should think the rest of them are above suspicion. Matron and the housekeeper have been here since before Edwin was born, and Lloyd Gregory too, if it comes to that. If he had it in him to turn murderer he'd have done it before now."

"And Mr. Birkett?"

"Oh, him! This is only his second term, but he hasn't the strength of character—he's quite harmless. Soft as they make 'em about Miss Tilling, but I don't hold that against him. She's not a bad-looking girl."

"Does he meet with any encouragement?" asked Beale. "He certainly said something about lending her a pencil this afternoon, but I don't remember seeing them together."

"You wouldn't—she doesn't fancy him. She'd very much rather have Lloyd Gregory, though it's hard to understand why."

"You dislike him too?"

"No, not especially, but he'll never get anywhere. He's thirty-five, and been here ten years all but a term. He has a degree, he's quite good with the boys, and his salary's £180, though I believe he also has a little money of his own. In my opinion, a man of his age and position who's content with that and his keep for eight months in the year can't have any ambition, and if you've no ambition and you're not over fifty you might as well be dead. If you're a man, anyway—it doesn't matter so much for a woman. They're not much good except for having children or nursing, and some of them aren't even good for that."

He fancied she referred indirectly to herself, but made no attempt to find out. Instead he reverted to the subject under discussion, with special reference to his recent idea.

"You said just now that if you were Lady Weekes, and wanted the cyanide, you'd have come downstairs to get it when everyone was asleep," he went on. "I wish you'd help me by going a little farther than that, and telling me what you'd have done when you had the cupboard door open."

She gave him a searching stare.

"Explain," she requested briefly. "What else should I do but take the bottle, shut the door, and creep back to bed?"

And then, as he still looked at her significantly and half smilingly, she spoke again.

"Oh, what a fool!" she cried. "What a fat-headed drivelling numbskull! Of course! Now I see just what you mean—why the devil didn't I think of that before? Excuse my language—it's lucky none of the boys can hear. Yes, Mr. Beale, now I'll answer sensibly, if you still think I'm worth listening to. I should have taken as much of the cyanide as I needed—say ten grains, to be on the safe side—and I should then have left the bottle precisely where it was before. Now why on earth didn't that happen? Why cause inevitable comment at some time or another by leaving nothing behind but a ring of dust?"

She regarded him intently, her blue eyes wide open.

"Go on, tell me," she urged, as he stayed silent. "You're a detective—you know why people do these things."

"I wish I did," he replied soberly. "As it is, one can only guess."

"Then guess; put yourself in the criminal's place, as all good detectives do. In books, at any rate."

"Very well, then either it never occurred to me to take the poison but leave the bottle—"

"Which isn't in the least likely, and a direct hit at me."

"Or something happened which made that impossible."

"Yes? What sort of something?"

"I might have dropped the bottle and broken it."

"Ah, I see; you think very thoroughly."

"Sometimes. There's another possibility, too. I don't imagine that anybody who was down here in the night would risk putting the light on. With a torch, or perhaps only a match, the state of the bottle might have been overlooked—its dustiness, I mean. I know you said the outside was corrugated, but that wouldn't apply to the part near the stopper, and quite possibly that would have been the only part to catch hold of it by if there were other things in front. Once the bottle was out of the cupboard, though, the question of fingerprints may have arisen in the mind of the person holding it."

Miss Charlotte pondered.

"But would that have made her take bottle and all?" she asked, refusing to be impersonal. "Wouldn't it have been a better move to dust it and replace it elsewhere? In the hope that by the time it was missed it would have acquired a second coat, of course. She knows how casual Herbert is."

"But apparently she didn't allow for the theft of the chocolates putting the idea of poison into his head. It's worth considering, though. In fact, there's no reason why we shouldn't explore the cupboard while we've got the chance and settle the point definitely, is there?"

She snatched at the last chocolate and rose.

"Yes, let's do that," she agreed. "You know, I don't believe anybody thought of looking anywhere else; the ring in the dust seemed so conclusive."

They found the missing bottle within three minutes, on the shelf below the one on which it was supposed to stand. It was hidden from view behind a broken pipe-rack, and confounded the expectations of both by appearing not to have been touched for weeks. It had certainly not been cleaned lately, and, more amazing still, when it was lifted out it left behind a clean circle in the surrounding grime identical with that on the shelf above.

VII

BEALE WAS AWAKENED the next morning by the persistent ringing of a bell. The sound was so loud, and went on for so long, that he began to think there must be a fire. Then there came a tap at his door, and a maid announced the presence of hot water.

"Breakfast is at eight o'clock, sir," she told him, and since the time by his watch was only 7.15 he decided that he could lie in bed for at least another quarter of an hour.

He had retired the night before with distinctly mixed feelings. The discovery of the bottle, coming after so much discussion and the supply of so much information from Miss Charlotte, had seemed something of an anti-climax. Herbert Weekes's apparently dumbfounded amazement had done little to remove the impression, while the Assistant-Commissioner's undisguised relief proved unexpectedly annoying.

'As if the presence of the blessed bottle need mean anything!' thought Beale now, still rather displeased. 'I'm prepared to agree it's probably the same one, but I shall want to be emphatically assured it still contains potassium cyanide, and also that there's enough of the stuff to make theft seem unlikely. It's no good relying much on Herbert—he's too careless. And who or what was responsible for the other ring in the dust? I could bear to be told. The man swears he never had two similar bottles, and I suppose he ought to remember.

'Then there are the chocolates, and nobody can explain *them* away. Chocolates just don't get on to old ladies' knitting-needles by accident. It was quite cleverly done, all the same. Whoever it was probably took just a few out with him, and had an odd glove in his pocket to avoid leaving his prints—there certainly don't look to be any on what were found. Then he merely seized any favourable opportunity to get rid of the things.

'Yes, somebody was amusing himself or herself there all right, but I hope I don't have to find out who. Unless that would be the same thing as finding out who took the parcel, where there are fewer people to choose from. The thief must have known what was inside, and it appears that nobody possessed that knowledge beforehand but Herbert and Charlotte and Lady Weekes. Herbert seems hardly worth considering—only a lunatic would deliberately invite investigation. His sister simply couldn't have done the distributing, in view of her position on the field and her lameness, and she doesn't strike me as the sort of woman who'd have an accomplice. What she did she'd do on her own, and in any case I doubt if she'd dream of committing murder; she'd have too much sense.

'That leaves Lady W., as she calls her, and that's where I may come unstuck. Lady W. has at least three contacts in the school which oughtn't to be overlooked: her son Maurice, Edwin himself, and Miss Tilling. The points for query are, how much control has she over the first two, and how well does she know the governess? Not that I shall find out, since I've got to be tactful above everything. They don't want a policeman here; they should have sent for a cross between a high-class shopwalker and a clairvoyant.'

He lay for a few moments staring idly at the ceiling, upon which half a dozen flies arranged themselves in ever-differing patterns. Then he reached out for his pipe and pouch, and his thoughts reverted to Miss Charlotte.

'Why should she take a fancy to me?' he asked himself as he stuffed in the tobacco. 'I'm sure I didn't go an inch out of my way to be nice to her. Of course, that may just possibly be the reason. Also, how reliable is *she?* Anyway, she's obviously got more go than Herbert, though I'd like to see him with the boys. If he's not more impressive with them than he is with grown-ups, I shan't think much of him as a headmaster. She doesn't seem to think much of him at all, which may be significant. Only if her opinion's worth anything, though, which brings me back to where I started.

'At any rate, her manner was convincing enough, even if the matter wasn't entirely above comment. For instance, she says that Edwin's disgustingly greedy, but one might justly accuse her of the same fault herself. I never saw anybody eat so many chocolates at a sitting, and apparently enjoy the last as much as the first. Still, I once smoked a quarter of a pound of tobacco in two days, so I suppose I mustn't point my finger.

'Anything else? If I were trying to crab her evidence? Well, she was very pat with her description of the bottle, and the date it was bought, and she admits to reminding Herbert about the cyanide. That might be a clever move in some obscure plot to arouse suspicion, allay it, and then administer the poison in peace and quiet. There's no policeman so armless as a satisfied policeman, they say, which probably accounts for all the jokes about cooks. As well, she was the one who ordered the chocolates in the first place, and as she said herself, a liqueur filling would be ideal for covering up unusual flavours. Again, it was she who told Lady Weekes about expecting a parcel from France, and what would be in it. Further, she didn't offer a shred of proof that her brother ever suspected the woman for a moment.

'Anything in all that, separately or collectively? I doubt it, even throwing in the apparent abandonment of her normal hostility, perhaps so that she could deliver a wad of inside information. She managed to insert quite a bit, too; that Lloyd Gregory drinks, though I happened to know that already, that the governess doesn't wear long enough skirts and ill-treats books and is keen on him, and Birkett on her, that boys mustn't go to other boys' lockers, and all the rest of it. That's probably in her favour, though. If she were trying to prime me with something she particularly wanted me to know, she wouldn't mix it with a lot of irrelevant news in case I got overloaded, and absorbed only half of what mattered.

'Yes, I think I can go by what she says, or at least feel sure she believes it herself. I expect the truth is that she saw a chance to play the detective for once instead of reading about detection, and took it in her stride. A queer old thing, and I dare say she could strike pretty hard with that tongue of hers if she felt like it; really hard, not the mere flicks she gave Barton.'

He arrived downstairs at what he imagined was five minutes to eight, overlooking the fact that school clocks are rarely correct and generally slow.

"Ha, good morning!" Herbert Weekes greeted him, as he stood at the foot of the private staircase rather uncertainly wondering where to go. "Sleep well? That's good. I don't mind telling you I did too—better than upon the two previous nights. I don't honestly recall that I was ever so relieved about anything as about the discovery of that bottle last night. I'm exceedingly grateful to you for your acumen."

'Good lord, what a word to use before breakfast!' thought Beale.

"Perhaps you'd better defer compliments till we've had the contents tested, sir," he said aloud, and the remark brought a momentary frown to the headmaster's carefully shaven face.

"Um! Yes, I suppose you're right—it won't do to be too precipitate. Still, the bottle hadn't been touched recently—a child could see that. The whole affair is most extraordinary. I wish I could think what may have made the first ring of dust—the one on the second shelf down which I took to mark the place where it had been standing. You know, it's a terrible thing to say, but I sometimes fancy my memory is becoming just the least degree defective. Is that attributable to the ravages of time, I wonder? I was fifty-four last birthday."

"When I attain that age we'll compare notes," suggested Beale gravely, but Herbert merely stared. He was dressed in a dark suit, and his visitor, realizing for the first time that it was Sunday, felt glad that he too was soberly clad.

"Well," said the head, glancing at a grandfather clock in the corner, "I'm about to take prayers—will you join us? And before breakfast I propose to enquire if any further discoveries have come to light. Or would you prefer not to be present?"

"I don't think I'd better," agreed Beale. "I might start asking questions before I remembered not to."

"Very well, perhaps you'll wait in the drawing-room, then. It would be better than walking in the garden—the boys might see you, and that would never do."

He walked away without offering to explain why, and Beale moved towards the appropriate door. Inside the room he had a surprise, for standing at the window in the sunlight was Lady Weekes.

She turned immediately, stared for a second from large brown eyes, and then smiled.

"Good morning," she said. "Have you solved the mystery yet, Mr. Beale? Or is that an indiscreet question?"

"Extremely indiscreet," he told her lightly, wondering how much she knew about him.

"Then I'm sorry, but I'm afraid discretion has never been my strong point."

She was dressed in pale green silk, and he saw that she was probably younger than he had supposed the previous afternoon. He also suspected that she was intelligent and alert; her manner made it seem likely.

"By the way," she went on, with only the slightest pause, "I had the misfortune to lose a box of matches yesterday. Would you advise me to employ a private detective, or to consult Scotland Yard?"

He smiled, gathering her meaning, and felt inclined to like her.

"Why not advertise and offer a reward?" he said. "Were they specially nice matches?"

"I don't know—I hadn't tried them. Which is why I want them back, of course. That's only sensible, isn't it? After all, why else should anyone bother about something which could easily be replaced? Perishable things, I mean, such as chocolates for example."

"Oh, there *could* be other reasons," he asserted quietly. "I don't think it would do for me to mention any, though."

'No? That's a pity—it sounds as if you aren't interested in my troubles."

He decided to be less cautious.

"Did you expect me to be?" he asked.

"Of course. I'd tell you why, if we had time, only they'll be out of prayers soon."

"And won't there be another opportunity?"

She shook her head, and her dark smooth hair moved slightly.

"I'm afraid not. I shall be out with my son all day, and this evening I'm returning to town."

"Really? I didn't know that."

"But why should you have known?" she countered quickly, and he saw that he had made a slip.

"No, I suppose not," he agreed lamely, hoping that she would not press the point.

"In any case you can always get in touch with me in London if you want to," she continued, smiling again. "And I admit it's a change from my original plans, but then, circumstances alter cases, as they say in the copy-books."

"Yes?" he murmured, and she laughed outright.

"So I'm not the only one who's curious!" she remarked, with an air of satisfaction. "Inquisitive, I mean, not peculiar. If you're really interested—this time—I'm going this evening instead of tomorrow because I haven't the least desire to spend another night here. And if you don't know why, perhaps it'll make it clearer to say that I shan't be returning alone, and that quite early in the morning I shall probably see a solicitor."

"Well, not absolutely clear," he said, "unless you mean on your passenger's behalf?"

"Yes, I see you've heard about the business. Ah, here they come,"—as the rumble of concerted footsteps reached their ears. "Don't forget to telephone me if you feel like another chat one day—I shall be in town till the first week in July. And good luck with the hunt. And don't forget to look out for my match-box."

The opening was too tempting to be missed.

"Now that wasn't what you said to begin with!" he reminded her, smiling. "A few moments ago it was a box of matches."

"Why, what's the difference?" she demanded, looking puzzled.

"Well, a match-box might contain spiders, say, or paper-clips or halfpenny stamps or aspirins."

For a second she frowned, then nodded.

"Thank you—that helps," she told him. "Yet those were real chocolates they found yesterday, weren't they?"

"Ostensibly. May I ask why you expect me to know?"

"It's obvious, surely. You came down with the Assistant-Commissioner, and you were the person they shouted for when things began to happen. You're a policeman right enough, so it won't be any use pretending you aren't—at least, not with me. Not because you've got big feet or look like one; I dare say you're one of the higher-ups, and I probably ought to have said police official."

"No, not official. This is a holiday, or supposed to be. I hope you haven't persuaded too many people to your way of thinking?"

"Of course not—it's none of my business who you are. All the same I'd like to know *why* you're here, as I may have hinted. And I'm not sure I couldn't make a pretty good guess, after your remark just now. Still, again it's none of my business, though it was certainly rather amusing yesterday. I was simply terrified I should find *I'd* sat on one of the wretched things!"

Then the door opened, and her face immediately became grave; all trace of her smile had gone, and the lines about her mouth were prominent. Herbert Weekes came in, to say that breakfast was ready. As the bell began to ring again he bade Lady Weekes good morning in a voice which was just too hearty; but he need not have bothered. She gave him the smallest of nods, and swept by as if she suspected him of being a leper.

After the meal, during which Beale was subjected to the constant and speculative scrutiny of the whole school, he had a short talk with Sir Francis and the headmaster. Two more chocolates had been found, one in the matron's work-basket in her sitting-room on the first floor and the other on the schoolroom mantelpiece, and it was decided that an effort should be made to locate the rest.

"Thirty-four, to be precise," said Herbert Weekes, and Beale sighed; he foresaw a dull day ahead.

"Do all the boys go out?" he asked.

"All but five; one of whom is my younger nephew, incidentally. I understood he was to have joined Lady Weekes and Maurice, but it appears I must have been mistaken."

And with that he wriggled his neck against his collar furiously, giving the impression that he could have said a lot more if he had chosen.

"What happens to the odd men out?" enquired Sir Francis. "Likely to be any use? And do they include Malcolm?"

"Why, no. I suppose you would wish to spend the day with him as usual."

"Oh, nonsense! For one thing I've no car here, and for another I'd call that shirking. Malcolm can jolly well join in too, if that's all right with you?"

Herbert Weekes assented with a gracious nod, and went on to suggest that the five boys he had mentioned were likely to be more hindrance than help.

"Oh, not necessarily," said Beale, anxious to enlist as many hands as possible. "At least they'd know their way about." Eventually it was arranged that the two elder ones, Lillywhite and Askew, should stay behind, while Mr. Birkett took the others, including Edwin, for a picnic.

"Strictly speaking, they ought to attend church first," observed the head, with an attempt at humour, "but I think that for once we may honour that custom in the breach."

"And the staff?" pursued Beale deliberately. "Miss Tilling and Mr. Gregory?"

He was given a cold stare which clearly implied that he asked too many questions.

"Ah, well, Mr. Gregory is naturally free to do as he pleases, being off duty. As for my governess, I think I had better be frank with you. She is—ahem, she has decided to leave me at ridiculously short notice. Briefly, she has informed me of her intention to return to London this evening with Lady Weekes. It's a regrettable affair, but any significance it may have is purely domestic in its bearing, and I feel I need scarcely trouble you with the details."

And, suddenly rather red in the face, he turned round and walked heavily away.

"Well, well!" murmured Sir Francis, gazing after him. "Know anything about it?" he added, to Beale.

"Yes, quite a bit—enough to appreciate his reticence over details. But I don't see why he wants to stump off like that—we haven't settled a blessed thing."

"No, I suppose we haven't. I'll go after him—any ideas?"

"Do you think you could get him to give us the run of this place and keep himself out of the way? We'd get on a lot faster, I shouldn't wonder, and I don't mind saying that the sooner I've finished here the better I'll be pleased. I want to find out what's in that bottle, and how much, and if that's satisfactory I hope you'll let me go back to real crime."

"He was promised a murder, and he's sore because it hasn't happened yet!" laughed the Assistant-Commissioner. "All right, provided we find the chocolates I'll let you off telling me who dumped them. Get anything from the old dragon last night?"

"Mr. Beale and I had a most instructive discussion," declared Miss Charlotte crisply from behind him; whereupon Sir Francis gasped, flushed violently, muttered, "Good God! I mean, good morning," and fled from the room.

VIII

"A MOST PECULIAR PERSON to hold such a responsible post," said the dragon, who had not appeared at breakfast. She spoke calmly, and was opening her familiar black handbag.

"Have a chocolate?" she added. "I hope you slept well? And I hope you're looking after that bottle?"

"It's under lock and key," he assured her. "For the time being its adventures are over."

"That's just as well. Have you heard about Miss Tilling?"

"Yes, your brother mentioned the matter just now, and so did Lady Weekes, indirectly."

"So you've met her! Well, Mr. Beale, there may be some small unpleasantness, but on the whole I'm greatly relieved. You see, Lady W. swears she'll never set foot in Anstey Court again as long as she lives, and after that it won't matter. In any event she would have only one more half-term available—I forgot to tell you that last night. Maurice will be leaving in a year's time, and since she comes every other term that would mean early next March. Have another chocolate."

He took one, and she smiled unexpectedly.

"It'll be a change from your pipe," she said. "Now, I don't suppose you'll be staying here a minute longer than you need. Some people telephoned this morning and invited me out for the day, so I probably shan't have another chance of talking to you. I spoke to my brother this morning about telling the staff who you are, and he says he did it because he particularly wanted to avoid their finding out by accident. That might very well have happened, he says, if you'd been the usual sort of plain-clothes policeman, and the discovery might possibly have led to the belief that he suspected one of them."

"Why?" asked Beale, as she paused.

"Well, I can't pretend I see the point myself in its entirety. Apparently he reasoned that they wouldn't expect a detective to bother about mere chocolates, *unless* those chocolates had been stolen by an adult."

"You mean that a dishonest member of the staff would have to go, whereas a dishonest boy could be walloped and put up with?"

"Exactly. Whether that was Herbert's real reason or not I naturally don't know—I pass it on for what you may think it's worth. And now I must go, if you've nothing else you want to ask me?"

"Only one thing, Miss Weekes," said Beale, glad that he had remembered. "How did you get hold of the French magazine which advertised the chocolates?"

"Oh, that! No mystery there, I'm afraid. It's a most respectable publication called *La Voix de France,* and I've been taking it regularly every month for the last ten years. No, you won't find much to help you in that direction. It didn't arrive suspiciously from nowhere with the advertisement underlined in blue pencil or anything."

"But the fact that you take the magazine is fairly common knowledge among your friends and relations?"

"Ha!" exclaimed Miss Charlotte, her eyelids drooping in what might almost have been a double wink. "I thought of that too, but the trouble is that Lady W. knows no French. Or so she says."

Sir Francis came back when Beale was safely alone again with the news that they were free to explore the school as they pleased.

"Only we mustn't take the boys anywhere they don't normally go," he said. "Just fancy that old wretch popping in then!"

He glanced warily round to make sure that she had not reappeared, and his smile was self-conscious.

"You're a detective," he remarked. "You might try to find out some time why she's got her knife into me—I simply can't imagine. By the way, the boys had no *Telegraph* on June 6th, so it seems that Herbert must have chucked it in the cupboard as she suggested. When d'you think you'd like to start?"

"As soon as everybody's out of the way," declared Beale. He walked to the window and looked out; in the drive were half a dozen cars, and several boys in grey-flannel suits obviously waiting to be collected.

"Well, I don't expect that'll be long—it's a glorious day."

"It might have been."

"Now, don't start repining—I'll make it up to you somehow. Ah, there's Lloyd Gregory—wonder where he's off to? A pub, I dare say. Will you want to see him? If so, better do it now, or you mayn't have the chance."

"I hope not," agreed Beale firmly, and went outside to where the senior master was chatting to three or four of the boys. At his approach they politely raised their speckled straw hats and departed with reluctant curiosity, while Gregory came forward smiling. He wore fight tweeds despite the heat, and had a camera slung over his broad shoulders. Remembering Miss Charlotte's remarks the previous evening, Beale scrutinized him closely, and decided that his face fitted in with her account of his character. The mouth was rather too full, the chin not quite firm enough; nevertheless, he seemed entirely pleasant in a slightly cynical way.

"Snatching a few hours off?" he asked, and Gregory nodded.

"One does while one can, in this game," he said. "I shall walk till I start steaming. Then I shall have a drink. Then I shall curl up under a tree somewhere and doze. After that heaven will doubtless direct, it being Sunday. Anything I can do for you before I go?"

"Only to say if you or the other chap mind if I rout round your rooms? I've got the job of finding the rest of those confounded chocolates, and I'm probably expected to do it thoroughly."

Lloyd Gregory laughed.

"Rather you than me! Yes, look where you like as far as I'm concerned. I shouldn't think there'll be many where I sleep—hardly anywhere to put a spare stud; nor in the masters'-room, but one never knows. Any use asking what it's all about?"

"Not much—I only wish I had an idea. Personally I believe it's a plot to spoil my week-end."

"Ah. You know what people are saying, I suppose?"

"No, but as a matter of fact I'd very much like to. The boys, do you mean?"

"Boys and staff. The current theory is that the chocolates were probably poisoned; otherwise there seems no reasonable explanation of your presence. Does the suggestion receive any marks?"

Beale hesitated, and then smiled.

"Seven out of ten, perhaps," he admitted, and the other nodded.

"That's a good percentage for Anstey Court," he observed. "Your turn for a question, I fancy."

"Thanks, then does the theory go into details at all? Deal with motive and villain and intended victim?"

"Only in an amateurish way. See that nemesia?"—pointing to a nearby flower-bed. "I mean the orange affair with the bare stem and cluster of blooms at the top. If they were all different colours it would be a perfect answer, the stem being the common idea and the flowers the lurid details. Everybody's got his own version, but most of 'em are too silly to take any notice of. The two principal schools of thought might interest you, though. One says the chocolates—poisoned, of course—were sent by some old-boy who particularly disliked Miss Charlotte in the hope she'd eat same and pass on. The other supposes she sent them to herself, or got someone else to do it for her, rather, and then pinched the parcel, and that if you hadn't butted in we'd all be moribund by now."

"Good lord!" remarked Beale, startled. "Do I gather she isn't popular?"

"Does anybody love the tongue which lashes him? Irrespective of height, size, colouring, or creed, so far as one can tell. The trouble with her—in confidence, of course—is that some fellow let her down badly when she was young, and she's never got over it. Not actually at the church door, but within sound of the bells as you might say. Anyway, that's how the story goes, though some declare it to be a fable on the ground that she could never have possibly been young enough.

"But it's too decent a day to talk scandal, and here's Mrs. Solomons,"—as an enormous Rolls swept towards the house. "A preposterous woman—mind if we walk the other way? I had too much of her yesterday, far too much. Last time she was here one of the kids' sisters trod on her toe, and you ought to have heard the language! Enough to give the poor child a complex for the rest of her life. Still, I said I wouldn't talk scandal. Sure there's nothing else I can do? Right, then I'll push along."

He smiled, turned to go, and then swung on his heel as if he had just remembered something; but Beale fancied the action was too studied to be genuine.

"I say, there's something you might be able to do for me, if you cared to," he remarked. "Don't answer if you'd rather not, but can you possibly tell me why our governess has been crying her eyes out? I tried to speak to her last night, but she dashed off sobbing, and this morning she looks like death."

Beale nodded, wondering how he could best reply; or if, indeed, he ought to do so at all. The girl was presumably capable of explaining the position to Lloyd Gregory herself if she felt inclined, and she might not thank a stranger to interfere in her affairs. But something in the senior master's manner indicated that, as well as being no mere afterthought, the matter might be important to him; that for some reason he found Miss Tilling's behaviour of considerable interest.

"Why do you ask?" he temporized, trying to look as if he had a good idea of the reason, and only needed confirmation to be informative.

Gregory shifted as though embarrassed, but his voice was still almost casual.

"Oh, I don't know. I don't like seeing people so obviously and utterly miserable. I—I wondered if there was anything I could do. Tell me what the trouble is, please, if you can. It can't be anything to do with those cursed chocolates?"

"No, nothing like that. All the same, the circumstances are a trifle out of the ordinary. Look here, I'll make a bargain with you. Give me your word that your enquiry's prompted by something more than just curiosity, and I'll see if I can persuade Miss Tilling to tell you herself."

By now his companion was regarding him intently, his face grave.

"I don't know why the devil I should tell you, but I happen to be quite fond of her," he muttered, glancing away as he spoke as if he were afraid his eyes might overrun his tongue.

"Thanks," said Beale. "If you wait somewhere round, I'll try to do my share."

With a friendly smile he walked away, entered the house, and immediately met the matron. Her identity was clear from her dress, though he had not been previously introduced. By the look of her, he thought, she was probably the sort of woman to whom Herbert Weekes would never bother to introduce anyone.

"Ah, good morning!" he greeted her genially. "Could you please tell me where to find Miss Tilling?"

Miss Wood stared at him with rather frightened eyes.

"Oh yes, of course," she agreed, nodding quickly. "She's upstairs—I'll say you'd like to speak to her. Or you could go up—she's in the junior class-room, and it's quite empty else. Shall I show you the way? I don't suppose you're learnt where all the different rooms are yet."

'Yet?' he thought. 'Good heavens, how long does she imagine I'm staying?'

Aloud he thanked her, and was led up a flight of narrow brass-bound stairs to a landing which seemed the focus of innumerable passages. At the far end of one an open door permitted him to see a row of iron beds neatly covered with white counterpanes.

The junior class-room was light and airy. It contained a blackboard and easel, eight small single desks, and one bigger one at which the governess was sitting. She looked up hurriedly at Beale's entry; then attempted a smile. For a moment he found it difficult to realize that she was the same girl who had talked to him so gaily on the field the afternoon before. Then she had been cheerful and quite pretty; now her blue eyes were slightly bloodshot, and her fair hair seemed dully lifeless.

"Looking for me?" she asked in a low voice. "Here's another chocolate, by the way—I just found it in the chalk-box."

She held it out, a *cognac* still wrapped in silver paper, and he took it with a smile.

Thank you—that makes one fewer to hunt for," he said. "Yes, I *was* looking for you—the matron told me you were in here. Do you mind very much if I ask one or two questions?"

"Of course not—I was going to find out if you wanted to, anyway. You see, I'm leaving today—going back to London with Lady Weekes."

He made no effort to pretend that the news surprised him.

"Yes, I was given to understand as much. Do you know her well, then?"

"Fairly; she was at school with my elder sister."

"I see. Naturally you're upset about going?"

"Because I've been crying? Don't take any notice of that. And I haven't been kicked out by sunset or anything. I *could* stay here till the end of term, only I don't think I want to. It's all because I smacked Edwin Weekes a fortnight ago; but I don't suppose you're interested in my troubles."

"I'd like to raise one point, though. I always thought that assistant masters—and presumably governesses as well—were entitled to half a term's notice the first term, and a full one thereafter."

She nodded.

"You're quite right," she said. "That's the normal arrangement, but not here. Mr. Weekes makes everyone sign a sort of form saying that half a term will be sufficient on either side at any time. Even Mr. Gregory's on the same footing, and he's been here ten years.

"Really? Do you know why?"

"No, just a fad, I suppose. He does odd things like that occasionally—I believe he thinks it impresses people. But that sounds thoroughly catty—sorry."

"I don't mind, so long as you aren't catty about me. Now, may I ask a personal question without having to explain why?"

"Certainly, but I don't promise I'll answer."

"Oh, you probably won't find it very difficult—I'm not trying to be purposely nosy. All I want to know is whether your leaving here today is your own idea or someone else's?"

She remained silent for a moment, looking at him wonderingly.

"It's a good job you put in the bit about not explaining," she told him with a smile, "otherwise I'd insist. To be truthful, the idea was chiefly Lady Weekes's. It's all a bit complicated, because after the smacking business Mr. Weekes first of all wanted to get rid of me on the spot. Not because he disapproves of smacking, but because it was Edwin—he simply dotes on the child. You could knock the rest of them about till their heads rattled—sometimes he does himself; but you mustn't lay a finger on darling Edwin, and of course he's the very one who needs it most. Somebody'll throttle the little wretch one day if he doesn't improve. But perhaps you've met him?"

"Not yet, but I've been told about him."

"I don't doubt it. Anyway, someone persuaded Mr. Weekes not to behave as if it was the end of the world—probably Miss Charlotte, because she's about the only one he'd take any notice of. Eventually he said the matter could drop, provided nothing like it happened again, and I've got a note from him to that effect. I agreed that it shouldn't, and of course it hasn't, in spite of the most terrific temptation; and then yesterday evening another note turns up saying he thinks I'd better go after all. At the end of a day like yesterday, when I'd been running round till my feet ached being sociable to a blasted lot of snobs, it was enough to make anybody sick. Lady Weekes maintains he can't possibly sack me after agreeing not to, and she's all for kicking up a fuss. It was her influence that got me the job here, incidentally, and I expect she thinks she ought to have been consulted."

"What sort of a fuss? Suing him for breach of contract or something?"

The governess stared glumly at her desk.

"If the solicitors approve," she said. "All the same, I'm not quite convinced it's a good thing to do. It might make it very hard for me to get another post, and—and—"

"And?"

"Oh, nothing. The truth is I'm not sure I want to leave. I mean, the pay's quite good, and I've been in worse schools."

But he knew that the reasons she put forward were not the real ones. Her bearing was suddenly too defiant, and a few seconds later she clearly regretted having spoken.

"But surely you could change your mind?" he suggested.

"Yes, I dare say, but I'd feel a bit of a fool, and anyway nobody seems to care much one way or the other."

Mentally he equated nobody with Lloyd Gregory, and had an unexpected vision of himself as an unofficial match-maker instead of as a professional sleuth hard on the trail of thirty-three missing chocolates. He made no move for the moment, however. Instead he became more businesslike.

"Now, about these things," he said, jogging the *cognac* up and down in his hand. "What's your own opinion, Miss Tilling? Who stole the parcel? Who's been spreading the contents round the school? Also, why?"

She laughed then, and at once looked younger and prettier.

"Anyone would think *I* was the detective!" she remarked.

"And why shouldn't you be? At least you've a lot more local knowledge to guide you than I have."

"Yes, that's true, but I can't really pretend I understand the affair a bit. At first I thought it must be one of the boys, for the sake of the French stamps—some of them are desperately keen. During the summer term they don't bother at most schools—they go in for butterflies or cricket averages or producing the biggest sunflower, but here they don't seem to slack off at all. If you went into the playground with a three-cornered Cape-of-Good-Hope in your pocket, and the boys knew, you'd probably get torn to pieces. That was my first idea, but now it doesn't seem so likely. I don't think a boy could have been responsible for scattering the chocolates round, and I'm sure none of them would have dared put one in Miss Charlotte's lap."

"Who told you about that?" he asked quickly, but she only smiled.

"Oh, I heard!" she said. "Not much can go on in a school that isn't common knowledge pretty soon. Why, if there was an exam about who and what you are, Mr. Beale, I think there'd be forty-one correct answers. Carmichael, one of the bigger boys, came up to me yesterday on the field and said 'Oh Miss Tilling, do you know if that man in the grey suit is one of the Big Four?' "

He laughed, rather relieved than otherwise at the news. It confirmed the hint he had already had from Lloyd Gregory.

Would that be inside information, or natural acuteness?" he enquired. "Or is it just that nobody could ever mistake me for anything but a policeman in plain clothes?"

"Oh no!" she told him quickly, shaking her head. "Why, you look quite ordinary. I think it's acuteness, as you call it. Boys *can* be intelligent, you know, so long as it's nothing to do with lessons.

"Well, I'm glad to learn how I stand—thank you for telling me. And now you can't make out who's responsible for the mystery?"

"No. And what's more, if I'm allowed to be perfectly honest, I can't for the life of me imagine why Scotland Yard should be interested."

"This part of it isn't," he answered firmly. "It's bored to tears, but unfortunately it has to do what it's told, and it's been told to find the beastly things. That comes of Assistant-Commissioners having sons and sending 'em to the wrong schools; and, perhaps, of having headmasters with no sense of humour. It strikes me at present that somebody's been taking a rise out of Mr. Weekes, and he doesn't appreciate the attention."

"Yes, it's possible," she agreed, apparently accepting his deceitful explanation of his presence. "Only, who?"

He shrugged.

"That's what I'm hoping somebody else will tell me," he said. "Detectives aren't magicians or thought-readers—not in real life. They have to go about pestering people for information and ideas and some sort of fuel to bite on. It's a pity; in a well-organized world I should merely have to sit down, smoke three pipes in absolute silence, and get up with an explanation that satisfied everybody including myself. It was all done by a left-handed Javanese who smoked Indian hemp and beat his wife with a snakeskin from 4.00 to 4.30 on alternate Wednesday afternoons.

"But I mustn't waste your time like this. Tell me one more thing, and I'll start work. Is there anybody at Anstey Court, boy or adult, who's suspected of being or known to be a practical joker?"

The governess answered without hesitation.

" 'Practical jokes are manifestations of a puerile or undeveloped intellect, and in the worst possible taste,' " she told him primly. " 'They are classifiable with puns and so-called funny stories about an Englishman, an Irishman, and a Scotchman, as among the lowest forms of humour yet invented. I shall be pained to discover any kindred activity among those present.' Rough quotation from beginning-of-term address by Herbert Weekes. The beginning of every term," she added, smiling, and then became serious.

"Does that qualify for help, Mr. Beale?" she asked. "Because if so, I wish you'd let me ask you a question."

"Of course," he agreed, expecting a further query about his presence; but he was wrong.

"Thanks. Then, if you were me—I mean I—would you go or stay?"

He at once recalled his promise to the senior master, and thought swiftly.

"That was partly what I came to see you about," he said, to her evident surprise. "If I were you, Miss Tilling, I shouldn't finally decide till I'd talked the matter over with somebody who's more than a little upset because I burst into tears and ran away when he asked me what was up."

"*Oh!*" she exclaimed, her face scarlet.

"You'll probably find Mr. Gregory in the garden," he added. "He asked me if I could help him. I very politely said 'Why do you want to know, and if it's curiosity you can go on wanting,' and he assured me solemnly that it wasn't, and offered a satisfactory reason, so I murmured something about suggesting to you that you might tell him yourself if you felt like it. I hope I wasn't too interfering?"

She shook her head, and he saw that her eyes were shining.

"What was the reason?" she asked softly.

"Oh, *you* must find that out," he said, moving towards the door.

"In the garden?" she repeated as she went by. "Thank you—thank you very much."

And, a moment later, he was alone.

IX

"COO, SIR!" EXCLAIMED ASKEW, as they searched the lockers.

"What's the matter?" enquired Beale. "Found another?"

"No sir, but young Heathfield's got my pen-knife. Look sir, there it is, and I've been hunting for it for weeks, and he *said* he never knew where it was. D'you think I could take it, sir?"

"Oh lord, don't ask me! I'm not even to know you ever had a pen-knife, you know. Couldn't you ask Heathfield himself later?"

Askew sighed, and then smiled cheerfully.

"All right sir—sorry. I'll say somebody told me he's got it, and jolly well make him show me his locker. That'd be pretty nearly true, sir, wouldn't it?"

"Pretty nearly," agreed Beale gravely. "Now, who inhabits No. 23?"

"Maurice Weekes, sir. Ah, Lily's found another one!"

"Under Marston's stamp album, sir," said Lillywhite, who had been given express permission to examine the belongings of the smaller boys by himself. He was tall, fair, and not unhandsome; more serious and rather less friendly than Askew, but probably more reliable, Beale thought. Both boys seemed to be enjoying the search, and so far he too was finding it less dull than he had expected. There was something novel in coming face to face with the treasured possessions of youth again: cameras and magnifying glasses and models of aeroplanes and racing cars; ancient copies of *The Cricketer* and fretwork sets; boxes of draughts and halma and decaying butterflies; miniature cannon which fired ball-bearings and were capable, according to Askew, of knocking down a small dummy tank.

There were more advanced items also: books explaining the principles and workings of internal-combustion engines, elaborate meccano sets, blueprints for the construction of simple wireless receivers. He suspected that he could have learnt a good deal from some of the pupils of Anstey Court, and wondered if the idea had ever occurred to Lloyd Gregory or Birkett or Herbert Weekes. On the whole he doubted it.

Nine of the fifty lockers were at present untenanted. They lined the sides of a passage which ran parallel to the big schoolroom, stretching from the rack in which the cricket bats were kept to a door which opened on to an asphalt playground. ('When it freezes in winter we flood it with water overnight and stick sandbags against the wall the other end and it makes a thundering good slide, sir.') On the left, between the fifteenth and sixteenth locker, came a break for the door of the senior changing-room. Each locker was numbered, and consisted of a cupboard two feet wide and about four feet deep. As far as Beale could tell they were allotted to the boys haphazardly, which did not surprise him. System was scarcely likely to be the headmaster's strongest point, he thought.

"Coo, isn't he tidy!" observed Askew now, surveying Maurice Weekes's ordered shelves. There was a tinge of envy in his voice, which was perhaps due to the fact that his own locker had proved chaotic.

"Doesn't look as if *he's* got any of 'em," he added, and prepared to pass on.

"There might be some in the biscuit tin," said Lillywhite, who had crossed the passage. "They're all in places that don't show. Shall I open it, sir?"

Beale nodded, in the midst of relighting his pipe, and the lid was taken off. Inside were roughly a thousand cigarette cards, and underneath them two *creme-de-menthe* liqueur chocolates.

"Another couple to cross off!" remarked Askew philosophically. "That leaves twenty-eight—not bad going. *Menthe—menthe;* what's it mean, sir? Name of a place or something?"

"Peppermint, fool!" Lillywhite informed him. "It's green."

"So're you!" was the unnecessary retort. "Peppermints ain't green, they're black-and-white stripes. Some are plain white, too," he added, "the ones that look like big aspirins. What's it mean, sir?"

"Lillywhite's quite correct. *Menthe* is mint, and in this case peppermint."

Askew opened his eyes wide.

"*Menthe*—mint," he repeated. "Of course—what an ass! A plant? Same as the stuff you have with lamb?"

"The same family of plants."

"Well I'm blowed! Wonder if it grows in England? Rather a jibe to ask for some peppermint sauce. And what are all the others, sir? *Kummel* and *cognac* and *maraschino.* Funny, that one—I always thought it was the name of a battle. It sounds as if it ought to be, sir, don't you think? One of Napoleon's, p'raps. The trouble with me is I'm unlucky, sir. When I don't know I think of all sorts of things to guess, but they're never any of 'em right. *What do you know of Thomas Burke?* for instance. That came in the half-term history paper, and I said he dug up bodies with a man called Hare and sold 'em to atomists, and it turned out it wasn't him at all but some old fool who made speeches. What's *maraschino,* sir?"

Beale explained as well as he was able.

"Coo, sir, we've been doing the Monks, too, but the Elk never said they made booze. 'Cording to him they luminated the bible and never spoke another word till they died and cut round bits out of their hair. Sir, could you get tight on those chocolates?"

"Of course not!" said Lillywhite scornfully. "You can't get tight by eating."

"Says you! What about De Thingummy? Opium-Eater—there you are!"

"But opium's a drug—'tain't the same thing at all."

"Oh, all right. Anyway, it's only made of poppies. I tried some once, only I didn't notice anything."

"Tried what?" asked Beale, smiling.

"Making opium, sir. I got a handful of big poppy-heads all full of seeds, the kind you shake and they rattle, and stewed 'em and stewed 'em, and then drank the juice. In the hols, that was."

"And you weren't even sick?"

Askew looked surprised.

"Oh no, sir," he said simply. "I'm never sick. I never have been. I wouldn't know what to do, even."

"Anyway," put in Lillywhite, returning to the matter in hand, "anybody who thinks young Maurice likes peppermint doesn't know much. He hates the stuff. Marzipan's what he'd go for—that and chocolate-drops; they're all he ever buys."

"And what about the other one?" enquired Beale, taking the opportunity. "Edwin, isn't it?"

"Oh, him! He'd eat anything that hadn't got maggots in it."

"But hasn't he any favourite flavours?"

"No sir, I don't think so."

"Yes he has," contradicted Askew, "toothpaste, 'specially *Maclean's.* You know the stuff. 'Did you clean your teeth today? Well, what do you think, chums?' I saw him wolf a whole sixpenny tube once—opened his mouth and put his head back and just squeezed it out like a long white worm."

Lillywhite shuddered.

"Ugh, horrible!" he said. "I hate worms and things with no legs."

And then, cautiously, he began to broach the subject which was clearly exercising his mind, and probably Askew's too, Beale thought, in spite of his chatter. Both boys had so far refrained from anything in the nature of a direct question about his identity or interest in the missing chocolates, and thus earnt good marks from him for their delicacy; but now the elder made a noticeable move.

"I wonder who it is that did all this," he remarked conversationally. "And anyway, what's the *sense* in pinching Miss Charlotte's blessed parcel and hiding the chocolates? That's what I should like to know. It seems a bit pointless, sir, don't you think?"

"Oh yes sir!" Askew broke in eagerly at once. "What *do* you think? What's it all about?"

And the two of them faced him suddenly, intent and hopeful.

He knew that with a word he could subdue them; that if he became in any way magisterial they would subside gracefully, perhaps disappointed but never again intruding their desire to learn what might be going on behind the scenes. Lillywhite would turn back into the tall fair-haired captain of the First XI escorting a stranger about the school, a stranger who must not be questioned nor made to feel that there was anything unusual or provocative in his actions; and Askew would play up, convincingly unconcerned and garrulous. Yet he preferred them as they were now, with upturned faces and alertly interrogative eyes. They were more human and more friendly, and made him feel that after all forty-four need not be quite the depths of middle age. So he failed to snub them, though not altogether throwing discretion aside.

"I can't tell you what it's all about because I don't know," he answered. "Your guess is probably every bit as good as mine. Incidentally, what makes you suppose I ought to know?"

"Oh, well, sir—" began Lillywhite uncertainly.

"Go on—I'd like to hear."

"Well, it's a bit hard to say, sir. Because—"

" 'Cos we think you're a detective, sir," declared Askew bluntly, his freckled face smiling. "Anyway, that's young Barton's idea. *Are* you?"

"Only in the very strictest confidence."

"Oh yes sir, of course!"

"Of course," echoed Lillywhite.

"Good!" said Beale cheerfully. "And now what about those guesses?"

After a little trouble the boys were persuaded that he seriously wanted their opinions, and gave them: that the chocolates were either poisoned, or contained diamonds. The latter suggestion came from Askew, and it made Beale laugh.

"The proceeds of some robbery, perhaps?"

"That's it, sir—a French one. It'd be an awfully good way of hiding 'em. And they were sent here by mistake, of course, and—and—"

"And that brings us back to the original question; what are they doing all over Anstey Court? Still, if we find any diamonds I'll let you know."

"There won't be any," said Lillywhite confidently. "He never guesses right—he told us so himself. And if it's poison, sir?"

"But what makes you think it might be?"

"Oh, sir, because chocolates that have been stolen are always poisoned. In detective stories, I mean."

"Exactly, which is why I'm here, roughly speaking."

"To find out?"

"Yes. You see, liqueurs are very highly flavoured, as I said just now, and quite a lot of poisons are too, and the point seems rather suggestive. I can't tell you all the ins and outs of things, of course, because that would be abusing other people's confidence. If you hadn't mentioned the word poison yourself I don't think I should have done it for you, but as long as you're not asleep I don't see any need to pretend you are. Not while I'm with you, at any rate."

"I wish you were a master here, sir," he observed with apparent irrelevance. "I should think you'd do all right."

"Thanks. And now we'd better get on with the search."

"But what *were* you going to tell us, sir?" persisted Lillywhite pleasantly as they moved on to the next locker. "Not the ins and outs, but it sounded as if you were going to say something. Or would you rather we shut up?" he added hastily.

"No, no. I was going to explain that at present my chief concern isn't so much with why these things are mysteriously distributed all over the school as with why they might be. In my job you automatically look on the worst side of the picture. If you see a coal-hammer lying about you think 'That's a blunt instrument—where's the body?' "

Again Askew laughed.

"And what you said to yourself this time was 'That's a stolen chocolate, what's inside it?' " he remarked shrewdly. "We did too, but only because of you. I mean, sir, we wouldn't have bothered twice about it else, much. Not seriously."

"Do you agree with that?" Beale asked Lillywhite, who nodded thoughtfully.

"We'd have said someone was fooling about," he declared.

"Good—that's where you may be able to help me. Forget I'm here, or rather that I'm a detective. Tell us what explanation you'd arrived at before I came, or would have arrived at if I hadn't."

"Oh lor, sir!" exclaimed Askew, grinning. "Sort of complicated, isn't it?"

"A bit—probably my fault."

"No, I see what you mean," Lillywhite assured him. "My own idea was that somebody pinched the parcel because of the stamps, and then perhaps got frightened and began pretending it was all a joke. Or perhaps he didn't get frightened—perhaps he did it just to be funny all the time. Jumbo's awfully against practical jokes. Oh sir! I mean Mr. Weekes is."

"That's all right; I wasn't listening. They're classifiable with stories about Englishmen, Irishmen and Scotchmen, aren't they?"

"I say, sir, who told you that?"

"Oh, I heard—it seems correctly. And your theory, Askew?"

But the younger boy shook his head with a disarming smile.

"Sorry sir—I was for diamonds right away. 'Fraid we're not much use."

"Don't despair. Had either of you any suspicions about the person responsible?"

But it seemed that they had not gone so far. On the whole they thought it was more likely to be a boy than a grown-up, but neither would suggest a name.

"Never mind," said Beale. "As long as there's no poison—or diamonds—I don't suppose anyone will suffer. All the same,"—and he became quite serious, "till that's proved by examination of all the chocolates, one can still speculate."

"Speculate?" repeated Askew.

"Sorry, I meant guess."

"Oh sir, d'you do that too? I hope you have more luck. I thought speculating was to do with stocks and things. I heard the mater telling dad off for it once, when he lost," he added sagely. "She never says anything when he wins, though. Well sir, what are we to guess?"

"Who did it," said Lillywhite. "But *I* don't know. I didn't, and that's as far as I can get."

"Quite the correct attitude," remarked Beale with a smile. "But I wasn't meaning that entirely. What I'd like you both to do, if you wouldn't mind, is to give me certain information, or certain opinions. Not because they'll help now, probably, but because it's just possible that they might in an emergency. It never hurts to lay in a store of information. It s like carrying an umbrella—often the rain keeps away, or seems to."

"I'll help if I can," Lillywhite promised quietly.

"Me too," agreed Askew.

"Thank you. Then, in the same strict confidence, who are the most unpopular boys here? Two or three will do, and I mean unpopular with the staff as well as with the rest of you."

"Oh sir, are you looking for a victim?" asked the elder of his assistants. "But people don't poison boys, sir, do they? It's usually rich old men who've just made a will."

Their first choices were unhesitatingly identical; Edwin Weekes, apparently loathed by everyone except the headmaster.

"And the other one, Maurice?"

"Oh, he's all right. He's quite funny sometimes, and he made a thundering good catch yesterday."

"Yes, I saw it. How does he get on with Edwin?"

Lillywhite frowned.

"He's blooming patient, sir, and that's a fact. Edwin's always going for him—you'd think he was his worst enemy. But Maurice pretty nearly always keeps his temper. He's a decent sort, really."

"And how does he get on with the head?"

"Oh, all right,"—from Askew. "He treats him about the same as the rest of us—it's only Edwin he prodigals."

"Does what?"

"You know, sir—kills the fat-headed calf for."

"I see. And one more question—possibly harder to answer. Who are the most unpopular grown-ups?"

"With us, sir, d'you mean?

"In the main, of course, but I dare say you'd notice if some of them didn't like others."

"Oh yes sir. Go on, Lily, you're older'n me."

But Lillywhite looked distinctly embarrassed.

"Rather not say?" suggested Beale.

"No sir, I don't mind—only I hope you don't talk in your sleep or anything?"

He laughed, then frowned, wrinkling his smooth forehead.

"It's a toss-up between Jumbo and Miss Charlotte, sir," he said. "I quite like her myself, but nobody else does much. And I don't care for Mr. Birkett a lot—he rather swanks."

"And I say the same three," Askew decided. "Only I put Miss Charlotte a long way first, 'cos she teases me and it isn't fair."

"Oh, that!" smiled Lillywhite. "She hasn't said anything about it for ages."

"She'd better not! I can't help it if my mater's got short sight."

Then, seeming to feel that an explanation was needed, he flushed unexpectedly and provided it.

"Two years ago I got landed here at the beginning of the summer term with half a dozen of my kid sister's nighties instead of cricket shirts, sir," he said disgustedly. "An' what's funny about it I don't know."

"Most awkward," agreed Beale tactfully, while Lillywhite shook with silent mirth. "And now we really must get on, or we shall be at it all day."

X

THE LOCKERS YIELDED FIFTEEN of the thirty-three chocolates still to be discovered; all, as Lillywhite had remarked, in places secure from casual observation. Beale felt sure they could not have been there very long, however, or their presence must have been noticed. The Assistant-Commissioner and his son, a thick-set boy whose owlish look seemed to belie his parentage, located nine more in the various classrooms. The big schoolroom was then searched by all five, without success, but the library provided four more hidden in sundry silver cups which adorned the mantelpiece. That left only five outstanding, and they sat down to lunch in good spirits.

"Boys been good?" enquired Herbert Weekes gruffly, grunted at Beale's affirmative reply, which earnt a dazzling smile from Askew, and said scarcely another word throughout the meal. He appeared distrait; his thoughts were plainly centred upon other matters, and probably unpleasant ones.

"And now where do we look?" asked Sir Francis, outside. "Let's get it over and clear off—that man gives me the pip. My brat and I will do the gym, shall we?"

Beale agreed to the suggestion, deputed the other two boys to scout round the changing-rooms and the dining-hall, and himself asked the way to the masters'-room. He found it to be small and untidy, its furniture two wicker armchairs, a small table loaded with exercise books and tobacco tins and a few novels, and a desk-flap under the window. Upon this lay a chessboard set out with a dozen men, and a remarkably dirty soft collar marked L.G. The grate contained a gas fire, and on either side were shelves filled with shabby text-books; rows of disused Latin grammars, several copies of *Meiklejohn's History,* and a battered set of a pre-war encyclopaedia. On the walls crookedly dangled three steel engravings which Beale supposed could have been worse; in a corner were a set of golf clubs and a shooting-stick. The hooks on the back of the door held two mackintoshes and a faded blazer; the mantelpiece was littered with cigarette ends, a tin of liver salts, and a pair of broken braces. Under the table was a typewriter and a duplicating machine.

Half an hour's search revealed two chocolates; one in the box which held the remaining chess-men and the other squashed neatly into the bowl of a cherry-wood pipe which was obscured by a *New Statesman.* He went downstairs again thoughtful; could any outsider, even Lady Weekes, possibly have had access to the room?

But in the gymnasium he forgot his worries.

"Three and two make five, then," Sir Francis told him. "It's good, isn't it? One among the Indian clubs, another on last year's cricket team—on the photo of it, I mean, and partly over the estimable headmaster's face at that; and your own two sleuths found the last being used as a plug in a wash-basin. It could have been a lot harder, you know. It might have taken us a week."

In the train Beale slapped his knee resentfully.

"Confound it!" he muttered, "I quite forgot to get Birkett's list of people."

"The ones he spoke to on the field before he found his pretty blazer spoilt? It mightn't have helped; they'd be the ones you wouldn't have to bother about, I expect."

"Yes, but we might have got a line, indirectly, by knowing whom to leave out. Still, I'm the last man to make trouble for myself. If that bottle's still full of death, the matter drops. That's the understanding, I believe?"

"And you aren't even curious about the whys and wherefores?"

"To a certain extent, perhaps. I don't feel I shan't sleep till I know who provided the fun and games, though."

"And you've positively no suspicions or suggestions or interesting ideas?"

Beale shrugged.

"I can tell you one thing, sir," he said. "The culprit was either an outsider trying to look like an insider, or an insider trying to look like an outsider trying to look like an insider. Involved, I admit, but not wholly without sense if you examine it."

"If I can remember it, you mean. Could it be put a shade more simply? For the benefit of a mere figurehead? I'm afraid I can't offer you a chocolate as a bribe, unless you care to sample one of the exhibits, but I've still a cigar or two left. Which is no thanks to friend Herbert. He had nine, all told, and my ambition now is to meet a Weekes who isn't greedy."

"Yes, that's strange," remarked Beale, branching off on his own line of thought. "Come to think of it, I never met the boys at all. I saw Maurice make his catch, but I don't believe I ever set eyes on Edwin, not to know who he was. Oh yes, of course I did! He was with Lady Weekes when you pointed her out to me. Ah, thank you, sir; I don't mind if I go back smelling rich."

He took a cigar from the proffered case, and attended to it absently.

"What I meant by that rigmarole just now," he continued, "was roughly this. If an outsider did the distributing of the chocolates, then I imagine that his or her aim would be to make the work appear that of someone intimate with the school—if possible of someone who lived in it. Hence the two secreted in the masters'-room, where outsiders wouldn't be expected to go. How it was done, if so, I can't say, but doubtless the room wasn't inaccessible for a determined person. That applies to the one in the matron's workbasket too, of course.

"On the other hand, an insider would naturally wish to be taken for a casual visitor; yet it wouldn't do to dump the things only where visitors could reasonably go—that would be altogether too crude. Hence, again, the workbasket and common-room. Or maybe it was done just to confuse the issue," he finished, smiling. "If so, it succeeded. In other words, I admit I don't know."

"But if you had to back your fancy?"

"I should risk my money on Lady Weekes, I suppose. Not so much because I'd put it past some of the others, but because I can't imagine why any of them should have wanted to play the fool. At least there's been a motive ascribed to her—very provisionally, of course."

"But only a criminal motive," objected his companion, for once dropping his pretence of mental torpor. "And if the presence of enough cyanide in the bottle removes criminality? Then I presume you overcome the difficulty by saying the business couldn't have been worth bothering about anyway? In short, you won't run after a bunch of rubber carrots."

"I don't overcome the difficulty, sir," said Beale, laughing. "I merely shirk it, and console myself with the reflection that I had to be on my best behaviour; that I could probably have found out everything if I'd been allowed to go round asking questions wholesale and looking in people's pockets and generally browbeating the entire establishment. At any rate, that's the kindest view.

"It also seems fairly certain, by the way, that the distribution in the school itself—in the buildings—took place very recently; in the night, perhaps. What we ought to have done, of course, was to go round *yesterday* without telling anyone; but I suppose that wouldn't have been feasible. What's your own opinion, sir?"

"Mine? I haven't one—what d'you think I took you with me for? But I wouldn't be surprised if Miss Charlotte did the whole thing herself."

"Really? On the field as well?"

"Why not? She pinched somebody's garters and made a catapult of 'em and amused herself taking pot-shots."

Beale laughed again.

"I know somebody who was short of a pair, too!" he said, remembering the fidgety schoolgirl. "But why did she waste good chocolates like that, sir? You'll have to provide a pretty convincing motive there."

Sir Francis shook his head.

"Can't think of anything better than spite, I'm afraid. Against Lady Weekes, maybe, or even against me. Or just out of spite; Miss Charlotte *contra mundum.*"

XI

(Letter from Sir Francis Barton to Herbert Weekes.)

June 30th, 1939.

Dear Mr. Weekes,

All the chocolate liqueurs found at Anstey Court the week-end before last have now been analysed, and I am happy to tell you that in none was any trace of poison discovered. The most thorough tests were made, by no means confined to cyanide of potassium, and you may rest assured that every one of the four dozen chocolates was completely innocuous. Further, the bottle which Chief-Inspector Beale took from the cupboard in your study has also been subjected to examination. It contained 123.4 (one hundred and twenty-three point four) grains of potassium cyanide in crystal form, in no way adulterated and in the condition one might expect from your account of its history.

I am most anxious to know if you consider the above amount sufficient for you to feel reasonably certain that none was abstracted from the bottle. You will, I am sure, realize the seriousness of the question, and give the matter your most earnest thought. I shall hope to hear from you about it by return of post.

Please convey my regards to your sister, and accept my own and my colleague's thanks for your hospitality.

Believe me,

Yours sincerely,

F. Barton.

(Reply from Herbert Weekes to Sir Francis Barton.)

July 1st, 1939.

My dear Sir Francis,

Let me tender you my most grateful thanks for the care you have bestowed upon the matter I lately brought to your notice. In answer to the specific query in your letter I will come to the point at once, and say that in my own mind I have not the slightest doubt but that the bottle, when found by your assistant, was as it had remained since I gave up the practice of photography many years past. The amount you mention corresponds almost exactly with my own estimate, and I am entirely satisfied.

Your information has proved a great relief to me, and to my sister also. I am now of the opinion that the disappearance of the parcel and the subsequent treatment of its contents was in all likelihood the action of some misguided practical joker, though whether boy or adult I am unable to determine. Provisionally I have decided to let the affair rest, now that it cannot be considered as bearing a criminal complexion. I hope this course will meet with your approval. Nevertheless I shall be more than usually alert for the rest of the term, and take certain precautions to safeguard my nephew, and indeed all the boys. For instance, I have requested the parents to refrain from sending further supplies of food or sweets in any form. Perhaps you will be kind enough to mention this to Lady Barton?

I cannot avoid the feeling that I owe you an apology, for had I not doubly erred, in carelessly permitting so great a quantity of so virulent a poison to remain at large and unheeded, and in misplacing my sister's parcel, there would have been no occasion to trouble you. In the circumstances I shall be glad if you will further oblige me by directing the enclosed cheque to any charity in which you may be particularly interested. I need scarcely say how grateful I am, both to yourself and to Chief-Inspector Beale.

Your son shaped well at the nets this evening, though in the match this afternoon he had the misfortune to be caught at the wicket without scoring.

Yours most sincerely, Herbert Weekes.

(Comment.)

"Good God, a guinea and a half!" said the Assistant-Commissioner in a dazed whisper, after much calculation. "It don't even pay for my nine cigars!"

PART II

THE VICTIM DEAD

XII

[Statement by G. Lloyd Gregory, B.A. (Lond.) covering the period June 18th to the morning of July 16th.]

I have been asked to contribute the following by Chief-Inspector Beale of New Scotland Yard, and have willingly consented, more especially because I have much to thank him for. But before I deal with that I think I had better give some idea of how the Great Chocolate Mystery was received by the school at large—as far as a mere master can tell, that is.

Briefly, then, the main attitude towards it was one of non-comprehension, which in turn led to fertile provision of the most fantastic explanations. I mentioned the two saner ones at half-term, but of the others, the wilder kind, I said nothing. Yet they were not unworthy of attention, if only by way of showing—I have always held it so—that nobody can be more genuinely imaginative than a small boy, provided he is the right kind of small boy. Perhaps that sounds nonsense, but only to a careless ear; one like Birkett's, say, who has not and probably never will have the least shred of understanding of the child mind. A boy is bound by no considerations of likelihood; his theories do not shuffle along earthbound. He doesn't give a rap for credibility, because he is doing his imagining deliberately, neither fooling himself nor seeking to fool others, sporting with his mental apparatus in the way a puppy sports with its immature legs and tail and teeth, for the sake of exercise and experience.

The pick of the more ridiculous explanations put about was Ingram's, I think. He declared with many a knowing nod, and in his always husky voice, that the parcel had been stolen and the contents dispersed by the headmaster himself; that before leaving them about he had injected into them a gland extract similar to that recently popularized in the world of professional football; and that the idea was to see if, the following term, Anstey Court could at last beat St Judes'. It is an event which has not occurred for six years.

"Then why organize a search for them?" somebody asked him.

"Oh, that's easy!" he answered. "He obviously put too much stuff in, or the wrong sort. Just think if we all started sprouting moustaches and singing bass in prayers!"

At all events the occurrence, together with Inspector Beale's visit, provided a topic of conversation for several days after half-term was over; almost for the proverbial nine. On the Saturday morning after next, July 1st, Mr. Weekes addressed the school and said that he had decided to take no further action in the matter. His demeanour was regretful, as if he were disappointed at not being able to thrash anyone. I considered it probable that he was attempting to mask his relief at the chocolates' harmlessness. He had told me of Sir Francis Barton's verdict privately after breakfast.

One thing I had better make perfectly clear, while I remember. At that time I knew nothing of the bottle of cyanide, never even having heard of its existence.

And now I will deal with the aspect of Inspector Beale's half-term visit which affected me personally. For some time past I had been greatly attracted by our governess, Patricia Tilling, but had taken the most scrupulous pains not to acquaint her with the fact. Why so? Chiefly for reasons of pride and pocket. To be quite open, I have always disliked poverty; not having quite enough clothes, or quite good enough ones, and being forced to economize on tobacco and beer and amusements. I experienced plenty of that sort of thing when I was younger, and I resolved long ago that I would never marry until I could count upon a certain income of at least £500 a year.

It never struck me then that I might be aiming too high. I had £120 a year of my own, and somehow that seemed almost half way. However, I soon found, or began to realize, that £380 isn't easy to earn as a schoolmaster, especially for anyone so unqualified as myself. It is true that I have a degree, but merely an ordinary common-or-garden pass, worth precisely nothing in the scholastic market. Further, I quite liked prep schoolmastering, but hated the idea of trying to get myself a post at a public school. Boys to me are interesting only up to the age of fourteen or so. After that they lose their freshness, and there is a distressing period till they achieve some sort of manhood. I'm aware that that is not the popular view, but then few of mine are.

Now there were two courses open to me. I could shelve my prejudices and go all out for a (comparatively) well-paid post, or I could drift along as I was, my highest hope as an assistant preparatory schoolmaster £250, say (and believe me, that takes some getting!), and my prospects of a headmastership, and a real income, dependent on miracles or magic. Perhaps to my shame, but also to my secret relief, I chose the latter, and found in fact that I could manage very comfortably on £300 all told and my keep for eight months in the year, provided that I gave up all thought of marriage. This I accordingly did, if not entirely, then with three-quarters or even five-sixths of my mind. And then came Pat Tilling to trouble the waters of contentment, and sternly I set my face against permitting her to stir them up too deeply. I couldn't help liking her, being a man and normal and not suffering from bad eyesight, but—I believed—I could help liking her too well, and I would.

By then, you see, I had got into set and pleasant habits. I smoked 5/- worth of tobacco a week, drank 10/- worth of beer, spent my summer holidays abroad and sometimes the Easter ones as well, did not deny myself the latest volume of Wells or Shaw or Faulkner or Agatha Christie. Marriage would spoil all that, I thought, and could imagine nothing from it which would go even part way towards making up my losses. As I am, I told myself, I can afford to pay 30/- for my grey flannels, but if I became entangled with Pat I might be reduced to something which irritated me at 17/6. As I am, I don't have to think twice if I fancy a decent seat at Covent Garden or a theatre at Christmas, but if I had a wife I might find myself queueing for the gallery, and that would be horrible.

It's amazing how stupid a man can be.

And then—I may say I teach French and Latin chiefly, not English, so my lapses of style must be forgiven—I met Pat that half-term Saturday evening, and saw that she had been crying, and with a sickly feeling between fear and pity I knew I was beaten beyond dispute. It was not love at first sight, nor anything like. It was a three or four terms' accumulation of repressed emotion. I asked her what was the matter, and she ran away from me sobbing, and that was queer, because I knew for certain that she liked me. For some time that night I lay awake wondering about it all, trying to persuade myself to leave well alone. My resolution to do so failed the next morning, however, and at half past ten I was kicking my heels in the garden, alone and waiting.

After that Pat came to me there and said she was leaving, and then my little selfish world was finally blown up.

What words we used I cannot now remember, or if I can I choose to keep them secret. It's enough to say that we walked out of Anstey Court as we were, I dressed for it and she not, and a mile or so till we found a secluded spot where we could enlarge upon our discovery. We talked, among other things, and by noon had reached the following conclusion. If Mr. Weekes would allow her to change her mind, and stay for the rest of the term, she would do so. Then we should either both leave, marry, and set about finding me a suitable non-resident post; or we would remain at Anstey Court as man and wife if he consented. On the other hand, if he insisted that she stick to her declared intention of travelling back with Lady Weekes that night, I would go too, forfeiting my salary and making shift as best I could. I was determined not to stay there another minute after she went. In my new-found plan of life I needed her company.

We tackled him in his study, issuing our various terms and conditions and ultimata to his astonished annoyance. His neck went up and down against his collar as if they both itched, and his hazel eyes glared at us.

"Really, Mr. Gregory, your suggestion passes the bounds of reason!" he observed in his most impressive voice. "You must surely be aware that no headmaster will tolerate the presence of mutually engaged members of his staff. It is an unwritten law that such things simply do not happen in scholastic circles."

"We could always dispense with the engagement," I told him. "Nobody but yourself need know how matters stand. Still, if you'd rather we went . . ."

"But you can't possibly let me down like that, at a moment's notice! How in the world do you propose that I carry on the school with only a single assistant, and an inexperienced one at that?"

"You can always get a temporary master from an agency, sir," I said, "and pay him with what you'll save on me. If I go today I naturally shan't expect my salary."

"Ha! I'm glad you're kind enough to reassure me on that point," he sneered. Then his manner changed, and he became to the smallest degree ingratiating.

"Nevertheless, your departure would cause a noticeable gap," he remarked. "You've been with me a long time, Mr. Gregory—ten years or thereabouts, isn't it? I think we have always got on reasonably well together—I shall be sorry to lose you."

He broke off for a moment, frowning, and I interrupted.

"Then why not let us stay as I suggested, sir?" I asked. "As we are this term, and as man and wife thereafter. I don't see why the arrangement shouldn't work."

But he shook his head doubtfully.

"It wouldn't be possible for you to live here," he said. "At least, I don't think so. I'm certain my sister would never hear of such a thing, and I know of no suitable house within several miles. I presume you weren't expecting me to build you one on the premises?"

It was the kind of offensively rhetorical remark of which he is master—taught by his sister, perhaps. I felt extremely inclined to take it up, but decided not to; less because I cared whether we had a row or whether we didn't, as far as the thing itself went, as because only by staying till the end of term could I hope to be paid, and £60 is a big item to throw away for the sake of a few sharp words. I pretended to treat his observation seriously.

"No sir, of course not," I replied. "Then the alternatives would seem to lie between your dismissing us now and our leaving at the end of term. I'm afraid we may have sprung this on you rather suddenly, but then I didn't know until an hour or two ago that Miss Tilling was going. Nor that I should mind so much about it," I added, not quite truthfully.

"I see, I see. A sudden heart attack, apparently? All the same I find it extremely precipitate, as I think is only natural. I wish my sister were here, but unfortunately she's away for the day. You had better give me a short while in which to consider the matter—if that is convenient to you both?"

We agreed that it was, and he promised to let us have his decision by three o'clock that afternoon. We thanked him, and went out to lunch at a very decent little pub half a mile away. For his part I understand from Lillywhite that he had scarcely a word for anyone during his own meal.

At the appointed time he received us in his study again, rather in the manner of royalty giving audience to persons of doubtful antecedents, and informed us that he was prepared to let us finish the term, and accept our provisional resignations. He would discuss the possibility of our staying on after we were married with Miss Charlotte, but could hold out little hope that she would ever agree to such a proposal. We had to give him our solemn word that we should be guilty of no unseemly behaviour, but to do him justice he didn't press the point objectionably. He said that as far as possible the engagement must be kept secret. The boys must certainly not be told, and he thought it better not to mention anything to Mr. Birkett or the matron. For his part he would observe strict silence.

Who told Lady Weekes, then, is a debatable point, but the fact remains that at eight o'clock that evening, soon after her return from taking out her son Maurice, she hunted out Pat in her room and went for her bald-headed. Not viperishly, as Miss Charlotte might have done, nor waspishly, as the head, but with apparently genuine indignation.

What had happened to Pat's self-respect, she demanded? How could anyone even contemplate staying a further six weeks under the same roof with a man who behaved like that? (If it be asked, Like what?) The answer would seem to be connected with his previous attitude to the face-smacking of young Edwin and his subsequent dismissal of his once-pardoned governess. But Lady Weekes trod very slender ground there, in my opinion. There was nothing in the dismissal note definitely referring to the previous incident. Herbert Weekes could have sworn he had forgotten all about the affair, and was getting rid of Pat because he found her generally unsatisfactory. All members of his staff have to agree, when he engages them, that half a term's notice will be sufficient on either side at any time. Why he makes that stipulation I am not sure, but I believe it is because he once found himself forced to endure for almost two terms a man who suddenly developed or displayed strongly atheistic tendencies.

In the end Lady Weekes went away, leaving behind the impression that if they ever met again it would be a deplorable accident. Pat was rather hurt at first, but soon got over it. After all, the woman was nothing much to her one way or the other. I know very little about her myself, but I can't say I was ever greatly attracted. That may be because she is a brunette, though, and I have never suffered from Shakespeare's complaint. Incidentally, I have often thought since that for some peculiar reason Miss Charlotte suspected Lady Weekes of being concerned in the Great Chocolate Mystery. She questioned me very closely about when and where I had seen her talking to Maurice the day the parcel disappeared. But I can hardly imagine that Lady Weekes would need to steal other people's sweets, nor that she would play the kind of practical joke which followed.

Then who do you think *was* responsible? it may be asked. I haven't the slightest notion, officially speaking, but if I wanted an outside bet I think I should choose Birkett. It strikes me as vaguely significant that the first of the missing liqueurs turned up in his blazer pocket, and he has always been inclined to despise my cherrywood pipe since somebody gave him a *Dunhill* for his birthday in May. Also, he is quite a clever amateur conjurer, an adept at sleight of hand and that sort of thing. However, I am probably wrong, and I make the suggestion in confidence only.

The term continued, neither more nor less interesting than other summer terms at Anstey Court. Several boys took their Common Entrance, most of those expected to pass duly obliging. Three sat for scholarships, and between them were awarded £100 worth of free tuition, which wasn't too bad however intrinsically valueless. The cricket team performed on Saturday afternoons, and sometimes on Wednesdays, and its members were thereafter exhilarated or depressed according as they had individually succeeded or failed. A child called Jenkins caused a mild diversion by punching another child called Opie on the nose in the middle of church one Sunday morning, and resolutely refusing to explain why. The mystery was never solved. Winkworth translated *Il n'y a que le premier pas qui coute* as *It is only the Prime Minister not (anyone) who matters,* which Miss Charlotte said was quite the most sensible remark she had ever known a boy to make.

And so we came to yesterday, Saturday July 15th, not of course realizing in advance that anything which happened then might later be important. To begin with, after breakfast we had one of the headmaster's typical conclaves. Just before grace he signified his desire that the whole school should assemble immediately afterwards in the schoolroom. His manner was aggressive, truculent. His eyes smouldered unamiably, and we felt that there was a row pending.

Privately I considered it about time, because since the half-term episode he had been singularly mild, passing over things with which he would normally have found fault, and not unduly disturbing himself or us about what could not be passed over. Trifles all, of course, for what matters in a school would be negligible in the outside world; but then I suppose the same is true of any enclosed community with falsely parochial values. The state of Europe is of less importance than the state of Smith minor's locker or exercise book, the Polish Corridor insignificant when compared with that which runs from Dormitory A to the fire-escape, and in which someone contrived to leave a blob of cold porridge.

However, to the point; the school assembled and the headmaster gave it a dispassionate glare, as if he loathed it separately and collectively. Then he selected a fresh stick of chalk from the box on the masters'-desk, called for a boy to clean the blackboard, and addressed us grimly. Yet I could see that he was not in one of his worst moods. After ten years one gets to recognize the signs and symptoms!

"This morning I was up early," he said, unnecessarily—he always is out and about before any of us. "I happened to visit the wash-room. Upon one of the walls I observed an inscription in pencilled lettering—to be exact, near the roller-towel opposite the door. I shall now copy that inscription upon the blackboard, in substance if not in form."

He proceeded to do so, turning his back on everyone and shielding what he wrote from sight with his body. Meanwhile I inspected the boys' faces. Often it's possible to detect a culprit before exposure; if generally known, because others are pointedly staring at him, for instance, or because he is looking thoroughly uncomfortable and fidgeting, or because he is unnaturally still and—on the surface—unconcerned. But this time I confess I failed. I could see no eyes which did not express either interest or annoyance, and as far as I could tell with entire genuineness. The interest explains itself, being based on the fact that from their own observation of the wash-room wall they knew what was coming, but the source of the annoyance may be a trifle obscure. It was anticipatory. The brighter boys were aware that if no one owned up, everybody might well be punished.

I then returned my attention to the blackboard, and repressed a smile at the legend upon it.

Edwin Weekes is a silly hog.

"And now the author of that sentiment will kindly stand up," commanded the headmaster, even more grimly. Yet it was speech, not a bark, which was a good sign.

No boy stirred, except to regard his neighbours covertly.

"I will make the request again," said the head, sourly. He hates what he terms the craven silence in which guilt seeks sanctuary.

No one moved.

"Very well!" he growled. "I shall act accordingly. The whole school uses the wash-room; therefore the whole school is implicated. Unless the boy responsible comes to me by lunch-time and confesses, I shall punish you all. Not, be it understood, because the subject of the statement I have just written up is my own nephew—I should do the same if it were any of you—but because I intensely dislike cowardice. No boy is perfect. Each occasionally does what he ought not to do, and in the nature of things his misdeeds are sometimes discovered. The only honourable course then is for him to own up. In general that happens in this school, and I am proud of it, for I can think of nothing more contemptible than for one guilty boy to acquiesce in the unjust punishment of the innocent, sheltering behind them. It is thoroughly mean and dishonest, and meanness and dishonesty are not qualities that I expect from any of you. Nor, in passing, is the habit of writing offensive remarks upon walls to be encouraged. Walls were never designed to take the place of writing materials, and rudeness of that kind betrays ill-breeding. Let there be no more of it."

As so often in the past, I felt tempted to ask him how he justified his readiness to punish all in order to be sure of punishing one, but I refrained. He is not the kind of man with whom one holds ethical discussions. What he does is in his own mind *ipso facto* correct.

At the eleven o'clock break for biscuits I witnessed a rather curious passage between Herbert Weekes and Lillywhite, the captain of the XL Virtually he is the head boy, or would be if Anstey Court knew such a distinction. But 'Titles produce dissatisfaction', to quote the law and the prophets in one of its less successful aphorisms; and less sincere too, I fear, for nobody could appear more gratified at being able to refer to his brother as 'Sir Robert' than the headmaster, especially when talking to parents.

He and I were reckoning the prospects of the match against Grove Park that afternoon when Lillywhite came up.

"Yes?" said the head.

"Please sir, about that—that inscription. It's old, sir, you know—it's been in the wash-room at least a week."

"Really? And you did nothing about it?"

"Me, sir? What ought I to have done, sir?"

"Oh, not brought it to my notice—I wasn't implying that. But I think you could have obtained a wet flannel and erased it."

Lillywhite looked suitably abashed.

"Yes sir—sorry, sir," he murmured, though plainly the idea had never occurred to him. Indeed, why should it have?

"In any case," continued Herbert Weekes, quite genially for him, "the age of the offence hardly affects the question of its heinousness, I fancy. It has been committed this term, for the walls were distempered at Easter, and I should be surprised to learn that one of the workmen was responsible. Consequently it has been done by one of you, and I wish to know by whom."

"Yes sir. Please sir, what will happen if nobody owns up?"

He was favoured with a superior omnipotent smile.

"That I prefer not to say—yet. You mustn't forestall nemesis, you know. The whole school will suffer, including Edwin, who is certainly not responsible. At least, I never heard of a boy publicly vilifying himself. Incidentally, that should serve to show you that it is the principle of the thing which counts, and not the opinion expressed nor the identity of the boy held up to ridicule."

"Yes sir," agreed Lillywhite demurely, and went away.

"But the hog *is* a hog!" I caught him whispering to someone a few minutes later.

After lunch Mr. Weekes addressed the expectant school again, this time in the dining-hall.

"I regret to say that the culprit has not thought fit to come forward," he informed us. "Originally I intended to treat the matter lightly; merely to make the offender delete the writing from the wall and perform nominal reparations—say two hundred copies of 'I must not deface school premises nor slander my fellows.' "

Miss Charlotte smiled bleakly from the opposite end of his table, opened her mouth, and snapped.

"Some would deny the interpretation of slander in that particular case," she observed.

Her brother said nothing in answer for a moment; he merely frowned the more severely.

"Tuck will be distributed as usual immediately after grace," he continued, "but none of it may be eaten until you return from church tomorrow. I shall feel at liberty to inspect any boy's locker in the interim to ensure that he has not disobeyed me. You had better be particularly careful, Edwin, in view of what has just been said. Grace, Watkins."

It was a light enough sentence on the whole, considering that his favourite was involved, and I heard one or two faint sighs. Miss Charlotte's interjection was characteristic, and by no means wide of the mark. There's no denying that Edwin Weekes, even on the most favourable view, was a positive little glutton. As a matter of fact, as Patricia told me later, something occurred within five minutes to prove the truth of that assertion.

Since half-term Patricia and I have both found ourselves being slightly imposed upon; not enough to complain of, but enough to notice. (Incidentally, it had been decided that we were to leave, but we had done nothing to offend him with reference to our engagement. She wore no ring, and we took the most exhaustive trouble not to let anyone suspect that there had been the least alteration in our attitude towards each other. But I have known Herbert Weekes on previous occasions to overwork those of his staff who were leaving.) For instance, I now have to take charge of extra (punishment) rolling-squads, though formerly Birkett did it, and I also have to do more than my fair share of indoor supervision on wet days. Similarly Pat has been landed with slight but annoying additional duties, one of which is to help Herbert distribute the tuck.

This is always done—and always has been, fair weather or foul, rain hail or snow—after lunch on Saturdays between approximately 1.45 and 2.00 p.m. The scene of operations is the schoolroom, and no boy is allowed to spend more than threepence at a time. Or rather, no boy had been so allowed prior to half-term; but after the affair of the chocolates the headmaster banned parcels of food from parents or friends, thus seeming to lend weight to my suggestion to Inspector Beale that poisoning might have been feared. The move was naturally not popular, and as a concession the boys were permitted to spend up to 6d each, though counselled not to in their own abdominal interests. Most of them bowed to this broad hint, but I don't suppose anyone seriously expected Edwin to, and no one was disappointed.

The supplies come from a firm called Marsh's, and on the whole their products are both cheap and good. In all probability they were recommended by Miss Charlotte, who possesses what must surely be a unique knowledge of sweetmeats and their varying merits. At all events, yesterday afternoon the tuck distribution took place as usual, and before many moments were past Edwin Weekes distinguished himself by pushing and shoving his way to the front. *En route* he trod heavily upon the foot of an infant named Bartholomew, who promptly began to howl. The head at once demanded to know what was the matter, and actually reprimanded his nephew in public.

"Go to the back and wait till last!" he ordered. "If you don't mend your behaviour, my boy, I shall begin to think you really are a hog."

Strong words for our headmaster, when applied in that direction, and only about three years overdue. Patricia reports that Edwin was very chastened.

No check is kept upon what each boy purchases, so it is not possible to give details. She remembers however that the takings in all amounted to thirteen shillings and fourpence, including a full 6d from the clouded favourite. What he actually bought with it she doesn't know, because as soon as she had his money, he as I said being the last, she went out at her own suggestion to see if Matron had given Askew a fingerstall. He broke a nail in the nets the other evening, taking one of his usual blind swipes.

The match against Grove Park duly took place, and was duly won, and at evening prayers the head reminded the school about not eating any tuck till after church the next day. (Prayers on Saturday evenings are at 7.00, I may say, but the elder boys do not go up to bed till 8.15.) Any disobedience would be severely punished, he said. He then departed, leaving me to carry on alone. Edwin went upstairs at 7.30, and I never saw him alive again.

At 6.20 the next morning, Sunday, he was discovered lying dead by the door of the downstairs changing-room, clad in pyjamas and dressing-gown and socks, two-thirds of a slab of chocolate cream in his left hand and a most dreadful expression of agony upon his face. Nearby was an electric torch on the floor, the glass cracked, and when he fell he had caught his forehead on the sharp corner of the door-post. There was a drop or two of blood, but not much.

I helped carry him upstairs after the maid—who found the body—had frantically told Mr. Weekes direct, and he had sent her up to wake me. The child's limbs were stiff, his flesh an unnaturally bright pink, and his fingernails blue. I should imagine that he had been dead for some considerable time, probably hours, and I have no doubt that he was poisoned. The chocolate cream—or more precisely marzipan block—I took charge of, Herbert Weekes being too dazed. I later delivered it into the care of the Guildford superintendent.

The headmaster was more upset than I would ever have believed possible. He was crying softly all the time, and his living features were almost as frightening to behold as Edwin's dead ones.

With regard to my own movements on Saturday from 2.00 p.m. till the time I went to bed, they were as follows. In the afternoon I umpired the 1st XI match, at home; was on duty afterwards till just after 8.15, and then went upstairs to the masters'-room. There I amused myself with last Sunday's *Observer* chess problem until Patricia returned soon after half past nine. We strolled round the playing-fields in the dusk, came indoors again a few minutes after 10.00, and I went back to my chessboard. Later I corrected some French exercises, and I was still there when Birkett came in between 11.00 and 11.30. We sat up talking, first about the European situation and then about my prospects of getting the kind of post I want. He knows that Pat and I are leaving, and I rather think he suspects why, but he has asked no direct questions and I have volunteered no information.

We went to bed at midnight after eating some cake and drinking some of the liquid which passes here for ginger wine. So far as I know, all the boys faithfully observed the headmaster's injunction not to eat any of their tuck. I haven't the slightest idea what Edwin Weekes bought, but later on Sunday morning, though before anyone else was down, beginning at 6.55 a.m., I and one of the maids collected all tuck from the lockers, Edwin's excluded. I thought I had better leave that untouched until the arrival of the police. The collection was done with Mr. Weekes's approval but at my own suggestion. My reason will be obvious—to prevent the possibility of any more sudden deaths. The detailed list I made, and the tuck itself, is already in the possession of the police.

I first learnt about the bottle of cyanide of potassium from Miss Charlotte later that morning.

It is understood that this statement has been made in the strictest confidence for Chief-Inspector Beale's assistance and personal use.

(Signed) G. Lloyd Gregory.

XIII

BEALE PUT ASIDE the statement, and sat thoughtful. He felt that Lloyd Gregory might easily prove tedious on closer acquaintance; yet interspersed among the laborious irrelevancies were several points in the narrative which he thought might help him. For instance, it was something to know that Birkett had ever been considered as a possible suspect, and also that Gregory had divined Miss Charlotte's attitude towards Lady Weekes.

It was Monday morning, and he had been at Anstey Court since early the previous afternoon; and, taking stock of the situation, he could not honestly say that he had made any great progress. That Edwin Weekes's death was murder, and murder of the most deliberately cold-blooded kind, seemed beyond dispute, but when it came to the question of the murderer's identity he found himself at once in difficulties. So far, he had no better guide than idle suspicion and surmise. In addition, the crime itself shocked him. It was the first time he had ever been called upon to investigate the death of a child, and somehow the victim's youth made the deed more vile. The fact that Edwin, by all reports, had been a greedy and objectionable boy did little or nothing to soften its brutality.

He had viewed the body, intensely disliking the task. What the senior master related about the expression of the face was if anything under-emphatic, and he felt that he could understand Herbert Weekes's breakdown. The man had obviously possessed strong feelings of affection for his younger nephew, though everyone else had loathed the boy, and he appeared inconsolable. Even Miss Charlotte unbent a little towards him in his grief, Beale noticed.

The school in general had been told no more than the barest essentials; merely that Edwin had died in circumstances which demanded police enquiry. No public statement was issued, and so far the matter had not reached the ears of the press. If it did, there would immediately be a rush of horror-stricken parents eager to snatch their sons away from a danger which was almost certainly non-existent, and Beale was not yet prepared for that. In any case there were only ten more days of the summer term left; he hoped to have settled the affair before the school dispersed.

He was sitting now in the morning-room, which had been exclusively set aside for his personal use. There was nothing to be done at the moment in the way of active investigation—that side of it had already been attended to by the local police before his arrival. Also, his own position was quite in order. In view of the special circumstances the chief-constable concerned had been readily persuaded to apply to Scotland Yard for his services.

Presently he picked up Gregory's account again, to verify the time of the tuck distribution; then he turned his chair towards the window and stared out at the gardens, at turf much greener than it had been at half-term, at white and pink and crimson standard roses in full bloom and beds of dahlias coming into bud. 'Flowers grow just the same, one murder or fifty,' he thought. 'I dare say it's just as well.' In the nearby class-rooms, he supposed, lessons were going on much as usual; Latin grammar, the congruence of triangles, the study of a well-pruned Shakespeare play. Yet in one, Miss Tilling's, there would be a noticeably vacant place, and in all, probably, an excusable lack of attention.

Later Sir Robert Weekes was expected. He had telegraphed his intention of travelling back from the continent by air. Meanwhile Beale had two immediate duties; to interview the headmaster if he had sufficiently recovered, and to see what he could make of the facts in his possession. After that he would be better able to tell what questions he needed to ask the school at large. That there would be several he felt certain.

And then, to his surprise, there came a knock at the door, and the maid announced a visitor.

"Mr. Purdon to see you, sir," she said, and Beale was on his feet in an instant. Anthony Purdon, assistant-editor of *The Stockbroker,* was his best friend, and his invariable companion when there was murder to be solved.

"Tony!" he exclaimed, moving forward with outstretched hand. "This is just what I'd have wished myself if I'd thought it would do any good. How did you know I was here?"

"They told me at the Yard," explained the newcomer, subsiding into a chair. He was tall, and his face pleasantly ugly; a bigger man than Beale, and a year or two younger. At the moment he wanted nothing so much as a drink, and was determined to say so at the first opportunity.

"Yes, I rang up about nothing in particular," he went on, "and a bloke with a fruity voice shoved me on to somebody else who kept sneezing, who pushed me up higher, and eventually I got a Commissioner or a commissionaire—I was never sure which. He said to look you up here—seemed to think you'd be lonely and glad of a face you knew."

"Really? That was uncommonly considerate of him, not to say intelligent. As it happens I'm all on my own and very glad indeed. This business has to be kept dark, or the place'll be besieged, and I hate working in a free fight."

Tony nodded; he knew probably better than anyone that his friend preferred calm and freedom from interference.

"Does this establishment run to beer before lunch?" he asked hopefully. Beale shook his head.

"Nor after. Nor during. In fact, it's not the sort of establishment you'll care about at all. Still, we can always go out for an hour—there's not much to do, really, bar speculate. I was going to have a word with Mr. Weekes, but he'll keep."

"Good, but before we go, just tell me who's dead. The kid you told me about—the greedy one?"

"Yes—I was forgetting you wouldn't have heard. He was found yesterday morning about 6.20 lying in a downstairs passage by one of the maids, clutching a slab of chocolate with a marzipan filling. His torch was on the floor close by, and there's no doubt whatever that he died where he was found. It had happened some hours before, the doctor says, probably about 2.00 a.m., but we can talk about all that later. Ah!"

The door opened again, this time without a preliminary knock, and Herbert Weekes walked slowly in. His features were grey and lined, his shoulders seemed bowed, and his clothes were vaguely untidy; he was no more than a shadow of the man he had been at half-term.

Beale introduced Tony, but the headmaster paid little attention.

"Of course, of course, anyone you like," he muttered, looking round with eyes which appeared out of focus. "I—I came to know if I could help, Inspector. My sister thinks you probably wish to ask me some questions. You have been very considerate."

"There are one or two points, certainly, but naturally I shall trouble you as little as possible."

"Had I better clear out?" asked Tony. "You have my deepest sympathy, sir," he added, feeling he ought to say something. Herbert looked at him for a moment, then nodded.

"Thank you. Remain if you wish—it makes no difference to me. Possibly you may be of assistance."

He turned to Beale, and straightened himself a little.

"Whoever did this thing must be found and punished," he declared, speaking slowly and passionately, "punished to the full. I place complete reliance upon you, Inspector—don't fail me. Poor Edwin may have had faults, but he also had virtues, great virtues. Character can be formed, but intelligence is a precious gift. He would have risen to the top in whatever walk of life he chose, had he been spared, and he must not go unavenged. And to think—to think that I of all men should be partly responsible for his death! It's cruel."

Beale decided that he had better not believe his ears.

"Responsible, sir?" he echoed gently.

"Yes. I should never have allowed my sense of danger to be lulled—I should have seen that he was taken away to a place of safety after what happened at half-term. I shall always reproach myself. Ask me anything you consider apposite, and if I can answer I will—my sister too."

He nodded again, then began to rub his neck against his stiff collar as he moved heavily towards a chair.

"I shall do everything I can, sir," Beale told him. "What I want from you now isn't so much information as corroboration of what I've already learnt from other people. For example, I understand from the matron that approximately since half-term your nephew slept in a room by himself instead of in a dormitory?"

"That is correct—I thought it better. I thought it would be easier to make sure he was safe in bed every night. You see, I've never forgotten those air-gun pellets which were fired at him last Easter—I mentioned them to you before, you'll recall. Thinking things over, it seemed to me possible that the affair of the liqueur chocolates was after all no practical joke, but an attempt on the boy's life which somehow failed of its purpose. Not that I believed that with any seriousness, mind you, or I should never have undertaken the responsibility of keeping the poor child here. However, I went so far as to arrange for him to occupy a separate room, one in which the curtains should be quite opaque and drawn every evening by one of the maids. I felt I was acting sensibly, in his own interests, but now—"

He broke off with a despairing sigh and sat silent. Beale too said nothing for a moment, having no wish to distress the man more than was absolutely necessary; yet it would be better to continue with his questioning now he had started. The sooner it was over, the sooner he and Tony could leave Anstey Court for a while and discuss things.

"I'm sure that whatever you did was for the best, sir," he murmured at last. "Another item of information I've been given is that both Miss Tilling and Mr. Gregory are leaving at the end of term. Is that so?"

"Yes, perfectly true," agreed the head, in the same courteous but dispirited manner. "They intend to get married, and I can't possibly accommodate them here even if it were desirable. In any case, this will probably mean the finish of the school,"—and he sighed deeply again. "The facts must emerge soon—that Anstey Court has been the scene of a brutal murder. What parent would dream of entrusting his son to my care thenceforth? It is the end."

Both his listeners made appropriate noises in their throats. It was really very difficult to find an adequate comment, thought Tony. Herbert Weekes was clearly in the depths, and with good reason; only time could soften the blow he had been dealt.

"Now, the one other point about which I must consult you at present is the question of the tuck," Beale went on. "Is it possible to obtain a complete list of what every boy purchased on Saturday?

The head shrugged faintly, as if to imply that it was a foolish enquiry.

"I cannot remember," he said. "Doubtless the boys themselves will tell you. The total amount spent was thirteen shillings and fourpence, if that helps, and I have already informed you what poor Edwin bought; one block of marzipan, two of peppermint, and three-pennyworth of liquorice all-sorts."

"I have your permission to find out full details from the boys?"

"Of course. You must feel at liberty to ask or do anything whatever which will clear up this terrible tragedy."

He leant forward slightly, and became more intense.

"How you set about such things I of course don't know," he said. "Nor do I know if you're accustomed to receive advice, or need any. It seems to me, however, speaking as one vitally affected and deeply moved, that we must face one unassailable certainty; *there is at this very moment a murderer at large in the school.*"

Since it seemed expected of him, Beale nodded.

"Very well, Inspector. You may have your own opinions, but to my mind it is inconceivable that any of the other boys should be implicated. They would possess neither the requisite cunning nor sufficient depravity. That at once narrows the field of exploration. Leaving aside my sister and myself—I can assure you we neither of us killed the child nor ever dreamt of it—there remain five adults; the matron, the housekeeper, the two assistant masters, and the governess. Or six if you include Mr. Elkington, my non-resident master, but I think he may safely be ignored, especially as he leaves at noon on Saturdays."

Pausing suddenly, he produced a cigarette case, but failed to share its contents.

"Considered one by one, my staff would seem to be above suspicion," he went on, speaking earnestly. "Yet in the circumstances we know that to be impossible. One of them *must* be guilty, much as it pains me to believe it. I presume I may rely on you to check their movements with the most exhaustive thoroughness?"

"You may," agreed Beale shortly. It was just like Herbert Weekes to be so long-winded about such an elementary matter, and though he could appreciate the other's natural desire for justice to be done, he still disliked being treated as if he were a small boy under instruction.

"Thank you—and forgive my pointing out what had perhaps already occurred to you. Yet it seems incredible—utterly incredible! How *can* it be one of them? And yet, how could it be anyone else?"

He shook his head, and made as if to rise.

"Finally, Mr. Weekes," said Beale quickly, "have you found your keys yet?"

"No," was the answer, accompanied by a grim contraction of the eyes. "Discover them, or rather who took them, and in my opinion you'll need to discover little else. I remain convinced that I had them in my trouser pocket when I went to bed on Saturday night, but since then I haven't seen them. They were definitely nowhere to be found when I searched at midday yesterday. The superintendent asked me for them. I sleep heavily, I believe, but I should not have thought it possible for anyone to visit my room without my knowledge."

Beale nodded, and took no notice of Tony's mystified expression. "You had visitors on Saturday evening," he remarked. "Your sister tells me you changed into a dinner-jacket suit. Can you be positive that you transferred the keys from the trousers you had been wearing earlier?"

"Good heavens!" exclaimed the headmaster, sitting up with a jerk. "I'd forgotten that! No, Inspector, to be quite truthful I can't. In all probability I left them in my bedroom. You think that may give you a useful hint?"

"I hope so. What time did you go downstairs after changing?"

"About 7.50, or slightly later. I went straight up after conducting prayers at 7.00. I dislike dressing in a hurry, and Dr. Armstrong and his wife are always punctual."

XIV

"WELL, WHERE SHALL I BEGIN?" asked Beale half an hour later. They were sitting in the otherwise deserted bar-parlour of *The Traveller's Rest,* a mile from the school, and Tony had just finished reading Lloyd Gregory's statement under a strict promise of secrecy. For a moment he said nothing; then smiled.

" ' All these years we had no interest in him ,' " he quoted from the end of one of Caradoc Evans's stories. "He writes rather as if he were telling his life-story—or at any rate as if he wished he were."

"Yes, but I'm partly to blame. I asked him to be as detailed as possible, though I'm certainly not interested in how much he pays for his flannels."

"The poison was cyanide, of course?"

"Yes."

"And the chocolate-block arrangement contained marzipan. Worth noting, that."

"Decidedly; it's about the one substance suitable for masking the almond nature of that particular poison. Even if Edwin were in the habit of breaking his chocolate blocks open and smelling them before he ate, he probably wouldn't have noticed anything wrong. But whether the poison matched the sweet, or *vice versa,* I can't say."

"Oh, I should think the marzipan was the starting-point. At least, I don't know. There'd been cyanide in the school for years, hadn't there? Any news about amounts and so on? Was the whole thing loaded, or only the part he swallowed, or what?"

"It's believed at present that about four grains had been inserted in each end. The blocks are in four sections, but the middle two seemed free. At any rate, that's what the analyst chap said—I brought him down with me. He only guessed at the amount, of course, but I dare say he wasn't far out."

"And Edwin ate one poisoned section?"

"Roughly speaking. He didn't have time to swallow it all, but that's what he'd bitten off."

"Good lord!" Tony was shocked. "Does cyanide act as quickly as all that?"

Beale nodded.

"The doctor thinks he probably didn't last more than a couple of minutes, for most of which he was unconscious."

"Ah well, I suppose that's something to be glad about. And he definitely took the stuff downstairs—no lugging of bodies around?"

"None; what Gregory says is quite reliable. Naturally there was only a little bleeding when he cracked his head on the door-post as he fell, because it would stop as soon as he died."

"Yes, quite. Presumably the poison was similar to what was in the bottle you found at half-term?"

"Yes, but that isn't to say that it necessarily came from there. Still, I shall provisionally assume that it did. I've started enquiries within a reasonable radius, but I'm not expecting any results. People can't get hold of potassium cyanide just by asking for it, and anyone who wanted some for criminal purposes would take especial pains not to rouse local interest."

"Probably," agreed Tony. "Now, tell me about this missing bunch of keys. Is it important?"

"I shouldn't be surprised if it proved one of the most important features of the whole affair, to date. Briefly, Herbert keeps the school tuck in a big black tin box, which in turn he keeps locked in a cupboard in what he calls the store-room. I've been in there; it's full of exercise books and graph paper and chalk and pens—enough for two or three years, by the look of things.

"But that's by the way. After distributing the tuck on Saturday he duly locked the box and put it back in the usual place. The key he keeps with his others on one bunch; about a dozen, all told. You heard him say he's lost it, or had it stolen, and the significance ought to be obvious."

"Even to me. So what?"

"So, according to Herbert, all I've got to do is to find who took it and I shall know who poisoned Edwin."

"Um! Does it follow quite so neatly?"

"Well, perhaps not. I can't say yet."

"And what are you doing about the keys?"

Beale smiled, and before replying drained his tankard.

"At the moment, nothing," he admitted.

"Nothing?"

"Nothing active."

"Why not? Because you don't want to, or because you can't?"

"Because I don't want to."

"Oh well, I suppose you know your own business best, but isn't that rather a handicap? I mean, it's all very fine just to sit down and wait till somebody rattles too much as he walks by, and then arrest him, and there in his trouser pocket, or in the equivalent place if he's a woman, there, I repeat, is the missing bunch, and a few odd grains of cyanide, and maybe a ticket to foreign parts. The point is, until he or she rattles how are you to know whether everything's in the box that ought to be, and if not, what isn't?"

Beale sighed.

"Do I really look like that?" he asked. "Simple, ingenuous, a sort of pale green pumpkin in a big strange world? I said a tin box, if you don't mind, not a safe deposit. Herbert's isn't the only bunch of keys in existence—I carry a pretty comprehensive one myself. I admit the lock wasn't the usual nonsense, though—I don't suppose anyone else at Anstey Court could open it without the right key."

Tony s face cleared.

"Well, how was I to know?" he demanded. "Never thought of it. The times I've been asked to see if I happen to have one that fits somebody else's suitcase or front door, and I never have had yet!"

But Beale was frowning, not smiling.

"If you didn't think of it, though, then other people may not have done," he remarked. "I wonder; perhaps I wasn't being too optimistic. At all events, I know what was inside the tin box at three o'clock yesterday afternoon, and I also spent an hour making an exact diagram of all fingerprints near the lock. Unfortunately photography was out of the question; it would have meant using powder first, and that would have given the game away."

"And back went the box, and now you're hoping that in due course there'll be a few extra prints."

"Well, hardly hoping; but if there should be, I won't be caught napping."

"And what *was* inside, if one may ask?"

"About a dozen other boxes, cardboard ones, containing various kinds of sweets. What interested me most was the marzipan blocks. Both Herbert and the governess say it was a new lot, and of the original four dozen there are now thirty-seven left."

"But you haven't asked the boys how many were bought on Saturday? So I gathered from your remarks earlier."

"Not yet; it's one of the next things to be done."

"So I should think!"

"Oh, it wouldn't have been wise to appear too anxious; that might suggest I'd already paid a visit to the tin box. In any case the marzipans in store correspond with Gregory's list of what he collected plus the poisoned one, and term doesn't end till Thursday week. Have another drink."

"Thanks—since there's no hurry. Any more news?"

"Nothing much in the way of facts. The fingerprints on Edwin's locker were his own, and on the torch, and the same is true of the chocolate block in spite of its contents. Whoever played about with it went very carefully—probably wore rubber gloves. The only other thing I can recall at the moment is that Edwin seems to have favoured the nocturnal consumption of sweets. There were quite two dozen toffee-papers under his mattress—the housekeeper was scandalized! But I don't think this case is going to depend a great deal on clues—I expect an arm-chair will be more useful than a tape-measure or a magnifying glass."

"In other words, rational contemplation?"

"If we're capable of it. That's not surprising, really, because we start with all the information which usually takes the time to discover in poison cases."

"Such as the nature of the poison and what it was given in?"

"Together with the method of giving it. You've no idea how difficult it is to find that out, sometimes; and then nine times out of ten it doesn't help as far as prosecution goes."

"Why not?"

"Lack of witnesses—most poisoners take care there aren't any. It never pays to make an unprovable allegation in court, however reasonable or probable. The defence at once accuses you of building your case on mere hypothesis, and may easily get the jury looking down its nose and sniffing. Here the poison was cyanide of potassium concealed in a marzipan block, the whole being put in Edwin's locker where he was bound to take it sooner or later."

"A sort of human mousetrap. And he took it sooner because he really was as greedy as everyone says he was."

"There can't be much doubt on that. He sneaked downstairs in the night, torch in hand, because he couldn't wait till after church the next day. Perhaps he felt hungry, and his tuck was the only food he could get at. Perhaps, too, he was peeved about being punished with all the rest for something it was quite obvious he'd never have done himself. Anyway, down he went. There was very little danger of discovery, and since he was Edwin, and his uncle's pet, he'd think that nothing much would happen to him even if he were caught. Though according to Gregory Herbert had spoken to him pretty plainly about his habits, certainly—I'll have to tackle Miss Charlotte on that. You'll notice how the single room contributed to the proceedings. If he'd been in a dormitory with a lot of other boys he mightn't have risked sneaking out."

"Which would merely have postponed his death, not prevented it. Still, Herbert must be feeling pretty sick—perhaps blaming himself out of all proportion. He rather gave me that impression. You know, I feel damned sorry for that man, Ted. He's quite without humour and full of long words and all the other things you said—I noticed a few of the words myself; yet you can see he's suffered, and probably will do more if the school goes pop. The kid may have been a squirt, but he inspired affection in that quarter all right."

"Yes, I'm afraid I agree with you," murmured Beale, and sighed.

"Afraid? What's that mean?" demanded Tony instantly. "There's no possible doubt. If ever a man was cut up, Herbert is—no play-acting there. If you think otherwise you're an ass."

"I don't, I don't. All I meant was that it makes me *feel* I oughtn't to suspect him, while at the same time I can't help *thinking* I ought to."

"Good lord! But surely you know if you do or not? And in heavens name why? I should call him the last possible person on any possible list."

"Which isn't always the safest place, remember. And I don't know if I suspect him—I merely think I should."

"D'you really keep your thoughts and feelings separate like that? And anyway, *why* should you? Or don't the thoughts translate into words?"

"It might—I'll try. To begin with, we've only Herbert's word for it that Edwin ever bought a marzipan block at all. He was the last to be served, remember."

"Don't keep saying 'remember'," objected his friend. "If I don't I'll remind you. Yes, that's true, but he could easily have mentioned what he bought to some of the others."

Beale smiled appreciatively.

"Another thing to find out," he said. "Next, if Edwin did buy a marzipan Herbert certainly knew, but that anybody else did is doubtful. Miss Tilling went away once she'd got his money—she didn't stay to see how he spent it. Admittedly she went at her own suggestion—that's generally agreed; but she did go, and it's highly improbable that she lurked outside the door listening. Then how, short of pumping Herbert or the boy himself, or going round the school asking most unusual questions, could any third person have discovered (a) what Edwin bought at all, or (b) that he'd bought anything suitable for poisoning with cyanide?"

"Don't know. Maybe it could be taken on trust; maybe he always bought marzipan."

"Perhaps, but it hardly seems likely. He bought less of that than of other things, which doesn't point to its being a special weakness. Now if it had been toothpaste! I'll ask, of course, but it sounds more like Maurice, the elder one, or so I was told at half-term. Marzipan's alleged to be one of his favourites, but fortunately his likes and dislikes don't count. It was Edwin who was threatened; even as far back as last Easter, so Herbert says."

"Now be fair!" protested Tony. "If you're suspecting the man you mustn't take any notice of what he says. For all you know he may never have been threatened at all."

"That's true; yet Herbert wasn't the only person to suggest the idea. I'm positive Miss Charlotte would never be in league with him, yet it was she who went all out for the notion of Lady Weekes trying to poison Edwin at half-term. I admit she didn't believe in the Easter business, though."

"And it's only your opinion that she wouldn't conspire with her brother."

"An opinion I stick to. Now, passing over the question of motive, mainly because I can't think of one, let's turn to the actual poisoning. Herbert had access to a supply of cyanide—nobody disputes that. He also had access to the medium used, and he could more or less make his own opportunity. It isn't too much to say that with regard to each of those points he was in a better position than anyone else in the school. That's why I should fancy him as a suspect if it weren't for his obvious grief.

"There's another question that's vitally important, too; which marzipan block was poisoned? The one Edwin bought on Saturday, or another which was later substituted for it? The absence of the keys seems to point to substitution, but it would be risky."

"Well, isn't the best way of finding out to consult the boys and check up on the thirty-seven marzipans left? If they say they bought eleven, including Edwin's, and since Gregory's list says the same, there'll be no more room for question."

"Yes, I shall do that by and by, of course. I don't think you quite see what I'm driving at—probably my fault. I should have explained that I'm still dealing with Herbert."

"What, assuming he pinched his own keys?"

"Temporarily. This is how I see things at present. If the block which Edwin was found clutching was the one he bought, then it was removed from his locker some time later than 2.00 p.m. on Saturday, tampered with, and replaced before 2.00 a.m. the next morning. He was just the child to notice if some of his tuck were missing; therefore—in that case—it's sensible to suppose that the removal and tampering would have been done *after* he went to bed at 7.30 and not before. If so, Herbert's the obvious person to turn to, because he was the only one who could have visited the locker without rousing comment."

"Why could he have?" asked Tony.

"Ah, so that's something you don't remember! Because he'd reserved the right to inspect lockers as a guard against any of the tuck being eaten before the return from church next day."

"What a memory! But how would he know what'd been scoffed and what hadn't, without a list to guide him? Gregory says they never keep one."

"A good point, with—I think—an equally good answer. Not to bother about a list would be typically Herbert; I mean, it's what everybody would expect, but he'd know what Edwin bought all right."

"Perhaps he even kept him till last on purpose! I'm not convinced. Do you go as far as suggesting that in order to be able to visit lockers on the level he bribed some wretched infant to write rude things about Edwin on a wall a week beforehand?"

Beale laughed.

"The devil must be hard up for advocates," he said. "You don't really imagine a headmaster couldn't find some excuse for punishing the whole school like that if he wanted to? It merely means he seized the first opportunity which came to hand. I admit that sounds just a little too smart for the Herbert I've met so far, but then I hardly know the man."

"Well, here's another objection—I hate to see fancy exalted above fact. Surely the point is, or ought to be, that however much you *think* you ought to suspect him you simply can't, because he was doing something else that evening; to wit, entertaining the punctual Dr. Strongbow and his wife."

"Armstrong. Yes, there is that—I must find out what time they went. You know, I think I shall get on a lot better now you're here—I needed someone to talk to."

"Splendid! But what about Matthews—couldn't he have come?"

(He referred to the detective-sergeant who usually accompanied Beale on his investigations.)

"He wanted to, but I thought I'd better be alone. This business has got to be kept quiet, and two strangers would stick out more than one."

"Then hadn't I better clear off at once?"

"Oh lord, don't be awkward! It hadn't occurred to me, and apparently not to Herbert either. You'd better be a prospective parent, I think, the same as I was going to be last time I came this way. If they invite you to stop, I mean; I shall try to get them to."

He took out a note-book, and scribbled for a minute.

"Find out when visitors left," he muttered. "Ditto if Edwin told anyone about his tuck. Ditto who bought what. Ditto if he usually went for marzipan. That's all so far, isn't it? The two peppermint blocks and the liquorice all-sorts were still in his locker, by the way, and thank heaven Gregory had the sense not to touch them. He made a very good job of the collecting, too—put down exactly what was in each boy's possession.

"Very well; we now come to the case where the poisoned block isn't the one Edwin took away from the schoolroom after lunch."

"Where Herbert sticks out like a sore thumb—even I see that, disbelieving as I do that he's in any way concerned. The man emphatically wasn't foxing this morning, and Lloyd Gregory doesn't seem to think he was foxing on Sunday. If it's going to wreck your life to kill your favourite nephew, why do it?"

"I can't imagine."

"Exactly; because it's unimaginable. Incidentally, here's something else to write down. One assumes it to be an inside job? I mean, Lady Weekes wasn't crouching in the laurels biding her time?"

"Hardly. She seems definitely out of it, in person, though I shan't overlook the possibility that she may have employed an agent. As a matter of fact, I'm rather surprised the idea hasn't been put forward yet by Miss Charlotte. I had quite a long talk with her yesterday, too."

"What was her attitude?"

"It's hard to say. She was mostly worrying about the effect Edwin's death would have on Herbert, and on Sir Robert Weekes, who's apparently in pretty poor health. She was also wondering how she could ever have been so mistaken at half-term, or how Herbert could have been—she didn't seem quite sure which."

"I see—not very helpful. Now, does this make sense? The murder was an inside job, and essentially an adult job, because it's unlikely that any boy could have done the inserting of the cyanide into the marzipan block. Remains to find out the movements of all adults resident at Anstey Court between 2.00 p.m. on Saturday and 2.00 a.m. on Sunday, as Herbert said. That covers both actual or substituted block; but—calling the two cases (A) and (S)—then I suggest that in (A) the important time-limits will be 7.30 p.m. and 2.00 a.m., and in (S) 2.00 p.m. and 7.30 p.m."

"Why?" asked Beale immediately. "Why the latter?"

"Because in the case of a substituted block the murderer presumably had his own all ready, and was merely waiting a favourable opportunity, till Edwin had a duplicate. Once that happened there'd be no point in delaying. The sooner the exchange is made the better, and if it can be done before the child goes to bed, when there are dozens of people coming and going, it seems to me there's far less chance of discovery.

"Yes,"—as Beale's eyebrows went up, "I know what you're going to say; that we're once more up against the difficulty of how anybody but Herbert *could* have known the opportunity had arrived. It's not going to be easy. The obvious source of enquiry would be Edwin himself, and that's one person you simply can't question. Still, that only ought to make it more interesting—for you. Not much satisfaction in an easy triumph."

"Rot!" said his friend. "I'm not looking for that kind of satisfaction. I want to solve the riddle and call it a day."

"Of course you will, even if it means calling it a week instead. Meanwhile, here's another point which occurs to me—I'm being exceptionally bright today, don't you think? We're fairly confident our murderer must be one of about half a dozen persons, and it would be making him very stupid to suppose he doesn't realize we know that. Then wouldn't a natural part of his plan be to throw suspicion on someone else? And, witness your own statements, isn't Herbert the best choice? And, with all due respect, doesn't the fact that your thoughts disagree with your feelings bear the suggestion out?"

"Ah! That's about the most intelligent thing you've said yet—with equal respect. This business has certainly been planned; though I don't suppose you could poison anyone in a passing fit of temper, really, or only very rarely, when you happened to have the means and opportunity ready to hand. But there's a drawback to the second part of what you say. No sensible person would pick on Herbert as scapegoat unless he knew of some convincing reason why Herbert could ever be thought of as disliking Edwin intensely, instead of doting on him. And if such a reason exists, then that would immediately remove all grounds for not suspecting Herbert."

"I say, that's rather clever!"

"We'll see. If there's anything in the scapegoat idea, applied to Herbert, then we'll hope the murderer's kind enough to provide us with a motive. Well, shall we go?"

"Have another drink first—I've one or two more intelligent remarks to unload."

"All right; but it's 12.30, and lunch is at 1.00."

"I'll be quite quick. First, is there any significance in the fact that the box of marzipan blocks was a new one?"

"Call that a remark? But it's certainly intelligent. The answer's doubtful. It seems that Marsh's, the firm supplying the tuck, failed to send any marzipan last time but one. I've got notes of all the dates and so on, and they assured me on the phone that it was a pure oversight. The truth is that between June 2nd—considerably before half-term—and the 14th of this month there was no marzipan at Anstey Court at all."

"Really? Then Edwin was killed the minute a fresh supply became available. That strikes me as highly significant. Also, it points to (A) rather than (S), doesn't it? In view of Gregory's list?"

"Apparently, but not necessarily. The murderer may have had a poisoned marzipan block ready for weeks, and not been able to use it because there were no genuine ones about. I doubt it, though."

"So do I. And would that matter, with a greedy boy like Edwin?"

"Not as far as the murder went, but there'd be a lot of speculation afterwards about how the child got hold of something that nobody else had."

"And what of that? Surely it would point to Herbert harder than ever."

"Well, perhaps the murderer was a bit dull there. Or perhaps he thought it would be making Herbert look too stupid. Or perhaps the murderer *is* Herbert after all, and my feelings are wrong."

"And perhaps not. Are these chocolate blocks wrapped up?"

"No, which leads me to discount the idea of a poisoned one being kept handy for weeks. Chocolate that's exposed soon gets stale, and Edwin would be the first to notice."

"Ah! No empty tins at Anstey Court?"

Beale laughed again.

"What have you been sharpening your wits on?" he asked genially. "Going back to the blocks, Marsh's sweets are cheap but good, as Gregory said; they don't waste money on fancy decorations. The names of the different flavours are stamped on the things; otherwise they all look alike. As I hinted just now, I've been on the telephone to them. They're mainly a north-country concern, and not a very big one at that. You won't find their goods in ordinary sweetshops, anyway not in this part of the world. I asked if they thought they could possibly date any particular block, meaning the middle sections of the one which killed Edwin, and they said they were pretty sure they couldn't unless it was very old and fusty. There was no question of that, of course. They also said that if it had been a lemon filling instead of marzipan they could practically have told me what o'clock it was made, because lemon is a new line. In their last parcel to Herbert they included a sample box of a dozen blocks. Any more intelligence?"

"That depends on your standards. Incidentally, *have* you checked the adult alibis?"

"I'm in process of obtaining them; the checking comes later. We'll sit down some time and work on them."

"That suits me. Well, here's one other question; is there any remedy against poisoning by potassium cyanide? If Edwin had collapsed after church yesterday, when the matron was about and plenty of people to call her, could anything have been done to save him?"

"The doctor doesn't think so. Cyanide works so rapidly; there really isn't much that anyone could do, caught unprepared. I believe artificial respiration and the use of a stomach tube are advised, but what chance is there of finding a stomach tube in a prep school?

"No, there wasn't any plot to lure the boy downstairs in the night so that he should die alone and unattended. He went of his own gluttonous volition—I'm certain of that. The precise time he died didn't matter. Once the poisoned block was in position he was as good as done for, being the kind of boy he was. I mean, there couldn't have been the least likelihood that he'd offer somebody else first bite."

"Do you really think the murderer took that into account?"

"Why not? He'd almost have to, because it would have spoilt everything if some other poor wretch dropped dead by mistake. There'd never have been another chance."

"No, not even for Herbert."

"Ah! Does that mean you're beginning to think you ought to suspect him too?"

"Not at all, but I wouldn't mind being given an alternative."

"Then why not go back to the half-term theory?"

"Lady Weekes? Through an agent?"

"Yes, and if so, almost certainly the governess."

"But they quarrelled," objected Tony seriously.

"Quarrels can be made up—in more senses than one. Staged for the benefit of Lloyd Gregory, say."

"It's an idea. You're making the place a perfect hot-bed of villainy, though."

"Well, villainy's in evidence."

"True. But is the governess that sort of person?"

"I don't know. From what I've seen of her I should say not, but I may be wrong."

XV

"THE HOUSEKEEPER'S definitely crossed off," said Beale. "She went into Guildford by bus, and wasn't here at all between 1.00 p.m. and 10.30, and after that I don't see how she could possibly have found out what tuck Edwin bought."

"Is that the small bustling woman who cut up some infant's meat at lunch with her own knife and fork? I discarded her long ago. All the same, what's the matter with opening the locker and looking inside?"

"Everything. I said she was gone by 1.00, which means she didn't stay for school lunch, which means she'd know nothing till next day about the boys being off tuck. Hence she'd have no reason to suppose Edwin hadn't already eaten all his. Satisfied?"

"Perfectly. I've nothing against her except that she doesn't seem too hygienic. And the matron?"

"She had bagfuls of opportunity, but I'm not going to waste my time with her till somebody shows me why I should. That leaves five persons whose movements have to be accounted for; Herbert, Charlotte, Lloyd Gregory, Birkett, and Miss Tilling. Excluding the domestic staff, of course. I've questioned them all, and they seem quite harmless."

Tony merely smiled, and Beale hastened to justify himself.

"No, I'm not getting slack," he said. "It's simply that they obviously had nothing to do with Edwin's death. It's most improbable that any of them had anything personal against the boy—anything nearly strong enough to inspire murderous feelings. I find it equally improbable, or a bit more so, that anyone would dream of employing them as assassins. Therefore, since they can't help by giving me any information, I shan't bother with them."

"All right, all right! I never said you ought to, did I? How does Birkett stand? Couldn't you dispense with him too?"

"I expect so, but I won't just yet. In a way he's linked with the others, or two of them. He's reputed to have been keen on Miss Tilling, who's now engaged to Gregory."

"Pooh! What does he say he did?"

"Briefly, he supervised the 2nd XI changing, escorted it to a place called Grove Park, about nine miles away, for a cricket match which he helped to umpire, returned here just before 6.00, had a meal, dashed upstairs for some money, cycled into Haslemere, joined up with a party of friends at 7.30, and spent the evening pub-crawling. He got back about 11.20, sat up talking to Gregory in the masters'-room till midnight, and then went to bed."

"Sounds innocent enough. By the way, how long a job would it be to doctor the chocolate block? Any block, of course, not necessarily the one that Edwin bought."

"As it happens I can tell you, because I tried myself yesterday," Beale answered. "How long should you think, at a guess?"

"Well, that's hardly fair—you've seen the thing and I haven't. Was it neatly done?"

"Very neatly indeed. There were no traces visible to the naked eye unless you looked closely."

"And did you have to remove some of the original contents before you inserted whatever you did insert? Which presumably wasn't cyanide?"

"No fear! I crushed up an aspirin. Yes, I did have to take out before I put in; not so much for lack of room as in order to concentrate the stuff—make sure it would all have taken effect together if it had been poison."

"I see. At a guess, then, quarter of an hour."

"Yes, that's about what I was expecting myself. With a safety-razor blade, though, and a pair of tweezers I managed it in five minutes after one or two practice shots."

"Did you now! And I thought I was underestimating. That rather mucks an idea I was having, that if it took a really long time you could discount the possibility of the poisoned block being the same as the one the boy bought."

"I was trying to find that out. I'm afraid we can't discount it, but all the same I don't think it's so likely as substitution. It needs two visits to the locker where the other needs only one. Now, we've five persons left, and statements from all but Herbert; but Miss Charlotte's covers his movements pretty fully. It washes out one of our questions from this morning, too, about what time their visitors left. You've already seen Lloyd Gregory's. Shall I read you the rest?"

"Yes, do. By the way, have you verified Gregory's where possible?"

"Yes, it seems trustworthy. For instance, the maid who found the body corroborates that after Herbert had been with it for a few moments he sent her up to wake Gregory and tell him what had happened."

"A matter of how long?"

"About four minutes. He's a deep sleeper, she says. Why?"

"I wondered; thought perhaps he might have been sitting up waiting. But then he wouldn't know Edwin had gone downstairs in the night—sorry, I'm getting muddled. Carry on with the alibis, and I'll see if I can spot flaws."

"If any; but I don't suppose there are. The difficult part of bringing home a murder like this is that it takes hardly any time at all to commit, and the person who does it needn't be anywhere near when it happens. To all intents and purposes Edwin's consisted of four separate actions, namely; (1) getting possession of the poison; (2) getting possession of a marzipan block; (3) placing one inside the other; (4) putting the finished article in the locker.

"The first was done at least as long ago as half-term, for a practical certainty; as I said, I don't anticipate the slightest success from enquiries at chemists' shops. The second may have happened equally long ago, or on the other hand may simply have meant a visit to the locker some time after 2.00 p.m. on Saturday. The third, by my reckoning, needn't have taken more than a few minutes, even remembering that both ends were loaded, and the fourth is only a matter of seconds. To attempt to discover who could and who couldn't have gone to the locker over a period of twelve hours, during at least two of which everybody was ostensibly in bed and asleep, is hopeless. Nor has the murderer any need to lie in his statement, except by omission. It's all darned difficult. We can only go at present by probabilities; rule out the housekeeper, for instance, and Birkett as well, I dare say.

"I won't read what he says because I've already give you the gist of it. In fact, I don't think I shall bother to read any of them in full except Miss Charlotte's. Here's the matron's comings and goings; in effect, none. She was on school premises all the time—didn't leave the place once. As well, she was alone nearly the whole afternoon except when she was digging a splinter out for one of the maids. She denies any knowledge of which boy bought what tuck, and admits quite frankly that she wouldn't have known what to do off-hand if Edwin had collapsed from cyanide poisoning in the daytime when she was about."

"Did she put that in off her own bat?"

"No, I'm afraid not. I asked her, and also about the tuck. That do for her?"

"More than enough. She's obviously innocent, or she'd have taken good care to be at least a mile away till the stuff worked. Still, at that rate they'd all be innocent, and that would never do. Let's hear about the governess; she's the one I'm supposed to be suspecting."

"Then don't get too excited beforehand. It was her half day off, so after she'd seen Matron about Askew's fingerstall—a mere excuse to get away from the schoolroom, she says—she got on her bike and went to Shottermill. That's a village a few miles away, and she has an aunt there. She stayed with the aunt till nine o'clock, and arrived back here soon after half past. After that she had her walk with Lloyd Gregory round the playing-fields as stated, then a couple of games of draughts with the matron, and went to bed about 10.45 with a book she wanted to finish."

"Pah!" said Tony disgustedly. "How can I suspect anyone on that? If it had been chess, perhaps; but no cold-blooded poisoner ever played draughts. What was the name of the book?"

"What in the world's that got to do with it?"

"Nothing, probably; I'm only looking for flaws. For instance," —and he reeled off the names of half a dozen recent novels. "If it was any of those, or millions like 'em, I'd know she was either a liar or a person of no taste, and in either case she'd be suspect.[1] Is Saturday always her afternoon off?"

"Always, except of course at half-term. Gregory has Tuesday and Birkett Thursday, and naturally all of them get various evenings and Sundays and so on."

"Shall you verify her visit to her aunt?"

"I don't suppose so. It doesn't seem to make any difference where she was so long as she could have found a minute to go to the locker, and she obviously could have done."

"And so could all the others, even if it meant sneaking down the same as Edwin did, only a bit earlier. I begin to feel that this business won't be easy. You can't hope to account for every minute of everybody's time."

"I said that just now. And if you could, in any particular instance, or it seemed as if you could, the fact would be highly sus-

---

1 The author regrets that the laws of libel do not permit him to give the names of the books in question; but guessing is still legal.

picious. Still, don't forget I told you almost as soon as I saw you this morning that this is an arm-chair problem. In any case the hardest part hasn't even been tackled yet, or not by you; or if so, not audibly."

"I suppose you mean motive? You don't seem to have harped on it much yourself. But then, the murderer's going to be kind enough to supply one for Herbert the scapegoat, which will then turn out to be the true one, and Herbert himself the murderer, and don't ask me what happens to him of the kind heart because I forget, if I ever knew, which I don't believe I did.

"Now read what Miss Charlotte says, and take the first opportunity of introducing me properly. By the look of her, and from what you told me after the half-term fiasco, she ought to be interesting."

"She is; even more so this time."

"Why?"

"Well, I definitely had the feeling then that she'd taken a liking to me; yet now, so far, she hasn't been nearly so friendly. Not rude or unpleasant, I don't mean. It's more that she treats me as a policeman pure and simple where formerly she treated me as a human being—offered me chocolates and didn't much mind what she said."

"Which may be significant."

"Every change of attitude signifies something," said Beale; "today's profound thought. It's always possible the murder's shocked her a lot more than she cares to admit, and that on that account she's behaving not quite naturally. Or perhaps she's genuinely sick at having slandered Lady Weekes—if she did; afraid it'll come out somehow."

"Or perhaps it was she who murdered Edwin," put in Tony. "She said to herself 'I'll show 'em whether he's greedy or not,' and substituted a poisoned marzipan for his harmless one. If it was still there by the time they set out for church then he was cleared, and she took her poison away again. If it wasn't, so much the worse for him. Any offers?"

"Not yet, thanks. Anyway, this is her statement. *"I remained indoors reading until half past three on Saturday afternoon. I then walked down to the cricket field for an hour to watch the match against Grove Park. My brother was there, having accompanied the boys. He came indoors with me for tea at 4.30, and then returned to the field. I did not go out again myself. Instead I went over the school accounts—not those connected with the house-*

keeping but the ones to be sent later to the parents. At 5.30 my brother came indoors, and as far as I know stayed in his study until he took prayers at 7.00. For my own part I changed between 7.00 and 7.30, then made sure that dinner would be ready at 8.15. We had two visitors coming, Dr. Armstrong and his wife from Ferndown. Their son was once a pupil here. Because of their visit neither my brother nor I attended the ordinary evening meal at 5.45. The only adults present, I believe, were Matron, Mr. Gregory (on duty), and Mr. Birkett, but he and the 2nd XI did not get back until about 6.00.

Dr. and Mrs. Armstrong duly arrived at eight o'clock, and after dinner we played bridge. They departed at 11.30, and soon afterwards I went upstairs to bed. My brother remained in the drawing-room, but said he would not be long, and I heard him close his bedroom door about ten minutes later—just after the grandfather clock had struck midnight. My brother, in great distress, informed me of what had happened about 6.30 the next morning.—Charlotte Weekes."

"It sounds all right," said Tony. "A bit jerky, but quite honest and straightforward—no labouring after effect. By the way, did Herbert himself tell you about the epitaph on the wall and the consequent embargo on tuck?"

"Yesterday."

"And did you ask him if he'd exercised his right to inspect lockers?"

"I haven't asked him yet. He mustn't get the least idea that I should ever be capable of suspecting him."

"But—supposing for a moment that he's your man—isn't it a question he'll be expecting, and mightn't silence be the one thing which would give him the right idea?"

Beale looked thoughtful.

"There's probably something in that," he agreed. "Always provided I do suspect him—I'm hanged if I know. I'll mention the matter next time I see him, to be on the safe side—thanks for the tip. Well, now you've heard everybody's movements, and I can't say I've been dazzled."

"Nor me; it's still extremely murky. Incidentally, it's five to four as well, and you're due to address the school when the clock strikes, in case you'd forgotten."

"Not exactly address it—ask a few questions and get the tuck list. Coming to help?"

"Who, me? I shouldn't be much good—I'm not used to hordes of small staring boys. Lunch was bad enough; I could feel eyes crawling all over me like spiders."

"You shouldn't be so sensitive. I'm not specially used to boys either, but I shan't let it worry me. They'll be much more frightened of you than you need be of them if you scowl once or twice."

"If I knew how to. I'll come if you want me to."

"Good—you can copy down all the things they say."

XVI

"MANAGE THEM ALL RIGHT, d'you think?" enquired Lloyd Gregory. "Or shall I stay?"

"There's no need, thanks," said Beale firmly. "I should go off and have a smoke if I were you. By the way, are there any particularly dull ones among them? Or deaf ones, for that matter."

"They're all dull," Gregory told him cynically. "None of 'em's an imbecile, though, if that's what you mean, and they can all hear well enough when they want to."

Beale thanked him; upon which the senior master nodded, smiled rather uncertainly, and walked out of the schoolroom door. He contrived to leave behind the impression that he wished he had not been so definitely dismissed.

Meanwhile Tony had been regarding the rows of small earnest faces from where he stood nervously on the platform which contained the master's-desk and the blackboard. His first thought was that their owners, in their uniform green jerseys and brown corduroy shorts, resembled a collection of parti-coloured frogs, or perhaps bright tropical beetles. His second thought was that after all Beale had been right; the boys *were* frightened, though not of himself. The reason dawned upon him almost the same moment; he felt surprised that it had not occurred to him sooner and quite forgot his own timidity. Only a fool would fail to realize that there was something very wrong with Edwin Weekes's death, and he remembered that his friend's identity as a policeman was reputed to be common knowledge.

'Good lord, it's only natural!' he told himself. 'The poor little devils are probably terrified out of their skins—I'm sure I should be. I dare say they've all got a pretty shrewd idea of what's really happened, and most of 'em probably read murder stories—'

He selected one or two faces at random, examined them more attentively, and became convinced that he was right.

'No boy ought to be as pale as that! He's frightened, that's what it is. He's suddenly come up against violent death, and can't cope with it.'

Almost without thinking he felt in his pockets for pencil and paper. Thus it was that a few moments later Beale was startled to find an old envelope being slipped surreptitiously into position on the desk before him.

Just struck me this flesh & blood business to kids he read. *You know—MURDER! ghosts, bogeymen, etc. Can you reassure porridge not poisoned will all be alive tomorrow?*

He nodded to show that he appreciated the note, and then turned again to the assembled school.

"I'm sorry if I'm taking up some of your spare time," he said. "I won't keep you longer than I need. The reason I've called you together like this is to ask you some questions, and I hope you'll give me all the help you can. Don't be afraid of answering freely and truthfully. I don't bite, and Mr. Purdon's equally harmless. Now, will any boy who didn't buy any tuck at all on Saturday please hold up his hand?"

Two were immediately upraised, belonging to a small fair child with a noticeable squint and an older thinner one with horn-rimmed spectacles and a wise expression.

"Thank you," said Beale. "That's a beginning."

He looked round the room, caught Lillywhite's eye, and almost imperceptibly beckoned to him.

"Hullo—mind helping me again?" he asked.

"No sir," said Lillywhite, with a faint smile.

"Thanks. Then will you please tell Mr. Purdon their names?"

There was a slight delay while Tony, who had forgotten to provide himself with adequate writing materials, remedied his omission, and then the questioning proceeded.

"Next, will those boys please put up their hands who bought marzipan blocks?"

This time there were several responses, and Tony's pencil became busier. Names were elicited, then sums of money spent and purchases received. After marzipan came peppermint; after peppermint, lemon. There followed details of such things as wine gums, liquorice all-sorts, chocolate drops and plain bars, toffees, bull's-eyes; the various commodities which constituted tuck at Anstey Court were enumerated by Lillywhite. The completion and checking of the list took half an hour, and at the end of that time Beale felt that he had the school both attentive and good-humoured. He had suggested that there was no need for silence while records were being made, but was grateful for the promptness with which the chattering ceased whenever he tapped on the desk. It appeared that the boys had been well trained.

"Right, that's half the work done," he said. "I'll finish with some general questions, and before I start I want to make one point quite clear. I'm not trying to persuade anyone to own up, and I'm not asking anyone to sneak. Whatever you tell me I shall keep to myself—that's a promise. I merely want information to help me settle a very serious matter, so please don't hold back anything you know. On second thoughts it may be better if you write your answers down—it'll save a lot of time and make what you say more secret. Mr. Purdon, could you tear up about half that exercise book?"

"If you guarantee I shan't get into trouble," agreed Tony; at which there was a general smile.

"There ought to be some paper in the desk, sir," observed Lillywhite. "We often have slip tests."

When everyone was ready, and it had been established that all could write with some degree of fluency, Beale continued.

"Spelling doesn't matter much," he assured the boys. "Number your questions in the usual way, and please put your names at the top of your papers. All in order? Then, first, what was Edwin Weekes's favourite sweet? If you think he had more than one, write them all down. If you don't know, say so."

Forty heads bent over forty desks, and forty pens and pencils moved scratchily. Tony smiled, took out his cigarette case, was frowned at by Beale, sighed, and replaced it.

"A penny saved is a penny gained!" he murmured obscurely, and began to study the geometrical theorem displayed on the blackboard behind him. He was soon frowning himself.

"Number two," said Beale; "if there were three chocolate blocks being given away, a peppermint and a lemon and a marzipan, which would you have expected Edwin to take? Only one choice allowed."

At this somebody sniggered, but was immediately rebuked by his neighbours. Anstey Court obviously considered Edwin's failings no longer amusing.

"Next, which would you have chosen yourselves?

"Number four—and don't be afraid of being honest here, because there's no possible question of punishment; did any of you disobey Mr. Weekes's order not to eat any tuck before you came back from church on Sunday? Answer yes or no.

"Number five; between the time tuck was given out on Saturday and the time each of you went to bed, did you notice anyone but Edwin going to Edwin's locker? Remember that if you did it won't be sneaking to say so, and to make that quite clear I'll include grown-ups as well. Did you see any other boy but Edwin, or any grown-up at all, go to Edwin's locker on Saturday afternoon or evening?"

Tony sauntered across.

"Suppose one of 'em went when there wasn't anyone else looking?" he asked in a low voice.

"I don't care if they all went," Beale told him, equally quietly. "It's only the grown-ups I'm interested in."

"Ah! You're too smart for me."

"So it seems. Number six; did Edwin ever exchange his tuck for other people's? I mean, did he sometimes alter his mind after buying a marzipan block, say, and try to swap it for a peppermint?

"Next, the same question a different way round; has he ever swapped any of his tuck because he was asked to by one of you? Answer for yourselves.

"Number eight; did he ever swap sweets of any kind for other things, such as stamps or cigarette cards? Answer for yourselves again, and if the answer's yes, give details.

"Next, did he ever give any of his tuck away, especially chocolate blocks or parts of chocolate blocks?

"Lastly, did any of you wake up in the night after you went to bed on Saturday, and hear any unusual noise? A door opening or closing, footsteps, a cry, a mysterious shuffle or rattle or bang? In fact, anything except a snore."

The papers were collected, and the boys told tactfully that they need have no fears for their own personal safety. Finally, anyone who thought he had other information of possible value was invited to visit the morning-room afterwards and share his knowledge.

"Now you can go," said Beale, after consulting Tony's writings; "and thank you for being so patient. I'd like Carmichael and Ridgeway and Askew to stay behind for a moment, though—and you too, Lillywhite, please."

The others trooped out and he took aside Carmichael, the tall boy with spectacles.

"D'you mind telling me why you didn't buy any tuck on Saturday?" he asked.

"No sir,"—very seriously. "I'm not allowed to, sir—the doctor says sweets are bad for me. I get spots if I eat them, sir."

"What rotten luck! Thank you."

Ridgeway, whose left eye looked inwards, proffered a different explanation for his abstinence.

"I'm off tuck, sir," he said. "I bust a window ages ago, and all my pocket-money went to mend it."

"What did you bust it with—a cricket ball?"

"Oh no sir, a catapult. It was a rotten boss shot, too—that's what comes of having a boss eye."

Beale laughed at the child's openness about his affliction.

"Do the other boys give you some of their tuck sometimes to console you?" he asked.

Ridgeway shuffled, then grinned.

"They're not supposed to, sir."

"But do they?"

"Well, some of 'em do—not very often, though."

"Did Edwin?"

"Oh no sir, never!" was the instantly emphatic answer.

Lillywhite and Askew received only one question, but it manifestly puzzled them.

"Have you ever seen any of the boys with a safety-razor blade?" queried Beale. Neither of them had, but they promised to make discreet investigations about the existence of such an article in their part of the school.

XVII

THE TWO MEN WORKED HARD on the information they had received, Tony checking the tuck and Beale attending to the slip-test. They finished within a minute of one another, and almost immediately came an interruption; a warning tap which made it clear that they were not being visited by the headmaster, and in the doorway stood a tall boy with dark hair.

"Hullo, come in!" said Beale, recognizing him. "You're Maurice Weekes, aren't you?"

"Yes sir."

"I thought so—I remember seeing you make your catch at half-term."

Maurice smiled, and both liked the look of him.

"Oh, that! An awful fluke, sir."

"I doubt it. And now you've got something to tell us?"

"Well, sir, I don't know. It isn't anything really, but Lillywhite seemed to think I'd better see you. It's about the torch, sir—the one Mr. Gregory said was found. It belonged to me, and Edwin borrowed it just before he went to bed on Saturday."

"Ah, that may be worth knowing," said Beale, "thanks. Did he explain why he wanted it?" he added, casually, and Maurice Weekes appeared troubled.

"That's the queer part, sir. He did tell me, but it couldn't have been the real reason. He *said* he wanted to read in bed, but—"

"But he went up at half past seven, and it wouldn't be dark for another two hours?"

The boy nodded eagerly.

"Yes sir, that's just it. I—I didn't see how it could be true."

"You noticed at the time?"

"Yes sir."

"Did you say anything?"

"No sir—I just gave him the torch. There'd only have been a row if I hadn't, and anyway there wasn't much left in the battery."

"No—I saw that for myself. Forgive me for asking, but you two didn't get on very well?"

"Not very—but I'm sorry he's dead. Sir,"—earnestly, his brown eyes intently surveying Beale's face, "do you know how it happened? Properly?"

"I'm sorry—not yet. But I shall find out."

"It couldn't have been an accident? I mean, he *was* poisoned? That's what they're all saying."

"I'm afraid they're correct; but please don't quote me, because I don't think I'm supposed to tell you."

"No sir, of course not. But what you said downstairs was right? There won't be any more of us dying suddenly like that?"

"I don't believe there's the least possible danger," Beale told him gravely. "And if ever I begin to, I shall take steps to prevent it. Don't be afraid, Maurice."

"No sir," agreed the boy, with a sudden frank smile, turned to go, and then halted by the door.

"I didn't know Edwin was going to use the torch to come downstairs with in the night," he said simply.

"A nice child, but a bit nervous," was Tony's verdict. "That finally disposes of any hocus-pocus, I suppose? It establishes Edwin's previous intention to feed himself at night?"

"If it needed establishing," said Beale, and picked up his papers again. "My results won't take long," he went on. "Shall I go first? Then to begin with Edwin's favourite sweet was apparently the one he was eating. There are six votes for marzipan, fourteen for peppermint, eight for liquorice, three for toffee, and the rest dither between coconut ice, wine gums, and nougat. Two boys have put 'Everything' in brackets. It doesn't really help much, except to show that the murderer probably couldn't have been certain of his buying marzipan. Next, which would he have chosen from peppermint, lemon or marzipan? Twenty-five say the first, three the second, and twelve the third. The lack of support for lemon is understandable, of course—last Saturday was the first time there'd ever been any here."

"Which makes it a bit odd that anybody should have chosen it, surely?"

"Oh, perhaps they once heard him say he liked lemon. It doesn't seem important. The third question was only meant to make the business sound more homely, so we'll skip that. No one tackled his tuck in advance, and so we're presumably in possession of everything that was sold on Saturday; except Edwin's, which went to be analysed. You agree?"

"I'm speaking next," said Tony firmly. "In any case, how do you analyse six ounces of liquorice all-sorts?"

"I can't imagine."

"Stew them and examine the juice, I suppose. And now comes the really critical question about the locker, doesn't it?"

"Yes, and the answer's unanimously negative. Nobody was seen going there, which is disappointing but only to be expected. The next three questions can all be taken together. Edwin never swapped his tuck, either at his own or anyone else's suggestion, and he never never *never* gave any away; seven answers underlined and two in capital letters.

"Finally, there were no startling noises in the night. A boy called Wilkins heard a dog bark, and another called Steede woke up towards dusk and couldn't get to sleep again because of two cats fighting.

"No, my questions have produced very little except nine ways of spelling marzipan."

"Really? I shouldn't have thought it possible."

"Nor I; but then, small boys have all the imagination, according to Gregory. And now it's your turn."

"Certainly, after I've asked a question. Wouldn't a good additional one have been 'What tuck did Edwin buy on Saturday?' Just in case we can't rely on Herbert or on what was found."

Beale nodded.

"I didn't overlook it," he said. "On the whole I decided to keep quiet, because it might get to Herbert's ears and start him thinking. In any case it's not very likely that the others would know, since Edwin was kept till last and nobody could have any expectations from him. I agree the matter isn't settled conclusively, but I shouldn't expect the murderer to risk having anything found in the locker but what the boy actually did buy."

Tony smiled broadly.

"You know, that's probably your worst failing as a detective," he remarked thoughtfully. "Not that it seems to handicap you much, though. But you may land yourself in a mess one day if you don't take care."

"What's my worst failing? Talking too much?"

"No, over-estimating other people's intelligence, particularly murderers'. 'Oh, he'd never have done this or that!' you say, time and time again. 'It would be far too stupid.' Yet people do do stupid things; murder, for example."

"Now don't start that!" remonstrated Beale.

"Murder's only stupid when it's found out and brought home, or when to a sensible man it isn't worth the inevitable risk that it may be. Call it anything else you like—wicked, anti-social, selfish; but not necessarily stupid. And don't say I'm contradicting myself, because murder's bound to be exposed—I simply shan't believe you. A good many are—the newspapers tell you that much. In addition, a few more escape public notice only because there isn't enough evidence to justify an arrest. Every now and again a murderer gets acquitted. Yet all those cases together don't total the same as the number of known homicides; which leaves entirely out of account the unknown ones."

"Are there any?"

"*I* think so. I think there are probably a considerable number of deaths which the police never investigate merely because there hasn't been enough rumour and suspicion connected with them, but which nevertheless weren't quite medically sound—not quite in accordance with the certificates. Or even that were, and yet constituted murder."

Tony frowned.

"How so?" he asked. "Doctors polishing off their patients? Shaw said that a long time ago."

"I didn't mean doctors. As an unoriginal example, the husband dying of pneumonia whose impatient wife lets out the fire and opens the window and so helps him on."

"Ugh! Do you really think much of that sort of thing happens?"

"Not a lot, but a certain amount. What's the annual death-rate? Somewhere about twelve per thousand, I believe. If you allow, for the sake of argument, that even only one death in every fifty thousand isn't all it should be, you immediately face the possibility of ten secret murders or manslaughters a year in England and Wales."

"So secret that nobody but you suspects their existence!"

"Oh no—I'm not quite alone in my views. But I don't expect you to agree with me blindly; why should you? For instance, you've probably never realized that it's just as much murder to kill a man with a weak heart by intentionally banging an empty paper-bag behind him as it would be to cut his head off with a rusty saw. 'The weapon, m'lud, came from the *Home & Colonial.*' It sounds silly; yet the act remains murder.

"Again, you've never seen for yourself how small a thing may start an investigation—a chance word in the right ear, and four or five months later out comes the black cap. Mr. and Mrs. Smith, we'll say, live next door to Mrs. Jones, who's an invalid with nothing better to do all day long than stare out of the window. She gets the idea that there's something between Mr. Smith and the girl in the flat opposite because she's seen them smile at one another several times; though the truth is that they could hardly do anything else after travelling to business on the same train every morning for years.

"Then Mrs. Smith dies, and after the funeral Mrs. Jones begins to look wise. Then, a month later, she thinks she spots Mr. Smith and the girl arm in arm, though actually it's two other people, and after that the fun really starts. She tells all her friends, and they tell all their friends; the story spreads, and becomes strangely positive and circumstantial, and one fine day Mrs. Smith is dug up.

"She's found to be rotten with arsenic, because that's what her husband poisoned her with; but not on account of a girl in the flat opposite or anywhere else—only so that he could get a little peace and quietness. The truth eventually comes out, of course, but only by accident—only because of one nosey parker's bad guess and bad eyesight. Yet what if Mrs. Jones had been blind, or charitable by nature? Some people are.

"The favourite answer to that—I make you a present of it—explains loftily how Providence kindly saw to it that she wasn't. Myself, I say it was bad luck on Smith, and I emphatically don't believe that all Smiths always have bad luck.

"Still, going back to what you said about me, I'm inclined to admit there may be a grain of sense in it. I can only answer that it's safer to over-estimate a criminal's intelligence than to under-estimate it. You must remember that nowadays murderers are usually amateurs, too, with occasional exceptions like Landru, and where crime's concerned the average amateur is cleverer than the average professional if only because he remains an amateur—because he knows when to stop.

"And now let's get on with this particular business. Does your list check with Gregory's?"

"Word for word and letter for letter, as far as the chocolate blocks go," said Tony. "So does the rest too, as far as I can tell, but I naturally won't swear that what Gregory calls a bag of wine gums, taken from Askew's locker, say, isn't one or two short of two ounces.

"The marzipans are all right, though. We can both account for ten, the one that killed Edwin makes eleven, and the thirty-seven you found in the box make the four dozen it originally contained. If you want details of the ten, here they are; two for Maurice, two for Perrin, and one each for Lillywhite, Dorland, Burnaby, Phipps, Stevenson, and Brown major. Further, the money adds up exactly. I asked the prices of the various kinds of sweets and worked it all out scientifically, and the result is 12s. 10d. exclusive of Edwin's sixpence; the same as Herbert and the governess say. By the way, she's got nice legs."

"Miss Charlotte doesn't think so," smiled Beale. "Well, very many thanks. So long as the marzipans are all right, nothing else seems to matter. We can now assume that the poisoned block was the actual one that Edwin bought. Of course, we may still be wrong; somebody may have had one waiting since before June 2nd, when the supply ran out, but I don't believe it myself."

"And can't we also explain the half-term business?" suggested Tony. "Despairing of ever getting any more marzipan, the murderer turned instead to Miss Charlotte's liqueur chocolates."

"Which brings us face to face again with all the old difficulties," said Beale. "If you remember, the persons who could possibly have known the contents beforehand were limited to Miss Charlotte herself, Herbert, and Lady Weekes. The same three persons knew, or could be suspected of knowing, that there was cyanide on the premises. Yet one of them couldn't have done the distributing, the second called for Scotland Yard, and the third seems right out of the present business, at any rate in person. It's all a confounded muddle."

"Lady Weekes could have told the governess about the cyanide. In fact, she could even have been responsible for the half-term amusements as a blind, and left a neat little packet of poison behind for future use under the smoke-screen of a furious quarrel."

"Which only took place because the governess decided to stay and not go."

"Nonsense! That was merely the excuse; I'm assuming it would have taken place anyway."

"Even though Miss Tilling went?"

"Oh, well, I don't know about that. Maybe she was fooling you and Herbert there too."

"And maybe not. All the same, I wish I knew *why* the chocolates were dotted round the place. It was a deliberate action, and so presumably had some reason behind it. Perhaps, as you say, it was meant for a blind, in which case it's succeeded with me. And yet—and yet—"

He broke off, frowning, while Tony watched in silence. He realized his friend was thinking hard—had perhaps had an idea which would throw light on the mystery. For his own part he saw at present no way through the tangle. He found his mind constantly reverting to the four separate actions of which the murder had consisted; the obtaining of the poison, the obtaining of a marzipan block, the deadly intermixture of the two, and finally the setting of the trap. How could any of those actions ever be conclusively brought home to one man or one woman? They already knew where the poison came from, and the source of the bait, they knew also where it had been placed and approximately when it took effect; yet none of that knowledge seemed to help. To him it looked very like a fool-proof crime.

Presently Beale spoke again.

"There's a possible answer," he said. "The question I ought to have asked myself a long time ago was 'What result did the half-term affair have, *as far as I'm concerned?'* That's making the assumption that what happened in the small hours of Sunday morning was in some way consequent upon what happened last time I was here, but I don't think that's unjust. Agree?"

"Certainly—I've been taking it for granted."

"Very well, then what *was* the result? As far as I can tell, that I went away conversant with the idea of an unaccomplished murder—you might almost call it an imaginary one—in which the victim would be Edwin Weekes, the author Lady Weekes, and the method poisoning by cyanide of potassium. That was in the middle of June, and here we are today, a month later, with the first and third of those conditions no longer imaginary but real. I now want to know if perhaps I'm expected to believe automatically that the middle condition is bound to be true also." Tony pondered the matter.

"There was never any intention of committing a murder at half-term?" he asked.

"None. The whole thing—I'm suggesting—was organized so that I could get one point firmly in my head. If Edwin Weekes died, and if he died by cyanide, then Lady Weekes killed him."

"And you want to know if that's sense? My answer is that it might be if Lady Weekes were here when he died; but she wasn't."

Beale nodded.

"And nobody's even hinted at it" he agreed.

"But you'll find out just where she was?"

"Of course. I was hoping to hear today—if I don't in the morning I shall ring up the Yard myself. Here's another thing that strikes me as significant now, though I can't honestly say it did at the time. There were four dozen liqueur chocolates going the rounds at this place during half-term; yet the interval between the discovery of the first in Birkett's blazer pocket and the last in the gym was less than twenty-four hours. As Sir Francis remarked, it might have taken a week. In short, it was too easy."

"That depends," said Tony. "Mightn't it be due to the thoroughness with which you searched?"

"I doubt it. We didn't have to be thorough. We looked in more or less the obvious places, and there they were—the ones that hadn't been thrust under our noses. There was no prodding the insides of bolsters, no tapping of table-legs in case they were hollow.

"You know, it would be a very *tidy* explanation, the one I just proposed." His friend laughed.

"Where Freeman and Hardy are gathered together, there shall Willis be also," he murmured. "All right, let's suppose something went wrong with the works, and when the real show came off Willis was unavoidably detained. The point seems to be, who put that composite idea into your head?"

"Miss Charlotte," was the immediate reply.

"All of it?"

"No, but two-thirds, and she could be reasonably sure her brother wouldn't keep quiet about the other, the identity of the victim. He told us of his fears for Edwin's safety—as she'd know he would; but it was she who suggested poison to him in the first place, and she was the one who went out of her way to make sure I didn't overlook Lady Weekes.

"At least, I think that's true," he added, less certainly. "Sir Francis did say something coming down in the train, though, and he couldn't very well have been prompted by her. Ah well, perhaps I'm being too fanciful; let's stick to facts for a bit."

"What facts? We seem to have used them all up. I propose we leave half-term, and get on to the question of motive. *Why* was Edwin killed? Tell me that, and I'll tell you who did it."

"Thanks for nothing; and anyway, that's a rash offer. Ignoring Latin tags for once, it's not too much to say that he was a greedy and objectionable boy with a tendency towards sneaking. As Gregory pointed out in his statement, the inhabitants of an enclosed community like this are apt to lose their sense of values.

Little things become enormously important, and big things are overlooked or taken for granted. Is it incredible that somebody found Edwin so intolerable that he grew to be obsessed with the urge to remove him and improve this narrow hemmed-in world of Anstey Court?"

"It doesn't strike me as likely, unless the boy was an absolute stinker."

"Which everyone but his uncle says he was."

"Even Lady Weekes?"

"Well, no, not that I've heard, though I don't suppose she's ever had much to do with him. But his father must have done, and Miss Charlotte told me he was no great favourite there."

Tony still looked dubious.

"Make him as objectionable as possible, and it still doesn't seem very strong," he said. "Not for murder, or only for someone who was already a regular misanthrope. Would Miss Charlotte fill the bill there?"

"I don't know—she might. She assured me herself that she didn't like one person in a hundred she met."

"Except chief-inspectors from Scotland Yard, apparently."

"And that perhaps only because it suited her purpose! The two other motives I can think of are, first, to benefit Maurice, and secondly to hit at Sir Robert."

"But you just said he didn't fancy Edwin," objected Tony. "Wouldn't it be more sensible to suppose that somebody aimed at hurting Herbert?"

Beale regarded him with interest.

"That's not half bad," he conceded. "Not that I believe much in this 'Hit-A-to-make-B-cry' business myself as a general rule, though if you remember we did come across a case of it once. Herbert certainly seems a better target than Sir Robert, but that by itself won't get us very far."

"No, we should have to set about finding someone with a deep grudge against the man. Any suggestions?"

"Lady Weekes doesn't like him much, though I'm not sure why. I don't think Miss Charlotte's particularly fond of him, either, but that's probably no more than the result of living with him for a few years. I know I couldn't stand much of him."

He smiled, got up, and looked out of the window.

"What about a breath of fresh air?" he suggested. "We've mugged indoors most of the time since you got here."

They strolled outside, and stood for a while watching the elder boys quietly practising in the nets; it was quarter to eight, and a fine clear evening. Presently Lloyd Gregory sauntered up.

"Getting anywhere?" he asked.

"Not yet," said Beale.

"Ah. It's a bad business. You wouldn't notice, of course, but there's only about a tenth of the usual noise."

"I thought they were being extraordinarily silent, for boys," remarked Tony. "Here, look out!"

He had perceived a cricket ball hurtling towards them. There came a warning cry of 'Heads!' from the nets, and a moment later a second cry of 'Well caught sir!' from Askew, the guilty batsman.

"You couldn't miss it, with hands that size," said Beale, not anxious to be catechized by the senior master. "Any objection to our joining in? It's a long time since I had the chance."

"Not a bit—not a bit. It'll give the kids something to talk about for the rest of their lives."

"Coo sir, are you any good?" asked Askew a moment later, adjusting his fingerstall.

"Not a scrap."

"Are you going to bowl fast?"—with an apprehensive glance at his unpadded legs.

"No, very slow—it probably won't even reach you."

Both of them enjoyed the next half hour; especially Tony, who with a tremendous swipe knocked a ball clean over the school buildings. After the feat there was a momentary silence; then Lillywhite spoke, seriously and critically.

"Good shot, sir—that would pretty nearly have cleared the pav at Lords!" he declared.

At nine o'clock Beale paid another visit to the store-room, his fourth since the previous afternoon. He returned rather disappointed.

"Nothing's been touched," he said. "I'm beginning to think maybe Herbert's keys are genuinely lost. Pretty soon I shall have to start looking for them."

Later they were invited to the masters'-room for a smoke and a chat. After consulting with Tony privately, Beale accepted. It probably meant that an attempt would be made to pump them, but he was interested to see how far the staff's curiosity would press. Thus the senior master's opening words were a surprise.

"I expect you'd rather not discuss Edwin's death," said Gregory. "We thought perhaps you'd like a game of bridge? Sorry the place is so beastly small, but I dare say we can manage."

"Bridge sounds ideal," declared Tony. "Sure we're not hindering you?"

As he spoke he nodded towards a pile of exercise books with a smile, which Birkett returned.

"Glad to give them a miss," he said, his pink youthful face amiable tonight. "Anyway, I don't suppose work matters much. The main thing is to keep the kids quiet, which is a darn sight easier than I thought it might be. Oh, and before we start not talking about this business,"—to Beale, "I would like just to ask one question. Has the head said anything to you about—well, about shutting this place down? It doesn't matter to Gregory much because he's leaving in any case, but if I'm to be out of a job I'd like to know as early as possible, and I hardly care to tackle the man point-blank."

"He's hinted at it indirectly," was the answer, "but I can't say if he's thought about things seriously. I'll try to find out, if you want me to."

"Thanks awfully—I would like to know. Oh lord, who's this?"

"Come in!" called Lloyd Gregory, and Miss Tilling appeared, in her hand a pile of large printed forms enclosed in pink blotting-paper.

"The reports," she explained. "Mr. Weekes just gave them to me, and says he hopes they'll be ready by the end of the week. I told the usual lies. Oh, and Sir Robert's just arrived, Mr. Beale, but he's too tired to see you tonight. In fact, he's going straight to bed."

"That's the political gent, isn't it?" asked Birkett. "What's he like?"

"Why, didn't you see him yourself last half-term?"

"No—I was in bed with flu, if you remember."

"Oh yes, of course. Well, he's tall and bony and looks shockingly ill. A thinner and more distinguished edition of Jumbo, really, only he's clean shaven and his eyes are like two deep blue stones—sapphires, perhaps, but with no sparkle in them."

"Lord, you're getting quite poetical!" remarked Lloyd Gregory with a lazy smile. "He's an old so-and-so, what I know of him. Last time he came he 'borrowed' my best walking-stick, but I don't suppose he brought it with him if he came by air."

"Why not?" murmured Birkett brightly. "Remember the Umbrella of Munich!"

A thought struck Beale, and he turned to Gregory.

"If it's a fair question, are they all like that?" he asked. "The Weekes, I mean, over borrowing and things?"

"If it's a fair answer, they are, every man jack of 'em."

"Only most of them are worse than the rest," added the governess with a laugh. "Miss Charlotte?"

"Thimbles and detective stories—you daren't leave either lying about or she finds them somehow."

"And the other boy, Maurice?"

"Oh well, he's not too bad, I suppose," admitted Gregory. "Not that I've ever seen him being specially generous—though it *was* his torch that Edwin had. I asked him—thought I recognized it."

"And one more question, if I may," said Beale. "Would you call Edwin a smart boy? I don't mean only over his work, but in general. Was he shrewd?"

"Where his own interests were concerned," replied the governess, and the other two nodded. "I've had him solidly all day long for four terms, so I ought to know, and that's what puzzles me rather. I mean, he'd have stood to gain a lot more by *not* eating his tuck in the night, after what Miss Charlotte said at lunch."

"Yet he did," Gregory pointed out. "You can't get over the blood where he hit his head when he fell. Or can you?"—to Beale.

"No. As you say, it's quite conclusive. I expect he felt too hungry to be shrewd for once. Thank you all very much."

"Not a bit. Going to stay and cut in, Miss Tilling?"

"No thank you, Mr. Gregory," she replied with equal politeness, though smiling. "I'll go and think up some acid remarks for this bundle of trouble."

" 'Still trying,' " murmured Tony, with memories of his own boyhood. "But the nicest one I ever had was for Greek; 'If marks were bruises, he'd look the same'."

After the governess had gone Gregory began to set the card-table. A few moments later Beale, who had discovered a dictionary in the shelf behind his chair, suddenly slapped his knee.

"Good lord, what fun!" he exclaimed; but resolutely refused to explain why.

XVIII

BEALE HAD MET Sir Robert Weekes once, years before, but he knew when he entered the drawing-room after breakfast the next morning that he would never have recognized the man. Miss Tilling's description—shockingly ill—had been an apt one. The former politician's gaunt frame and laboured breathing betrayed the state of his health, and his fingers felt like cold wax. He bore some resemblance to the headmaster, his brother, but his manner seemed infinitely more frigid and overbearing than Herbert's was ever likely to be at its worst.

"Good morning, Inspector," he said, bowing slightly. "I shall be glad to hear what progress you have made in the case. I saw the Home Secretary before coming down here yesterday, and he assures me of your capabilities. Charlotte, do please sit still! It irritates me to have people rustling papers near when I'm talking. Still eating chocolates? One might have supposed this affair would cure you of that."

And, to Beale's surprise, Miss Charlotte obeyed without protest, though he fancied that she was a little put out at the directness of her brother's speech. He braced himself for possible unpleasantness, but before he could speak Herbert Weekes came into the room; a shambling listless hulk of a man with, today, a faintly apologetic air.

"Ah, you're here," he said, unnecessarily.

"It would appear so," retorted Sir Robert, evidently in no mood for small talk. "I have asked the Inspector if he has made any progress."

"A certain amount, sir," Beale answered. "I haven't discovered the murderer's identity yet, however, and until then I should prefer not to go into details. I'm sure you'll appreciate my reasons for saying that."

It was clear at a glance that Sir Robert did not, but he nodded as if in an attempt to insinuate that he himself had counselled caution.

"But you're entirely satisfied that it *was* murder?" he asked.

"Entirely; though perhaps an unusual one."

"Yes?"

"I mean, sir, that it will probably be difficult to build up a convincing case against the person responsible, even when we know that person's identity. For instance, you're probably aware that the poison employed was cyanide of potassium, and until half-term there had been enough of that lying about casually in Mr. Weekes's study for years to account for twenty murders. Again, it's not too much to say that every adult resident here—and every boy too, if it comes to that—had ample opportunity to visit Edwin's locker between the time he received his tuck on Saturday afternoon and the time he died about twelve hours later; more than once if necessary, in secret, and without leaving a trace."

"You've made sure there were no fingerprints?" asked the other, and Beale smiled.

"I think that would come under the heading of capabilities," he suggested mildly.

"Yes, of course—quite. But I presume you don't seriously include the boys in your reckonings?"

"No sir. I merely wished to emphasize the difficulty of proving anything with regard to means or opportunity, particularly the latter."

"What you're really driving at, Inspector," interrupted Miss Charlotte, "is that every adult at Anstey Court automatically comes under suspicion. Hence, of course, your reluctance to tell us how you're getting on."

"To some extent, yes," he admitted.

"But that's preposterous!" exclaimed Sir Robert. "D'you mean to sit there and tell me to my face you suspect my own brother and sister?"

"Well sir, I'd rather put it the other way round and say I'm not yet in a position to exclude them from suspicion. In short, as I mentioned to begin with, I don't yet know the name of the person I'm looking for."

"And you're not even prepared to explain what steps you're taking to find out!"

Beale sighed.

"For one thing, it would waste a couple of hours," he observed quietly. "For another, I certainly couldn't do so without first consulting the chief-constable and my own superiors at Scotland Yard. I may be in charge of the investigation, but that doesn't mean I have a completely free hand to conduct it how I like, sir."

Sir Robert grunted; the argument was one which appealed to him, as Beale had thought it might.

"Well, is there anything I can do to help?" he asked gruffly.

"Yes, sir; you can be good enough to answer some questions. Just now I spoke of means and opportunity, but there's a third factor of vital importance where murder's concerned, and especially so when it's a planned murder. I mean motive. Have you considered that point at all, sir?"

"Ah. Hum. Suppose you give me your own views first."

"Nonsense!" said Miss Charlotte tartly from her chair by the window. "Really, Robert, you mustn't make his job harder than it already is. He's just told you he doesn't want to discuss his own opinions—he wants to know yours."

The elderly man snorted, his thin face angry.

"Please be kind enough not to interfere, Charlotte!" he requested.

"Thank you, I shall speak my mind when and how I please," came the swift answer; and, very deliberately, she rustled in her box for another chocolate.

"No good quarrelling," put in Herbert Weekes heavily, rousing himself from his brooding silence. "If you can give the Inspector even the smallest degree of help, Robert, do please do so. Why was Edwin killed? Why should anyone commit a vile brutality like that?"

"Good God, how d'you expect me to know?" exploded his brother. "Confound it, I wasn't even in the country when it happened!"

"But what has being in the country to do with anything?" demanded Miss Charlotte. "The motive generally precedes the crime; isn't that so, Mr. Beale?"

He agreed that it was, and turned again to the irate man opposite.

"Perhaps I had better make one or two suggestions," he said; "and perhaps you'll all be kind enough to give me your opinions. There are numerous motives for murder, but in this case they can be reduced to three which seem at all applicable. In the first place, it may be that Edwin was poisoned because someone felt for him an intense and overpowering hatred. Does that idea strike any of you as worth consideration?"

"No," replied Herbert instantly, glaring and jerking his head up and down rapidly. "The boy may have had his faults, but who has not?"

"There are faults *and* faults," remarked his sister. "However, I had best say nothing. I don't wish to hurt anyone's feelings, and I think Mr. Beale already knows my views."

Herbert made no answer to that but to look at her for a moment as if he detested her from the bottom of his heart. It was Sir Robert who spoke next.

"Frankly, I shouldn't care to dismiss the suggestion out of hand," he said steadily. "But perhaps you can give us a better one, Inspector?"

"Secondly," continued Beale, "it may be that Edwin was murdered in order to benefit someone financially, that person not necessarily being the murderer. Whether or not that was the object of the crime, sir, can you say if it has been achieved to your knowledge?"

"When the time comes, Maurice will naturally inherit more than he would otherwise have done; but I am a comparatively wealthy man, and there would have been ample for them both. It goes without saying that Maurice would take the title in any event—I am a baronet, of course, not a knight. I've no reason to think that anyone else will be a penny the better off for Edwin's death, now or ever."

He stared at Beale bleakly with his dull blue eyes.

"It seems that we must ask you for your third motive, Inspector," he said.

"Very well, sir; it is that Edwin may have been killed in order to inflict pain upon yourself. Is that too fantastic?"

"In other words, Robert, have you any bitter enemies?" enquired his sister with what appeared malicious clarity; but as she spoke she looked not at the man she addressed but at Herbert, once more huddled in his arm-chair with legs crossed and one hand cupping his chin. Her glance plainly passed unnoticed. The headmaster of Anstey Court might have been in another world, thought Beale; perhaps one where Edwin still breathed in safety, secure from poison or the threat of poison. He felt a pang of sorrow for the man; there could be no slightest doubt about the depth of his sorrow. He suddenly remembered Birkett's query of the evening before, and reminded himself that he had yet to ask if anything had been decided about the future of the school. But Sir Robert was speaking again.

"Anyone who has occupied a high position in public life," he said, rather as if he were still in parliament, "as I think I may suggest has been the case with myself, and who is not a time-server nor a panderer to all men's favour, as I know I have never been, must inevitably make enemies. I can only tell you what I believe to be the truth; that I know of none bitter enough to have ever conceived such a method of satisfying their baser feelings."

"Baser?" repeated Miss Charlotte acidly. "What's base about honest dislike, pray? Or d'you mean only when it's dislike of you?"

"I see no necessity for quibbling," was the equally acid retort. "My meaning was clear enough, and if revenge is not a base instinct, I should be glad to learn what is."

"Revenge!" echoed Herbert, coming back to life. "That's what it must have been! I—I'm afraid I have not succeeded in thinking very clearly about things yet, but there seems to me no doubt that you have hit the mark, Inspector."

"Very well then, revenge," said his sister, sitting up as if she were tired of vagueness. "The question is, revenge against whom? No one in his senses would poison Edwin in order to strike at *you,* Robert."

"I beg your pardon? Why not?" he inquired, turning his head towards her. She looked at him from under drooping lids, somehow resembling a black parrot about to peck hard.

"Because only a fool could suppose you ever cared *that* about the boy!" she told him, snapping her fingers with surprising violence. "Why,"—as he began to expostulate, "look at the way you've behaved since you got here last night! Have you expressed one word of sorrow or regret that your own son's lying cold and stiff in some mortuary having his inside cut out and stared at? Not in my hearing. Have you shown any other feelings than peevishness and bad temper and a most almighty sense of self-importance? Not an inkling."

"How dare you!" spluttered Sir Robert, his blue eyes for once animated.

"Oh, stop it, stop it!" growled Herbert Weekes. "You're not the one to talk, Charlotte—everybody knows you disliked the poor child."

"Who didn't, except you? All this idiotic humbug! Death doesn't automatically involve saintliness, you know. I've never pretended I liked Edwin, and I shan't start now. All I'm objecting to is the idea of Robert smugly preparing to suppose that anyone in the world could imagine *him* feeling affectionate—that's the truth of the matter. If there was the slightest intention of revenge then it was against you, Herbert, and no one else."

And then, with a startling change of manner, she turned to Beale.

"You mustn't take any notice of our wrangling," she said. "Doubtless it's extremely bad manners, but the circumstances are rather exceptional. Now, let us all keep cool and discuss things with some approach to decency."

"It would be an admirable improvement!" agreed Sir Robert scathingly. "I resent your remarks more than I can say. I am no more a hypocrite than yourself, and to imply that I lack normal affection is not only a deliberate insult but a gross travesty."

He was still furiously angry, and his tone stirred Miss Charlotte from her recent good resolution.

"There can be two opinions about that!" she snapped. "I marvel the doctors can think you have a weak heart. A better diagnosis would have been that you have no heart at all."

"Stop it!" cried Herbert, more loudly, and moved in his chair as if he were about to get up and walk between them. But it was too late; Sir Robert had passed beyond control of his tongue. He sat livid for a moment, his thin lips moving without sound. Then the storm burst.

"You ignorant wicked hell-cat!" he screamed, his face contorted and his voice almost treble. "Why should I care tuppence about Edwin? Eh? Tell me! Ha, you can't! Then let me tell you—let me give myself that pleasure after all these years! Humbug, eh? No heart, eh? Listen, you chocolate-stuffing shrew; Edwin was a nasty deceitful little pig—*just like his father!*"

And, in the stunned silence which followed, he stared malevolently at the headmaster of Anstey Court; at Herbert Weekes, who sat open-mouthed and dumb that his secret was discovered. But then something went wrong with Sir Robert's stare. In turn his mouth too opened, he half rose, swayed, and a moment later fell heavily backwards with his hand to his heart.

No one, not even Beale, had noticed the drawing-room door move; but there standing quietly by the grand piano, dressed in cool blue linen and a wide-brimmed hat, was Lady Weekes.

XIX

THE CHAOS HAD SUBSIDED SOMEWHAT. Miss Wood, the matron, came hurriedly; a doctor was telephoned for. Herbert Weekes and his sister remained together in the drawing-room, white-faced and shaken and resolutely not encountering one another's eyes, while Beale took the new arrival into the morning-room. They had it to themselves, since Tony had gone up to town for a luncheon engagement.

"Well, *well!"* said Lady Weekes, and sat down. "Do let me get my breath before we start talking. I feel like somebody who's been turned inside out and put back all wrong. Have you a cigarette, please? Forgot to buy any."

Beale managed to find a tin of Tony's, and filled his pipe in silence. Then he smiled.

"Recovered yet?" he asked. "I dare say you found it a bit of a shock."

"A bit? I'd as soon have believed Charlotte takes drugs and goes off for week-ends to Brighton. Imagine Herbert of all people having an illegitimate child! And by his own brother's wife at that! I'm sorry, I just can't grasp it properly yet."

"But you've no doubt it's true?"

She looked at him sharply, her cigarette daintily poised between her fingers.

"Not after I saw his face," she replied. "There was guilt all over it—guilt and surprise. Why, have you any doubts?"

He shook his head.

"No, none; but my case is rather different from yours. You see, I was prepared for something of the sort."

She laughed, a little sceptically.

"If you really mean that, you must be an extraordinarily clever man!" she remarked. "Unless someone told you, which hardly seems likely. Charlotte certainly didn't seem to know."

"Yes, I got that impression too," he agreed, frowning. "Nor did I, if it comes to knowing, not definitely, but I had suspicions. As a matter of fact, I can establish that much,"—and taking out his note-book he showed her an entry he had made in bed that morning.

Shouldn't be surprised if Edwin not Sir Robert's son at all, but Herbert's; would explain favouritism, etc. Did C. try to tell me at half-term?

"C. being Charlotte?" queried Lady Weekes. "Whatever makes you think that? She didn't know—I'm sure of it. And,"—with a smile—"why so anxious to impress?"

It might have been an offensive question, but she put it quite casually, and the seriousness of his reply was in marked contrast.

"Not just to show off," he assured her. "I should like you to believe I'm a good detective, because presently I'm going to give you some advice which I particularly want you to take. You'll be more inclined to if you've some reason for thinking that my judgment's occasionally right. If you don't mind, I'd rather not say why I wrote that in my note-book. Quite possibly I wasn't justified—that remains to be seen. You can state quite positively that you yourself never had the least suspicion?"

"Never."

"Is it like Sir Robert to have concealed his knowledge of his brother's secret all these years?"

She wrinkled her forehead at that, and thought for several moments.

"Perhaps I'm prejudiced," she said at last, "but I shouldn't have expected him to. Unless—yes, that would be it. If you ask me, he kept quiet because it would have hurt his vanity to speak. I mean, his first marriage had ended disastrously—nobody knows that better than myself. He probably felt he'd get laughed at if people heard his second wife had been a failure too. Not that he'd have hushed anything up if she'd lived—I don't believe that for a minute because I know how spiteful he can be. But she didn't; she died when Edwin was born. Which makes one wonder how he ever got to know at all, when you think of it. I'm certain Herbert wasn't aware he did."

Beale ignored the possible digression.

"And is it like him to have given the secret away to a stranger?" he pursued.

"Well, he did, didn't he? Surely the question of whether it's like him or not doesn't arise."

"I'm sorry, I don't agree. For all I know, Sir Robert may have informed me purposely."

"Oh, rot! He was far too angry to be deliberate. He blurted out the truth because he was so beside himself he didn't care a damn what he said so long as it hurt. You must have seen the state he was in."

"Yes, he certainly didn't look as if he was carrying out a plan."

"Good heavens!" she exclaimed. "You're not trying to believe that Robert killed Edwin, are you?"

"Of course not; he was on the Continent. Has he a temper? Does he often lose control like that?"

"About three times a year," she said, after consideration, "and nearly always when he's had a shock or is already under some emotional stress. Edwin's death would be bound to affect him, because it would involve publicity of quite the wrong sort. I'm glad you don't suspect him, though—not that you could very well. But you don't know who did do it?"

"Not yet, Lady Weekes. Tell me, how long had you been in the drawing-room?"

"About a minute, or a little more."

"And how did you get in without our noticing?"

"That's easy—by opening the door very quietly. Why? Because I simply couldn't resist it. I knew some kind of a row was going on, and I fancied I heard Robert's voice, and I'm afraid I'm a very inquisitive person. Perhaps I'd better explain what I'm doing here at all, and then you may understand. Principally I came to see you, Inspector, and I didn't come bearing olive branches."

Beale's comment was a mild one, since he could see that she was no longer in aggressive mood.

"Dear me! I hope I shall be able to pacify you."

She laughed.

"I hope so too!" she agreed. "Yes, I wanted to see you, to ask for an explanation. Yesterday a most preposterous person called Symonds came to interview me from Scotland Yard. Where were you on the night of the 16th inst.?—you know the sort of stuff. It was ages before I could even get him to tell me what it was all about. His reluctance, and his general foxy manner, gave me the ridiculous idea that somebody thought I might be a murderess, and it wasn't an idea I relished. I learnt you were in charge of the case—and here I am."

He nodded complacently.

"That was clever of Symonds," he remarked, to her intense amazement. "It was precisely the idea I wanted him to leave with you."

"Wanted him to? Why?"

"So that I could see what you'd do next, Lady Weekes. Action and reaction, you know; stick pins in people and they jump—unless they've carefully padded themselves beforehand so that they shan't."

"I see; and Symonds was the pin. Does that mean I *am* suspected, then?"

"Not necessarily. Put it that you seem to be one of the few persons who could have had an adequate motive for preferring Edwin dead."

She frowned deeply, got up, took another cigarette from the tin, tapped it briskly against the mantelpiece, and sat down again. As he struck a match he saw that she looked suddenly older—nearer forty than thirty.

"Because of the divorce?" she suggested presently, gazing at him through a cloud of grey smoke.

"That was one reason."

"I see. May I ask the others?"

"I think so. The motives attributed to you—hypothetically, of course—were hatred of Sir Robert and desire to benefit your son Maurice."

"Thank you. I won't pretend I don't follow the first, because I'm not quite a fool, but the second doesn't seem much sense. In what way is Maurice better off now that Edwin's dead? Except that he won't have to put up with his beastly nature any more."

"He'll inherit a correspondingly greater proportion of Sir Robert's wealth," said Beale, and she gasped.

"Good lord, what incredible ingenuity! And how hopelessly misplaced! I solemnly assure you I never had such a thought in my life."

"I'm glad to hear it; and—in confidence—not terribly surprised. It never struck me as very convincing."

"I should think not. Who invented it—Symonds?"

He shook his head, smiling. "I'm afraid I can't tell you. In fact, I'm not even sure it wasn't myself. I do a lot of speculating at times independently of the evidence—what's called envisaging all the possibilities."

"Ah! I recognize that language, but I never knew anybody actually did it."

"Sometimes. It sounds the longest way round, but often it isn't. For instance, if you're worrying at a crossword, and you want a five-letter fish beginning with T, you can either try to build it up from the other clues, or you can make a list of all the suitable fishes, consider them one by one, and so perhaps throw light on the surrounding words.

"There are two kinds of detection, Lady Weekes. One kind tries to fit a framework of reason round known facts, the other to insert those facts into a preconceived framework. Both are all right so long as you remember, if anything goes wrong, to scrap the faulty framework in each case. In general, the reason is safer than the imagination, but sometimes there isn't enough material to reason with, and that's particularly true with motive. When the victim of a cold-blooded poisoning is only a child, most of the usual motives clearly can't apply, or a great many of them. Accordingly one guesses, and then tries either to verify or disprove; always bearing in mind, of course, that possession of motive doesn't settle the question of guilt."

He broke off, smiling again.

"Sorry about the lecture," he said. "But I hope I've shown that it wasn't entirely stupid to consider you? Nobody else had such *apparently* strong grounds for disliking Sir Robert, and since you didn't know he wasn't Edwin's father you might easily expect him to be far fonder of him than of Maurice."

But she shook her head.

"It's funny, but I never did think so," she told him. "It always puzzled me, because from the way he treated me I felt that he ought to have loathed Maurice."

"Then I was wrong. But in addition there was the half-term business, you know."

"What, all those chocolates flying about? So you did mean to imply they might be poisoned?"

"When we talked about matchboxes? Yes, I think it was a natural implication, in the circumstances."

As he spoke he watched her with extreme if covert attention, but could discover nothing false in her manner.

"I don't remember anything special, except that you and Sir Francis Barton were here," she remarked. "Was that what you meant?"

"No—far from it. I referred to the theft—or at any rate the temporary disappearance—of the bottle of cyanide."

"Cyanide?" she echoed uncertainly. "But that's what Symonds said Edwin died of."

"It was."

"And you say a bottle was stolen at half-term? Where from?"

"The study."

She stared at him blankly.

"What *are* you talking about?" she demanded. "It's all riddles. What on earth was a bottle of cyanide doing in the study?"

"Nothing in particular—that's the silly part. It was a relic from the days when Mr. Weekes was an ardent photographer. He used it for deepening prints or something."

Her face suddenly cleared, and rather to his surprise she burst out laughing.

"Oh, how perfect!" she gurgled. "That was Charlotte—I bet you anything you like it was! Still, perhaps I'd better not talk too much."

"Why not? It won't do you any harm. What makes you say it was she?"

"Because it's just like her, somehow. Mentally she lives on detective stories the same as bodily she lives on sweets. And she never liked me at any price. I am right, aren't I? You see, when I was married to Robert we used to come here in the holidays, and I sometimes helped Herbert with his messing about. It was something to do. Yes, I see just how she worked it out."

"Do you remember the bottle in question?"

"My dear man, there were thousands of bottles. I certainly don't remember any cyanide, if that's what you mean. But then, to be quite truthful I never did have more than the vaguest notion of what I was doing. I simply followed instructions and tried to look intelligent. And you say the stuff's been in the study for years? How like Herbert! But what happened to it at half-term?"

Beale told her as much as he knew, and she frowned again.

"The theory presumably being that I took the wretched thing?" she said. "But where did the chocolates come in? Did I take them too?"

"Yes, you were told by Miss Weekes of their expected arrival, and after that you hung about waiting for the postman."

"Well well! I wish I knew if you're serious or not. If you are, I can only assure you you're dead wrong. And anyway, what does half-term matter? Surely it's Saturday and Sunday that count, and till midday Sunday I was at Cowes—for a full week before."

"Can you prove that?" he asked.

"A dozen times; only—only I'd rather I didn't have to. Not hour by hour, anyway—unless you're discreet as well as clever?"

"I *can* be discreet. And you weren't quite correct in what you said just now. It wouldn't really matter where you were."

"Ah, so you *don't* suspect me! Then why not say so earlier?"

"Earlier? I haven't said so at all, yet."

"But I don't understand—"

"Then I'll explain, on one condition. You must give me your word not to mention anything I tell you to any other person."

"Well, that would be easy; but how do you know I keep my word?"

"I don't; I shall have to take a chance. Do you promise, Lady Weekes?"

"Certainly, Inspector."

"Thank you. The explanation's very simple, really. It's equivalent to pointing out—what you doubtless know already—that in order to put a particular five-pound note on a Derby runner with a particular bookie five minutes before the race, you don't have to be at Epsom yourself. You can employ an agent."

Her brown eyes stared from a dead-white face.

"It's utterly fantastic!" she told him, her voice not quite steady. "You mean Maurice, of course?"

"Not at all; I mean Miss Tilling."

"Pat! My God, I never thought of her! Still, it's better than the other idea—that would have been loathsome. But do you really suppose I'd dream of employing her or anyone else to do a murder for me? And spend the rest of my life worrying in case she gave me away?"

"Well, that's only the surface aspect," he objected quietly. "Ignoring the fact that she couldn't afford to give you away unless she wanted to be hanged with you, just imagine for a moment that you did do that, Lady Weekes. If only for the sake of argument, accept that you took the bottle of cyanide at half-term, removed some of the contents, put the bottle back, played about with the liqueur chocolates, and came to a secret verbal understanding with Miss Tilling. Then, to throw other people off the scent, you appeared to quarrel with her, and after that you went to Cowes.

"Miss Tilling duly commits the murder as soon as the circumstances are favourable, and I may say that it would need no special skill—merely caution and a level head. Very well; convinced that that's what happened, we'll further suppose that I take my first step by arresting her; whereupon she breaks down and tries to implicate you. The point is, exactly how does she do that? How *can* she, so that anyone will place the slightest reliance on what she says?"

He paused, but she made no reply.

"By swearing she got the poison from you?" he went on. "Your answer is that you haven't the least notion what she's talking about, and perhaps she'd care to substantiate her remarks? Which, of course, she can't do. By pointing out that you're the likeliest person to have wanted Edwin dead? You retort that Edwin was responsible for her dismissal, and that she obviously bore him a deep and disproportionate grudge. You appeal to Mr. Weekes to agree that she was extremely upset at half-term, threatening to leave on the spot, and he bears that out. She then asks why she should behave like a lunatic when she's going to be happily married in a month or so. You gently hint that she never intended to be; that she regretted her decision to leave because she was overcome by desire to exterminate Edwin at all costs, and hence made use of Lloyd Gregory so that she could stay on to carry out her fiendish plan.

"Finally, of course, she stops trying to drag you in, and instead challenges me to prove she did it; and that's where the story breaks down, because I can't. That's beside the point, though. What you must remember is that even if I could, you'd be quite safe from anything but mud-slinging, and by no one more reputable than a convicted murderess at that; *although every word she said about you might be true.*"

"But it isn't true!" cried Lady Weekes despairingly.

"Well, she hasn't said it yet—I haven't arrested her."

"Oh dear, you do make it all sound sinister! Are you going to?"

"Not at present."

"But you really think she did it?"

Beale smiled.

"What I think at the moment isn't evidence," he said. "If you'd come into the drawing-room a quarter of an hour earlier you'd have heard me say that I've grave doubts if I'll ever be able to *prove* anything against anybody. That's not quite the same thing as not knowing who did it, of course, but pass that by. All I can say now is that Miss Tilling was apparently as well off as the next person for opportunity, and rather better in that it was she who helped Mr. Weekes distribute the tuck on Saturday. The poison was administered in a marzipan block which was either the one Edwin bought, or a replica of it, in case you don't know."

"I didn't."

"And the block, once poisoned, was put in his locker, so we believe. The whole school, incidentally, had been forbidden tuck till after church on Sunday, but Edwin couldn't wait. He crept downstairs in the night and was found dead next morning near the changing-room door by a maid."

"How horrible!" said Lady Weekes softly.

"It is," agreed Beale; "and someone living here was directly responsible. I suppose you can't help me?"

"Not in the way I think you mean," was the firm reply. "I had no 'understanding' with Pat at half-term, and I haven't corresponded with her since, and in any case she's not the sort of girl to do a frightful thing like that. Tell me; you're sure it was a grown-up?"

"Reasonably sure. Then, leaving yourself and Miss Tilling out of it, which of the remaining people here is the sort? One of them must be."

"So it seems, but I'm afraid I can't help. You see, Charlotte and Herbert are the only others I've ever had much to do with, and I wouldn't slander either of them to that extent. I don't like them, and I don't mind saying so, but it would take a great deal to convince me they were capable of murder."

"Yes, I was forgetting you wouldn't know the rest of the staff. In any case, Mr. Weekes would scarcely wish to poison his own son, and he's extremely upset by Edwin's death."

"Yes, he really was fond of him," she declared. "I always wondered why, because he wasn't a nice child at all, even if I oughtn't to say that now. In fact, what I overheard in the drawing-room explains a lot of things I never understood."

"Yes?"

"For one, why Herbert spent so much of the holidays at Moor Cross—that's Robert's place in Hertfordshire—particularly as they weren't especial friends of late years. Robert changed a lot after the divorce, people say, and again after the death of his second wife; which is also explained now. Obviously Herbert wanted to be near Edwin, and in circumstances where he needn't even keep up the pretence of treating him the same as the others."

Beale nodded.

"Would that be the reason for your hostility towards Mr. Weekes at half-term?" he asked, and saw that the question surprised her.

"In a way," she admitted. "The spark was his behaviour to Pat, but the tinder had been waiting a long time; the fact that he was more and more favouring Edwin at Maurice's expense. Mind you, I'm not making out Maurice to be an angel and Edwin a devil. I expect I should naturally prefer my own son, but I think that most people who knew them both would tell you they liked Maurice better. He's not perfect by any means, though. I ascribe his faults to Robert, of course," she added, rather bitterly, "and I don't doubt he ascribes them to me. What it is to have been unhappily married! Still, we won't talk about that now.

"I was going to say that Herbert isn't fair to Maurice. Not so much over any one thing as an accumulation of little things. He punished him when he wouldn't even have scolded Edwin, and that kind of behaviour rankles. Last summer he wouldn't let Maurice take the history prize in his form as well as the English one; he said that the primary object of awarding prizes at all was to encourage the also-rans. Yet he let Edwin walk off with three in *his* form!

"Oh, I know it must sound petty to bring up trifles like that now, with Edwin dead and poor Herbert robbed of the only thing he had to love—I'm only trying to explain how I used to feel. Now I can understand, and perhaps even sympathize a little, but then it used to make me boil. Why, even at half-term—But no, that doesn't matter any more."

"It might," suggested Beale. "Anything about half-term interests me—now. I'm afraid it didn't at the time, though."

She smiled suddenly.

"I guessed as much," she told him. "You looked so very forlorn that Sunday morning—I was quite sorry for you. I was only going to say that I offered to take both boys out, and Herbert was really objectionable in his stuffy way because I wouldn't run down to Portsmouth and show Edwin the *Victory.* On half-term Sunday afternoon—imagine it! That was on the Saturday morning, and then Pat told me her news at night when I got in, and after that I felt devilish. Not that anything happened beyond a few backbites," she added hastily, "and that I didn't take Edwin out after all. I wouldn't have trusted myself with him. Oh dear, that seems a terribly incriminating thing to say! Do understand."

He laughed, and for some moments they sat silent.

"And what are you going to do now?" he asked presently.

"Me? I don't really know. Go back to town, I suppose—if I'm allowed to?"

"Of course. But please remember your promise."

"I will. If you like you can escort me to the gate, to make sure I don't speak to Pat. Ought I to enquire after Robert, d'you think? After all, if I'd come in like a Christian he wouldn't have had the shock of seeing me suddenly. I—I wouldn't like his heart to give out on my account, though to be honest I'd forgotten all about him, sitting here talking to you."

"I shouldn't intrude if I were you," he advised. "You can always send a note saying you're sorry, and it's unlikely that Mr. Weekes or his sister will feel very sociable. There's Maurice, though—you'd probably like a word with him?"

"I should, yes, if it can be managed. Especially as I let him down about Friday."

"Eh, what's that?" demanded Beale abruptly, sitting up. "What about Friday?"

"Oh, nothing to get excited about!" she smiled. "It was his birthday, that's all, and my turn to visit him. After the divorce the lawyers made the most complicated arrangements about when I might and might not see him every other Christmas and Easter and birthday and so on. Robert was quite generous there, I will say. Anyway, after I'd sworn at half-term that I'd never set foot in this place again I wrote and told Maurice I was sorry but I wouldn't be able to manage this year. He wrote back begging me to come, and almost immediately I had a letter from Charlotte. As a matter of fact I brought it with me, as a sort of passport."

The letter was short, and inscribed in a forceful up-and-down hand.

> *Dear Cynthia, My brother asks me to say that if you care to visit Maurice for his birthday on Friday the 14th, and stay the week-end, you will be very welcome. He has taken your remarks about favouritism to heart, and wishes to convince you that he is not as black as you painted him. We understand from the boy himself that you have decided not to come, but he is clearly most disappointed. Could you not change your mind? We were all a little upset at half-term, I expect, with chocolates and policemen everywhere. I repeat, you will be welcome on the 14th or at any other time.*
>
> *Yours sincerely, Charlotte Weekes*

"Thank you," said Beale, and sat staring at his shoe.

"But you didn't change your mind?" he asked, a moment later.

"No. By then I'd made other arrangements, and half-term wasn't so easy to forget, and there was Pat to be considered too. I'd been a bit cutting over her affair with Lloyd Gregory—he doesn't strike me as much of a catch, somehow."

He shrugged.

"I wouldn't know," he murmured. "Where does the passport idea come in, exactly?"

"Why, in the last sentence. 'Or at any other time'—that would cover today, wouldn't it? But I'd never have come if I'd dreamt Robert was here so quickly, not even to get things straight with you. Of course, the maid ought to have warned me, but she didn't think to. You see, I came in by the school entrance as usual, and saw her laying the tables in the dining-hall through the open door. I asked where Mr. Weekes was, and she said in the drawing-room and should she show me the way? I told her I knew it, and went on up. It's queer how things happen."

"Very queer," he agreed, and shot a surprise question at her.

"By the way, Lady Weekes, were you anywhere near Moor Cross at Easter?"

She took it calmly.

"Part of the time," she answered. "Why?"

"I wondered."

"Why? There was nothing wrong in it. I mean, I wasn't trying to kidnap Maurice or anything. Who told you?"

"Nobody. Who did you think might have done?"

"Maurice himself, perhaps. You see, I met him by accident in St Albans once with Herbert, and we all had coffee together. I asked them not to tell Robert, to avoid giving the wrong impression."

"I see—thank you. And one more point; how did Edwin and Maurice get on?"

She shook her head.

"Edwin—peace to his soul and all the rest of it—was a beast over that. What he had against Maurice I could never discover, but he behaved shockingly. Once he poured ink over some particularly favourite butterflies, and another time he tore some stamps in half. I needn't go on, need I?"

"No, that'll do. Did Maurice ever retaliate?"

"Not to my knowledge—he's quite a sportsman. Oh, and what about my seeing him? Can it be done?"

He looked at her very steadily.

"Earlier on I threatened to give you some advice," he reminded her. "You may find it apposite, Lady Weekes."

After he had finished she got up slowly, whiter than at any time before.

"I'll take it," she told him, almost in a whisper. "Yes, indeed I will. Thank you, Inspector—I'm very grateful to you."

XX

IT WAS ALMOST MIDDAY when Miss Charlotte came to disturb Beale's thoughts.

"Alone?" she enquired. "Good—I want to see you!"

She sat down, her black bag on her lap, and stared at him coolly. It seemed that she had recovered from any shock she might have experienced earlier.

"Well, now you know what the Weekes family's really like!" she observed grimly. "A pretty fine lot, aren't we? But it's not much good apologizing, and anyway you probably wouldn't thank me to."

"How is Sir Robert?" he asked.

"Oh, as well as can be expected; the doctor thinks he'll pull through. But he's not strong—his heart's in the sort of state when he might die practically any time. I take a lot of the blame for this morning, of course—I shouldn't have roused his temper. But then, he shouldn't have roused mine. We've always been like that from the time we were children, though it seems to have grown worse in the last few years. We can scarcely sit in the same room without snarling at each other. And then that woman suddenly appearing like a ghost put the finishing touch. What's happened to her? Has she gone?"

"Yes."

"And what did she want? And why creep in without even knocking?"

Beale explained briefly, and Miss Charlotte sniffed.

"Well, the harm's done now," she said. "In any case, I didn't come to talk about her, I came to talk about myself. The fact is, I'm in a most difficult position entirely through my own fault, and I can think of nothing better to do than be perfectly open and throw myself on your mercy, Inspector. Herbert's told you he's lost his keys, hasn't he? Well, I know where they went to."

"Really? Please tell me."

"I'm going to. They were taken out of his trousers pocket on Sunday morning while he was downstairs with the body; half past six, say. I know all about it, you see, because I took them myself."

Beale was genuinely startled.

"*You* took them!" he exclaimed. "Well, that's something I'd never even thought of."

The elderly woman laughed.

"Why, who were you putting it down to?" she demanded.

"I'd rather not say, but certainly not to you. Have you the keys here?"

She nodded, felt in her bag, and handed him the bunch.

"Thank you. Has any use been made of them since Sunday morning?"

"None whatever."

"Then why did you take them?"

"Because I fully intended to use them, but later changed my mind. I'd better tell you the whole story, and then you won't need to keep asking questions. In case you don't know, my bedroom is opposite my brother's. On Sunday morning I was woken up by somebody knocking at his door; the time by my clock was just after 6.20. Now, that was a most unusual thing to happen, and I naturally listened to find out what was the matter. There was no difficulty about hearing—if you doubt that you can easily verify the fact for yourself.

"What the maid said, as near as I can remember, was 'Oh Mr. Weekes, sir, wake up! Wake up! Master Edwin's lying dead downstairs, oh sir it's horrible!' After that she began to cry, but not loudly enough to prevent me catching Herbert's answer. He said *'Master Edwin!'* in a sort of agonized yell—'Good God! All right, go away.' I heard her shut the door and walk down the passage, still crying, and then less than half a minute later he came into my room in his dressing-gown.

" 'Charlotte!' he said. 'Edwin's dead downstairs—poisoned. I'm going to see—you stay here.' Then he went out, leaving me with a lot to think about. You see, I was positive the maid had never mentioned the word poison."

She looked at him expectantly, and he nodded.

"That roused your suspicions?" he asked.

"Immediately. I began to think, and somehow I found myself thinking extraordinarily fast. Poisoned? But how could Herbert possibly know, *unless he did it?* And downstairs—what could the boy be eating there in the night? Well, the answer to that was easy, if a little unexpected—his tuck. Of course, he *might* have sneaked down to the pantry, but I considered it unlikely. He'd been caught doing that a term or two ago, and punished; I insisted on it."

Beale muttered under his breath.

"That was something I forgot to ask about," he explained, dissatisfied with himself. "Please go on, Miss Weekes."

"Well, as I was saying, the idea of tuck occurred to me, and at once I started to wonder if it were possible to check what was left. You must realize that part of me was thoroughly ashamed of my suspicions, and I couldn't imagine *why* Herbert should have wished to harm Edwin. It seemed against nature; as of course it was, only I didn't know that then. At all events I decided to borrow my brother's keys, and did so. It all happened much quicker than it takes to tell; it was just after half past six when I went into his room. You see, it had to be then or never, and that may have helped me to make up my mind."

She sighed, as if regretting her action.

"And then I began to have doubts," she continued. "For one thing, Herbert was so utterly grief-stricken; nobody in the world could suppose that Edwin's murder was anything but the most profound shock to him. For another, I realized for the first time that if he were responsible, then it would have to be he who played all those tricks at half-term, which to say the least of it was extremely improbable. He loathes practical jokes of any kind.

"All the same, I think I still might have visited the store-room but for two considerations. First, he missed his keys almost at once; as soon as he dressed properly. Secondly, I saw what had escaped me before, that it would be little good knowing what was in the tuck box unless I could also find out what had been sold on Saturday, and I didn't think I could do that without causing comment. On the other hand, I couldn't very well explain what I was doing with the keys, and of course I hadn't bargained for the police suspecting they'd been taken by the murderer. That was the Guildford superintendent's view, and for all I know it may be yours too. If so, I can only say you're wrong. I admit borrowing them—or stealing them, even, if you choose to call it that; but I emphatically don't admit having had anything whatever to do with Edwin's death."

"Of course not," he said soothingly, for she was becoming just a little agitated. "All the same, you behaved very foolishly, Miss Weekes."

"Yes, I admit that too—it was ridiculous. What are you going to do about it?"

"Do?"

"I mean, shall I have to tell my brother the truth? I will if you say so, but I'd naturally very much rather not."

"I think it could be arranged. I gather you no longer suspect him?"

"No. I don't believe in murders without a motive. Yet in a way I still feel I was justified, you know."

"Yes, I see that. But wasn't it a rather drastic explanation? After all, what happened at half-term was quite sufficient, in view of your brother's statement that Edwin had been previously threatened, to implant the idea of poison firmly in his head. He tells me that his reason for giving Edwin a separate room was because he couldn't satisfy himself completely that the business of the disappearing cyanide and the liqueur chocolates wasn't an abortive attempt at murder."

"Yes, I understand now how stupid I was. I should like to say that I very much regret any trouble I may have caused."

He smiled, suspecting that that was the nearest she would ever approach a direct apology.

"We'll forget that side of things if you'll answer some questions," he said. "You may find some of them rather pointed, but I think I'd better make myself quite clear. First, from which pair of trousers did you take the keys?"

"From his ordinary ones—not those he wore with the dinner-jacket."

"Thank you. Next, did you know before this morning that Edwin was not Sir Robert's son?"

Miss Charlotte shook her head firmly.

"I never dreamt of any such thing," she assured him. "The more fool me, I suppose! However, I know all about it now—I insisted that Herbert tell me. Do you require details?"

"No, I think not. You can't give me any idea of how long Sir Robert had known the truth, I suppose?"

"As a matter of fact, I can; he explained that point not half an hour ago. You see, Inspector, he's now extremely sorry he ever said anything, and begged me to tell Herbert as much. He's been aware of the truth ever since Edwin's birth—his second wife confessed to him on her death-bed. Quite why he allowed Herbert to remain ignorant that his secret was no secret at all from the one person who mattered, I can't say. It may have been because she asked him not to make trouble, or it may have been that he wanted the truth kept quiet for his own sake. Anyway, that's how things stand."

"I see. Now, Miss Weekes, who do you think killed Edwin?"

She looked startled.

"I'm sorry, I don't know at all. I simply can't imagine. It wasn't any of us, and it couldn't have been Lady W., apparently, and that leaves only the staff. Teaching staff, I mean, not household and domestic—they're not worth considering for a moment, and nor are the housekeeper or matron. Three persons, two men and a woman, and I prefer not to make a choice."

He smiled again.

"But somehow you don't think it was a man," he suggested, and saw her move slightly.

"*I* didn't say so!" she retorted. "If you care to put words into my mouth, that's your concern."

"I'm sorry; and disappointed. You aren't as helpful as you were at half-term, you know."

She stared at him very steadily.

"That was different," she declared. "That was merely a problem without any particular consequences; this is a hanging matter."

"Well, I see your point, but I'm not at all sure I agree with you. It seems to me that your nephew's death is almost certainly a direct outcome of the other business; which therefore did have consequences."

"But I wasn't to know that at the time, was I? At least, that isn't quite true. I really mean that I wasn't seriously afraid of anything happening—I never honestly believed in the murderous side of it."

"You treated it more as an intellectual exercise?"

"Exactly—provided women are capable of intellect!"—and she chuckled as if she had scored off an enemy.

"Oh, I think so, Miss Weekes. Now, going back to the keys for a moment, where have they been since half past six on Sunday morning?"

"Oh, I couldn't possibly tell you that!" she replied. "On my person—put it that way; and wrapped up in cotton wool, incidentally, so that they shouldn't rattle. Nobody could have re-borrowed them from me, if that's what you're worrying about."

"Yes, it was. Now, some minutes ago you said that the idea of Edwin eating his tuck in the middle of the night was unexpected. Why, if he was so greedy?"

"I meant because of something that happened at lunch on Saturday," she replied, gave him a résumé of the information contained in Lloyd Gregory's statement, and then frowned.

"He was a coward as well as a glutton," she said. "I can't think what possessed him to risk Herbert's anger like that. I—I suppose he *did* go down? Alive?"

"Without any possible doubt. In fact, he borrowed Maurice's torch before he went to bed. Finally, Miss Weekes, here's a somewhat odd question. Your brother gave up photography because a clumsy boy broke his best camera; can you tell me what make it was, how much it cost, and when and where he bought it?"

She stared.

"Why?" she asked.

"That doesn't matter, please. Can you tell me?"

"Very well, be mysterious if you must—I suppose it's a detective's privilege. It was a *Una*—what's called a hand-stand camera, I believe, though I never understood the reason. The price, if I remember, was fourteen guineas—second-hand, of course—and he bought it in London during the Easter holidays in—let me see—yes, in 1928."

"Thank you. Your memory appears to be excellent."

"Of course it is! Good heavens, was that what you were trying to find out?"

He nodded, smiling.

"You were so precise about the missing bottle at half-term," he explained, "what it looked like and when it was bought."

She smiled too.

"What it is to have a suspicious mind!" she remarked. "But one oughtn't to joke, I suppose. You know, it's a shocking thing to say, but I feel as if I were in church all the time, and the unpleasant part is that I can't imagine how to stop the feeling. Any more questions?"

"You don't know how much cyanide the bottle originally contained?"

No, I'm sorry. I don't think Herbert ever told me."

"I see. Well, that's really all, but I'd like to repeat one question even at the risk of offending you."

"By all means—I've nothing to hide now."

"Thank you. Then are you absolutely positive you didn't know, or even suspect, that Edwin wasn't Sir Robert's son but Mr. Weekes's?"

She frowned at him.

"Absolutely. What makes you think otherwise?"

"Something you said at half-term which came back to me yesterday. I don't know if you remember, but when you were talking about your brother's attitude towards Edwin you said that favouritism leaves a nasty taste in the mouth, especially when it's nepotism of the most literal sort. Why the word suddenly returned to me last night I can't tell you, but it did, and brought with it a vague feeling that I wasn't entirely sure of its meaning. As I happened to be near a dictionary I looked it up. Now, Miss Weekes, what does nepotism mean?" She still frowned.

"Favouritism applied to relatives at the expense of other people," she answered. "And *nepos* means a nephew in Latin, so it certainly seems to fit."

"And you believe that to be the full definition?"

"Well, isn't it?"

"I used to think so—until last night. However, this is what the C.O.D. says—I copied it down afterwards; 'Undue favour from holder of patronage to relatives (originally from Pope illegitimate sons called nephews).' "

"Well I'm blessed!" exclaimed Miss Charlotte. "They say truth will out, but I didn't know it did it like that! And you thought perhaps I was giving you a hint if you were sufficiently well informed to take it? I'm sorry—I wasn't. In any case, Popes should be celibate."

XXI

"ANY NEWS?" asked Tony, when he returned at three o'clock. Beale told him in outline, and enjoyed watching his friend's expression.

"Well, I should never have thought *that* of Herbert! It was pretty bright of you to work it out."

"Sheer luck—it was an entirely false assumption."

"And how do things stand now? D'you believe Miss Charlotte's explanation about the keys?"

"Yes."

"Then that lets her out. And Herbert keeps her company, because he could have had no conceivable motive."

"Well, don't exaggerate; how do you know he didn't set out ten years ago to have a son he could insure for a fortune and then poison? Still, I agree I'm convinced that Edwin was the last person in the world he'd have wanted to murder."

"That's what I was humbly trying to say. Similarly Lady Weekes joins the band because of absence at Cowes, and Sir Robert because he was on the continent. Though he could have had a motive, you know."

"Yes, that's the trouble with this case, looked at casually. The people who might have wanted the boy dead weren't here, and the ones who were here don't seem to have wanted it enough, or in Herbert's case at all."

"What about the governess woman?"

Beale shrugged his shoulders.

"Think what you please," he said amiably.

"May I? Thanks. Then I think,"—very deliberately—that the murder was done by someone we haven't even considered yet."

"Sorry; there isn't anyone. At any rate, no one who could possibly have done it that *I* haven't considered. I can't speak for you, of course, but I think I know whom you mean, and if so you're wrong. In fact, you couldn't be wronger. Incidentally, I've a quarrel with you."

"Me? What have I done?"

"It's what you didn't do. You assured me the tuck checked, but it didn't."

"It did!"

"Not entirely. I gave you a note of the contents of the tuck box as seen by me on Sunday afternoon, and one item was five lemon blocks out of the dozen in the sample box. Yet Gregory's list—I ought to have spotted that for myself earlier—and the one you compiled from the boys' answers each only accounted for six."

"Good lord! I'm sorry," said Tony. "But you did say that only the marzipans really mattered, you know."

"Did I? Then I'll share the blame. Not that I mind now, because I've had an explanation."

"From whom?"

"Herbert. He came in here after lunch to tell me he'd forgotten to mention that he took a lemon from the box on Saturday to give Edwin, because he'd just spoken harshly to the poor child. That shows his habitual attitude—understandable now, I suppose, in a way; yet he made him promise not to eat it till the next day, to show he could be trusted. We looked for the thing, and found it in his blazer pocket—blazers are collected after use and hung in a special cupboard in the linen-room. Herbert was painful to watch. He dithered between pride that Edwin hadn't broken that particular promise, and regret at the undisguisable greed which took him downstairs in the night. If I ever have a son, legitimate or otherwise, I hope I don't make a fool of myself over him like that."

"If you don't hurry up about it," remarked Tony, "I'm afraid you'll never survive his infancy. How did Herbert react to your knowledge of his secret?"

"As you might expect. He was a bit embarrassed, but trying hard to look as if I hadn't been in the drawing-room at all."

"He didn't attempt to excuse himself?"

"To me? Good heavens no—why should he?"

"No, I suppose not. Any more news?"

"Not much. I talked to one or two of the boys, and Lillywhite reports there aren't any safety-razor blades about. I also learnt that Herbert didn't inspect the lockers. He was going to do it after church, he says."

"And now what happens?"

"What I foretold yesterday," said Beale with a smile. "I'm going to sit down and endeavour to solve this business by thought. I'm pretty sure I'm on the right track at last, too, so do you mind breathing quietly?"

"Not a bit. You're positive it wasn't—well, anyone we haven't discussed?"

"That wasn't the word you used just now; but I'm still positive."

Half an hour later Beale got up, walked over to the black tin box which now rested on the morning-room table, unlocked it, took out a block each of lemon, peppermint, and marzipan, examined them carefully under a lens, and then proceeded to eat them all. Tony stared.

"What's up—hungry?" he asked. "Or has Miss Charlotte been getting you into bad habits?"

"Maybe. These things aren't half bad for a penny, you know."

"What penny?" enquired his friend rudely, but Beale ignored him.

"The marzipan's a bit wiggle-waggle, as Dr Johnson might say, but the peppermint's better value—really powerful, in fact. The lemon's quite life-like, too—have one?"

"No thanks—and do be careful! You make me nervous, stuffing away like that when the beastly things might be poisoned."

"I don't think so. If they were, I'm dead."

He locked the tin box again, and put it on the floor. After that he gazed out of the window, now and again consulting his watch. At last, apparently satisfied, he turned to his companion.

"Well, if it's all the same to you it's about time we started," he said.

"Started? Where to?"

"London, of course—I've finished here. I took the liberty of packing your bag while you were out, just in case, and if we go now we'll escape unseen."

"But what do you mean, you've finished here?"

"Just that; I've solved the problem. The next step is to get in touch with Sir Francis, and see if he thinks anything can be done."

"Done?" Tony was still at sea.

"Do stop behaving like an echo. I know all about everything to my own complete satisfaction, but I'm not very certain I can prove my case strongly enough to justify any action. That being so, I must ask advice. Will you or won't you run me up to town?"

"Yes, of course, but I don't understand a bit. You suddenly tell me without a moment's warning that you've finished here, thank you very much, and expect me to take it coolly. Who's your chap? And how long have you known?"

"I've strongly suspected since this morning. I sat down just now to make sure it checked, and it did."

"But who is it?"

INTERLUDE

It is suggested that before going on the reader should answer Tony's question for him. As Chief-Inspector Beale has said, inability to prove a criminal's guilt need not by any means be the same thing as ignorance of that criminal's identity. Who killed Edwin Weekes may be determined from the evidence supplied in the preceding chapters; if not with that certainty required by a court of law in a capital charge, then with sufficient thoroughness to condemn him or her on paper with a clear conscience. In this particular case there ought not to be much difficulty, but those who find it necessary are invited to pause again at the end of the first break in the next chapter.

XXII

"I'LL TELL YOU who did it later," Beale promised. "When we're safe from any possible interruption." Tony sighed.

"All right," he agreed. "But I don't really believe you know. You mean you can unequivocally supply me with the name of the person who put the poisoned marzipan block in Edwin's locker? That's my definition of the murderer."

His friend's answer was accompanied by a smile so broad that it verged on laughter.

"Then you're in for a big disappointment!" he observed. "You see, there never was such a person. The thing never happened."

They drove back to town slowly, so that Beale would have time to explain.

"There were three improbabilities connected with Edwin's death," he began. "First, if he intended to eat his tuck in the night, he would have taken it to bed with him instead of coming down again for it hours later.

"Second, if he decided to eat some in defiance of Herbert's orders he wouldn't pick a chocolate block which could be checked at sight, but a handful of his liquorice all-sorts, which couldn't. Five ounces spread out look as much as six, but you can't possibly make two chocolate-blocks look like three. Incidentally, both Miss Charlotte and the governess remarked on the fact that he should have chosen to defy his uncle so openly. I mean his father, of course—I was forgetting. The third improbability was that, being the kind of boy who worshipped his stomach, he'd ever leave sweetstuff in his blazer pocket. For all he knew, anything might have happened to it, since blazers are collected and temporarily put beyond reach.

"Have you grasped those three points clearly? I think I'll repeat them to make sure; separately, and adding opinions.

"(1) Edwin would have been more likely to take his tuck upstairs with him to eat in the privacy of his own room than to leave it in his locker and fetch it later. The toffee-papers under his mattress show that he wasn't unused to eating in bed. But we know he died where he was found, by the evidence of the blood on the door-post, and everything else pointed to his previous intention of sneaking down in the night, particularly what Maurice told us about the torch. A tentative suggestion can be made; *that he may not have been able to take upstairs with him at 7.30 the precise articles of tuck he meant to consume later.*

"Because he feared that Herbert might examine the lockers that evening? Nonsense; he was far more likely to do that the next morning. The only reasonable inference from that suggestion is this; *Edwin wanted to eat not his own tuck but that belonging to some other boy who went to bed after him.*

"(2) If, nevertheless, Edwin had proposed to visit his own locker, he would more probably have taken some of his six ounces of liquorice all-sorts than one of his three chocolate-blocks. The reason hardly needs explaining; because Herbert had warned him particularly and publicly and personally about his greediness—witness Lloyd Gregory's statement and Miss Charlotte's repetition of what happened at lunch on Saturday. We have the word of all the staff that he was a sharp boy, not in the least likely to overlook his own interests.

"Again, and more confidently, it may be suggested that he never had the slightest intention of taking what belonged to himself. If we accept Herbert's story about giving him a lemon block and making him promise not to touch it till next day, the suggestion is strengthened. How could he show he kept his promise unless he produced *four* blocks? Still, I won't labour that point.

"(3) It would be unlike Edwin to leave tuck in his blazer pocket, since he was an exceptionally greedy boy and exceptionally interested in things to eat. Here the inference is different; that he never had an extra lemon block to leave there—that Herbert's story is a fabrication. In passing, it seems significant that although the question of what sweets Edwin did or did not possess became of extreme importance from the moment he died, we hear nothing of this alleged free gift until today, more than forty-eight hours later. That *may* have been due to forgetfulness, but one doubts it."

"Whose forgetfulness?" Tony put in. "Mine or Herbert's?"

"His. Our failure to notice the discrepancy ourselves, that one lemon block couldn't be accounted for, was sheer carelessness, yours and mine.

"Now, we'll leave (3) for a time, but return to it presently. Let's go back to (1) and (2). Briefly, Edwin appears to have been acting both in and out of character. His behaviour was greedy, and yet anything but shrewd; *unless* you suppose that he borrowed Maurice's torch for the purpose of coming downstairs in the dead of night to steal someone else's tuck. Please note, too, that he'd no great reputation for honesty; otherwise he wouldn't have been previously caught robbing the pantry, as Miss Charlotte said.

"Now, is there anything to recommend that idea beyond its agreement with two—or three—sides of his reported character instead of one only—that it's consistent instead of contradictory? I think there is; the further fact that he particularly disliked his half-brother Maurice. Lady Weekes gave me instances this morning, and I heard the same thing from Askew and Lillywhite at half-term. He continually behaved badly towards Maurice, and Maurice, perhaps foolishly, didn't retaliate but put up with him patiently."

"Gosh!" muttered Tony. "And he was my secret suspect!"

"I thought as much. To go on, if Edwin wanted to get his half-brother into trouble, and at the same time satisfy his greed, here was a heaven-sent opportunity. All he had to do was borrow the torch, pinch some of Maurice's favourite marzipan, and then wait for Herbert to inspect lockers. And if Herbert forgot, who but his little favourite Edwin would come sidling up to remind him, bristling with integrity and darkly hinting that others mightn't be so pure? A nasty deceitful little pig; those were Sir Robert's words, and the stories of the mark-book and the boot-boy confirm that view.

"A most important question now arises; can we find reasons for believing Maurice a more suitable victim of a murder by poisoned marzipan than Edwin? For you will have seen that, on this reckoning, the person meant to die wasn't Edwin at all but the rightful owner of the stolen tuck. I suggest two, which I shall elaborate; that there would be a better motive, and also a better explanation of the use of marzipan at all.

"Take motive first. We couldn't—or I couldn't—feel happy about suspecting Herbert Weekes of deliberately killing Edwin because it seemed the last thing in the world he'd ever want to do. Put Maurice for Edwin and accidentally for deliberately, however, bear in mind that Herbert was Edwin's father and not his uncle, and the difficulty disappears. How would Maurice's death benefit Edwin? By ensuring with reasonable certainly that one day he'd be Sir Edwin, as Sir Robert's sole heir. Herbert, remember, had no suspicion that Robert knew the truth about the boy's parentage. In fact, he believed the secret was his alone.

"And now for the marzipan. I sampled the stuff myself—by the way, it couldn't have been poisoned—and I found it rather feeble. The peppermint, on the other hand, was definitely strong, and so would have been quite as good a medium for disguising the taste of cyanide. In any case, I think we over-estimated the need for disguise. Cyanide acts so rapidly, and so little's required, that the risk of its effect miscarrying must have been very slight. Now, we learnt from the boys that more than twice as many would have expected Edwin to choose peppermint as to choose marzipan—twenty-five votes against twelve. He evidently liked it better, and so I suggest that it would have been a safer bait for him. But not for Maurice, who wouldn't touch peppermint at any price. I was told at half-term that he hated the stuff. In short, we now get a really sensible reason for the murder taking place directly marzipan became available; *Maurice would be sure to buy some.*

"Very well; let's take it that Edwin came downstairs about two o'clock in the early morning of Sunday, stole a poisoned marzipan block from Maurice's locker, and died a minute or so later. Leaving the part played by himself out of account, can we indicate *without reference to motive* who was responsible for his death? Again, I believe we're not flying too high.

"The significant fact is that Gregory's list of what he found in the lockers, starting to look at 6.55 a.m., corresponds exactly with what the boys themselves say they bought. That means only one thing; previous to 6.55 a.m. someone replaced the poisoned block of marzipan missing from Maurice's locker with a harmless one. That's true even if Gregory himself did it, because he couldn't have afforded to be caught out by the maid who helped him. But no one, innocent or guilty, had the faintest reason to expect Edwin to behave as he did. Hence we can assume that only three persons saw the body lying downstairs where it had fallen; in order, the maid, Herbert Weekes, and Lloyd Gregory; and we can further assume that the fact of death was unknown before the maid's discovery. Until 6.55 Miss Charlotte was the only other person to be told, and she couldn't have come downstairs to the lockers unobserved. Accordingly we can say that the substitution I mentioned just now was done either by the maid—out of the question—or by one of the other two, Herbert and Gregory; and only Herbert had a suitable opportunity."

"When?" asked Tony quickly.

"During the two or three minutes the maid was waking Gregory. And remember this; whoever effected that substitution, whoever filled up the empty place in Maurice's locker, was the murderer, *for only he would know where the poisoned block had come from.*

"We now face the further point; can we choose between Herbert and Gregory on any other ground than opportunity? My answer is that we can, without hesitation."

"Because he used the word 'poison' when he told his sister, I suppose?"

"Partly; but I've a better one than that. Since the maid who woke Herbert was clearly innocent, her evidence would be held reliable. Thus Miss Charlotte would never dare tell me her brother said anything in answer to the news—'Oh! sir. Master Edwin's *lying* dead downstairs!'—but what he did in fact say. And what was that? Did he exclaim 'What!', or 'What, dead!', or just plain 'Dead!'? Not a bit; he accepted that part of it without comment. His first words, 'in an agonized sort of voice', are '*Master Edwin!* Good God!' That, to my mind, indicates the most intense surprise; but not so much that anyone is dead as that of all people in the world it should be Edwin.

"And now I think I'd better outline what I believe to have been Herbert's plan. In a few words, it was to spread the idea of threats against Edwin, and then to kill Maurice in such a way as to make us assume it was still Edwin who'd been aimed at; by Lady Weekes, of course.

"We've all sorts of reasons for preferring Herbert to anyone, if only we can provide him with a sound motive. From half-term we get the following points.

"He said the missing bottle of cyanide was blue, but it was green.

"He knew that Lady Weekes had heard about the expected parcel of liqueur chocolates—may even have led up to the subject by 'talking about the post-office', as Miss Charlotte put it.

"He knew—I strongly suspect—that the parcel had been noticed in the hall, because a boy called Burnaby told me today that he thought Herbert had seen him looking at it.

"He knew Lady Weekes was going to say goodnight to Maurice before she went out, and he knew she'd been near Moor Cross at Easter.

"He could have done the business of the air-gun and the bicycle brakes himself.

"He was in as good a position as anyone for distributing the chocolates, and who would ever suspect a man known to detest practical jokes? Certainly not his sister.

"He was apparently most reluctant to draw attention to Lady Weekes as the possible author of possible threats to Edwin, though he could be confident that the notion would arise.

"He himself told the staff I was a policeman, to prepare the way for the gravest suspicion and the wildest speculation, and so—later—help to establish the probable existence of previous attempts on Edwin's life.

"It was he who estimated the amount of cyanide in the bottle, and therefore he alone who could mislead us. Further, he would have an excellent shield; his well-known absent-minded carelessness, which I don't doubt was exaggerated.

"Some of those points are stronger than others, but in the aggregate they strike me as pretty convincing. From more recently we get similarly suggestive facts.

"Miss Charlotte says he missed his keys soon after she took them, but his own version implied that he didn't notice their absence until midday, when the Guildford superintendent asked him for them.

"After half-term Miss Tilling was roped in to help with the tuck; in order, I suggest, that Lady Weekes could seem to have a possible source of knowledge concerning what Edwin bought. His plan was either to make it appear that she put a poisoned marzipan block in the wrong locker—that she meant to poison Edwin but muddled the numbers; or that she actually did put it in Edwin's locker—reckoning that the dead can't swear to what they bought—and that Maurice stole it. That of course would be what you might call the mirror-image of the real murder; if so, the shock to Herbert must have been even more ghastly."

"But are you quite sure he meant to shove it on her?" asked Tony.

"Quite sure. You see, there's that letter he got his sister to write, asking Lady Weekes emphatically to change her mind about not visiting Maurice on his birthday and to stay the week-end. To my way of thinking, that clinches it. Both the half-term 'threat' and the actual murder were designed to fit in with her movements."

"Then why on earth carry on with his plans when he knew she wasn't coming?"

"Because he simply *had* to—because it was probably his last chance. He might never get another, with the woman refusing to visit the place again and Sir Robert liable to die at any time and so ruin the whole scheme."

"Oh lord, now I see it all!"

"And are you convinced?"

"Absolutely."

"Well, let me finish—there's a bit more. Herbert, we suppose, was able to produce a genuine unadulterated marzipan at a moment's notice to put in place of the poisoned one. Yet he couldn't have got it from the tuck box because Miss Charlotte had his keys—I told you I believed her evidence about them. The explanation must be—there's no other—that he didn't poison one of those Maurice bought but prepared his bait at leisure. He probably did that in his study between the time he came in from the cricket match against Grove Park and the time he took prayers. His sister says in her statement that he was alone there then. Later, just before going to bed, he substituted it for a harmless one, which remained in his possession; but not in the tuck box because the key to that was upstairs in his other trousers.

"After the maid's delivered her frightful news the next morning he goes downstairs, realizes what's happened, and sends her up to wake Gregory. The moment he's alone he rushes to his study, gets hold of the untouched marzipan, returns to the lockers, puts it back in Maurice's where it had originally come from, and out of Edwin's three intact blocks takes one at random. There he made the first of his serious mistakes; he took a lemon, which could be checked because it came from a new box, instead of a peppermint which couldn't because it came from an old one.

"He need do nothing else, except assert untruthfully that Edwin bought two peppermints and a marzipan instead of two peppermints and a lemon; but he found himself left with the latter, and he couldn't replace it in the black tin box because his keys were gone. Sooner or later, when he realized that lemons could be counted, he must have expected us to ask him about it, and he probably worried himself sick wondering why we didn't. In the end he decided to 'remember' having given it to Edwin and making him promise not to eat it till next day, and that was silly. If he'd said the boy devoured it on the spot, we'd never have been a scrap the wiser. He wanted to be all open and above-board, though, to produce the actual block and show there was no fake, and so he planted it in the blazer. Like so many people do when they're twisting, he tried too hard. He left me facing a third improbability, and I couldn't swallow it.

"To finish with, here are a few miscellaneous points.

"Maurice was three years older than Edwin, and would naturally go to bed later, which meant that his tuck couldn't be stolen safely *en route.*

"The writing on the wash-room wall was probably done by Herbert himself—as you almost suggested once. He would consider he was the last possible suspect for the authorship of disparaging remarks about Edwin. No boy would own up, because no boy was responsible. He'd be free to inflict whatever punishment he cared, and he chose one which would make it extremely difficult to know when the setting of the trap took place. His first concern was to kill Maurice; his second to divert attention from himself. After that, nothing mattered particularly, though I'm certain he did his best, at any rate earlier on, to provide a murderess as well as a corpse."

"And the intended victim's own mother at that!" remarked Tony, which made Beale stare.

"Good lord!" he said. "Do you know, I'd never thought of that! How deeply he intended to involve Miss Tilling, as a substitute scapegoat for Lady Weekes, it's hard to be sure. In any case he managed that part of it badly. By keeping Edwin till last, and—perhaps—not being able to think of an excuse to detain the governess, he let her go away ignorant after all of what he particularly wanted her to know. Due indirectly to the boy's greediness, of course, as his death was—he could scarcely have spoilt his father's plans for him more effectively if he'd been really trying.

"If you notice, though, the mistakes which mattered happened after Herbert had had the appalling shock of finding he'd killed his own beloved son. It was enough to put any man off his stroke, and the subsequent broadcasting of the truth about Edwin's birth must have made him afraid to do or say anything much in case he gave himself away. As, in fact, he did, over the lemon block.

"Well, what do you think?"

"You've satisfied me," declared Tony. "It's morally certain that Herbert was responsible; but what do you mean by agreeing with me this afternoon that he wasn't?"

"I beg your pardon—I was extremely careful to do nothing of the sort. I merely said, quite truthfully, that Edwin was the last person Herbert would ever have wanted to murder."

"All right—sorry. But can you prove it to a jury?"

Beale frowned dubiously.

"Perhaps I won't need to," he answered. "I told you rather mysteriously that I presented Lady Weekes with some advice this morning, but I didn't give you details. It amounted to this; that if she wanted to ensure Maurice's continued safety she'd better get him away from Anstey Court."

"A good move."

"Yes, and one which fulfilled my promise to him. Incidentally, I can't help wondering why it was Maurice who seemed especially afraid. Is it so impossible that he dimly suspected the truth? I must ask him one day. We arranged that he should go out of class that afternoon on the usual excuse and meet her at the gates. I waited till I saw him safely away, and then we followed. If you'd been driving faster we might have caught them."

"But what's all that got to do with not needing proof?"

"Oh yes. Before the boy left he put an envelope on the hall table addressed to Herbert. Inside was a note, very short and pointed and in his own writing.

> "*Dear Uncle, I feel I had better run away before you really do manage to kill me. It was a pity you forgot how greedy Edwin could be, don't you think? Maurice.*

"That was composed at my dictation, of course, and you'll probably consider it a bit heartless. He did himself—almost refused to write the thing. Still, heartless is a kind way of describing Herbert's intentions, and we shall see if anything results."

It did; had done by the time they reached Scotland Yard. Sir Francis Barton informed them, in shocked mystification, that the headmaster of Anstey Court had committed suicide.

"How?" asked Beale.

"By cyanide," was the answer. "He left you a message, by the way—an open letter which his sister read over the telephone."

Dear Chief-Inspector Beale, it said, *You are quite correct; I killed Edwin, and am now about to make what amends I can. I know you must be aware of the truth by the phrasing of Maurice's note, since all boys here are taught never to begin correspondence with the personal pronoun 'I' Two things I desire to say. I should not have harmed Maurice now, the incentive being absent, and you need never feel in the slightest degree responsible for my death. I could not much longer have borne the intolerable empti-*

ness of life without Edwin; I have literally nothing left to live for. Goodbye.

Yours sincerely, Herbert Weekes.

THE END

RAMBLE HOUSE's

HARRY STEPHEN KEELER WEBWORK MYSTERIES

(RH) indicates the title is available ONLY in the RAMBLE HOUSE edition

The Ace of Spades Murder
The Affair of the Bottled Deuce (RH)
The Amazing Web
The Barking Clock
Behind That Mask
The Book with the Orange Leaves
The Bottle with the Green Wax Seal
The Box from Japan
The Case of the Canny Killer
The Case of the Crazy Corpse (RH)
The Case of the Flying Hands (RH)
The Case of the Ivory Arrow
The Case of the Jeweled Ragpicker
The Case of the Lavender Gripsack
The Case of the Mysterious Moll
The Case of the 16 Beans
The Case of the Transparent Nude (RH)
The Case of the Transposed Legs
The Case of the Two-Headed Idiot (RH)
The Case of the Two Strange Ladies
The Circus Stealers (RH)
Cleopatra's Tears
A Copy of Beowulf (RH)
The Crimson Cube (RH)
The Face of the Man From Saturn
Find the Clock
The Five Silver Buddhas
The 4th King
The Gallows Waits, My Lord! (RH)
The Green Jade Hand
Finger! Finger!
Hangman's Nights (RH)
I, Chameleon (RH)
I Killed Lincoln at 10:13! (RH)
The Iron Ring
The Man Who Changed His Skin (RH)
The Man with the Crimson Box
The Man with the Magic Eardrums
The Man with the Wooden Spectacles
The Marceau Case
The Matilda Hunter Murder
The Monocled Monster
The Murder of London Lew
The Murdered Mathematician
The Mysterious Card (RH)
The Mysterious Ivory Ball of Wong Shing Li (RH)
The Mystery of the Fiddling Cracksman
The Peacock Fan
The Photo of Lady X (RH)
The Portrait of Jirjohn Cobb
Report on Vanessa Hewstone (RH)
Riddle of the Travelling Skull
Riddle of the Wooden Parrakeet (RH)
The Scarlet Mummy (RH)
The Search for X-Y-Z
The Sharkskin Book
Sing Sing Nights
The Six From Nowhere (RH)
The Skull of the Waltzing Clown
The Spectacles of Mr. Cagliostro
Stand By—London Calling!
The Steeltown Strangler
The Stolen Gravestone (RH)
Strange Journey (RH)
The Strange Will
The Straw Hat Murders (RH)
The Street of 1000 Eyes (RH)
Thieves' Nights
Three Novellos (RH)
The Tiger Snake
The Trap (RH)
Vagabond Nights (Defrauded Yeggman)
Vagabond Nights 2 (10 Hours)
The Vanishing Gold Truck
The Voice of the Seven Sparrows
The Washington Square Enigma
When Thief Meets Thief
The White Circle (RH)
The Wonderful Scheme of Mr. Christopher Thorne
X. Jones—of Scotland Yard
Y. Cheung, Business Detective

Keeler Related Works

A To Izzard: A Harry Stephen Keeler Companion by Fender Tucker — Articles and stories about Harry, by Harry, and in his style. Included is a compleat bibliography.

Wild About Harry: Reviews of Keeler Novels — Edited by Richard Polt & Fender Tucker — 22 reviews of works by Harry Stephen Keeler from *Keeler News.* A perfect introduction to the author.

The Keeler Keyhole Collection: Annotated newsletter rants from Harry Stephen Keeler, edited by Francis M. Nevins. Over 400 pages of incredibly personal Keeleriana.

Fakealoo — Pastiches of the style of Harry Stephen Keeler by selected demented members of the HSK Society. Updated every year with the new winner.

RAMBLE HOUSE's OTHER LOONS

A Shot Rang Out — Three decades of reviews from Jon Breen
The Time Armada — Fox B. Holden's 1953 SF gem.
Sideslip — 1968 SF masterpiece by Ted White and Dave Van Arnam
The Triune Man — Mindscrambling science fiction from Richard A. Lupoff
Detective Duff Unravels It — Episodic mysteries by Harvey O'Higgins
Mysterious Martin, the Master of Murder — Two versions of a strange 1912 novel by Tod Robbins about a man who writes books that can kill.
The Master of Mysteries — 1912 novel of supernatural sleuthing by Gelett Burgess
Dago Red — 22 tales of dark suspense by Bill Pronzini
The Night Remembers — A 1991 Jack Walsh mystery from Ed Gorman
Rough Cut & New, Improved Murder — Ed Gorman's first two novels
Hollywood Dreams — A novel of the Depression by Richard O'Brien
Six Gelett Burgess Novels — *The Master of Mysteries, The White Cat, Two O'Clock Courage, Ladies in Boxes, Find the Woman, The Heart Line*
The Organ Reader — A huge compilation of just about everything published in the 1971-1972 radical bay-area newspaper, *THE ORGAN*.
A Clear Path to Cross — Sharon Knowles short mystery stories by Ed Lynskey
Old Times' Sake — Short stories by James Reasoner from Mike Shayne Magazine
Freaks and Fantasies — Eerie tales by Tod Robbins, collaborator of Tod Browning on the film FREAKS.
Five Jim Harmon Sleaze Double Novels — *Vixen Hollow/Celluloid Scandal, The Man Who Made Maniacs/Silent Siren, Ape Rape/Wanton Witch, Sex Burns Like Fire/Twist Session*, and *Sudden Lust/Passion Strip*. More doubles to come!
Marblehead: A Novel of H.P. Lovecraft — A long-lost masterpiece from Richard A. Lupoff. Published for the first time!
The Compleat Ova Hamlet — Parodies of SF authors by Richard A. Lupoff - New edition!
The Secret Adventures of Sherlock Holmes — Three Sherlockian pastiches by the Brooklyn author/publisher, Gary Lovisi.
The Universal Holmes — Richard A. Lupoff's 2007 collection of five Holmesian pastiches and a recipe for giant rat stew.
Four Joel Townsley Rogers Novels — By the author of *The Red Right Hand: Once In a Red Moon, Lady With the Dice, The Stopped Clock, Never Leave My Bed*
Two Joel Townsley Rogers Story Collections — Night of Horror and Killing Time
Twenty Norman Berrow Novels — *The Bishop's Sword, Ghost House, Don't Go Out After Dark, Claws of the Cougar, The Smokers of Hashish, The Secret Dancer, Don't Jump Mr. Boland!, The Footprints of Satan, Fingers for Ransom, The Three Tiers of Fantasy, The Spaniard's Thumb, The Eleventh Plague, Words Have Wings, One Thrilling Night, The Lady's in Danger, It Howls at Night, The Terror in the Fog, Oil Under the Window, Murder in the Melody, The Singing Room*
The N. R. De Mexico Novels — Robert Bragg presents *Marijuana Girl, Madman on a Drum, Private Chauffeur* in one volume.
Four Chelsea Quinn Yarbro Novels featuring Charlie Moon — *Ogilvie, Tallant and Moon, Music When the Sweet Voice Dies, Poisonous Fruit* and *Dead Mice*
Four Walter S. Masterman Mysteries — *The Green Toad, The Flying Beast, The Yellow Mistletoe* and *The Wrong Verdict*, fantastic impossible plots. More to come.
Two Hake Talbot Novels — *Rim of the Pit, The Hangman's Handyman.* Classic locked room mysteries.
Two Alexander Laing Novels — *The Motives of Nicholas Holtz* and *Dr. Scarlett*, stories of medical mayhem and intrigue from the 30s.
Four David Hume Novels — *Corpses Never Argue, Cemetery First Stop, Make Way for the Mourners, Eternity Here I Come*, and more to come.
Three Wade Wright Novels — *Echo of Fear, Death At Nostalgia Street* and *It Leads to Murder*, with more to come!
Four Rupert Penny Novels — *Policeman's Holiday, Policeman's Evidence, Lucky Policeman* and *Sealed Room Murder*, classic impossible mysteries.
Five Jack Mann Novels — Strange murder in the English countryside. *Gees' First Case, Nightmare Farm, Grey Shapes, The Ninth Life, The Glass Too Many.*
Seven Max Afford Novels — *Owl of Darkness, Death's Mannikins, Blood on His Hands, The Dead Are Blind, The Sheep and the Wolves, Sinners in Paradise* and *Two Locked Room Mysteries and a Ripping Yarn* by one of Australia's finest novelists.

Five Joseph Shallit Novels — *The Case of the Billion Dollar Body, Lady Don't Die on My Doorstep, Kiss the Killer, Yell Bloody Murder, Take Your Last Look.* One of America's best 50's authors.
Two Crimson Clown Novels — By Johnston McCulley, author of the Zorro novels, *The Crimson Clown* and *The Crimson Clown Again.*
The Best of 10-Story Book — edited by Chris Mikul, over 35 stories from the literary magazine Harry Stephen Keeler edited.
A Young Man's Heart — A forgotten early classic by Cornell Woolrich
The Anthony Boucher Chronicles — edited by Francis M. Nevins
Book reviews by Anthony Boucher written for the *San Francisco Chronicle,* 1942 - 1947. Essential and fascinating reading.
Muddled Mind: Complete Works of Ed Wood, Jr. — David Hayes and Hayden Davis deconstruct the life and works of a mad genius.
Gadsby — A lipogram (a novel without the letter E). Ernest Vincent Wright's last work, published in 1939 right before his death.
My First Time: The One Experience You Never Forget — Michael Birchwood — 64 true first-person narratives of how they lost it.
Automaton — Brilliant treatise on robotics: 1928-style! By H. Stafford Hatfield
The Incredible Adventures of Rowland Hern — Rousing 1928 impossible crimes by Nicholas Olde.
Slammer Days — Two full-length prison memoirs: *Men into Beasts* (1952) by George Sylvester Viereck and *Home Away From Home* (1962) by Jack Woodford
The Golden Dagger — 1951 Scotland Yard yarn by E. R. Punshon
Beat Books #1 — Two beatnik classics, *A Sea of Thighs* by Ray Kainen and *Village Hipster* by J.X. Williams
A Smell of Smoke — 1951 English countryside thriller by Miles Burton
Ruled By Radio — 1925 futuristic novel by Robert L. Hadfield & Frank E. Farncombe
Murder in Silk — A 1937 Yellow Peril novel of the silk trade by Ralph Trevor
The Case of the Withered Hand — 1936 potboiler by John G. Brandon
Finger-prints Never Lie — A 1939 classic detective novel by John G. Brandon
Inclination to Murder — 1966 thriller by New Zealand's Harriet Hunter
Invaders from the Dark — Classic werewolf tale from Greye La Spina
Fatal Accident — Murder by automobile, a 1936 mystery by Cecil M. Wills
The Devil Drives — A prison and lost treasure novel by Virgil Markham
Dr. Odin — Douglas Newton's 1933 potboiler comes back to life.
The Chinese Jar Mystery — Murder in the manor by John Stephen Strange, 1934
The Julius Caesar Murder Case — A classic 1935 re-telling of the assassination by Wallace Irwin that's much more fun than the Shakespeare version
West Texas War and Other Western Stories — by Gary Lovisi
The Contested Earth and Other SF Stories — A never-before published space opera and seven short stories by Jim Harmon.
Tales of the Macabre and Ordinary — Modern twisted horror by Chris Mikul, author of the *Bizarrism* series.
The Gold Star Line — Seaboard adventure from L.T. Reade and Robert Eustace.
The Werewolf vs the Vampire Woman — Hard to believe ultraviolence by either Arthur M. Scarm or Arthur M. Scram.
Black Hogan Strikes Again — Australia's Peter Renwick pens a tale of the outback.
Don Diablo: Book of a Lost Film — Two-volume treatment of a western by Paul Landres, with diagrams. Intro by Francis M. Nevins.
The Charlie Chaplin Murder Mystery — Movie hijinks by Wes D. Gehring
The Koky Comics — A collection of all of the 1978-1981 Sunday and daily comic strips by Richard O'Brien and Mort Gerberg, in two volumes.
Suzy — Another collection of comic strips from Richard O'Brien and Bob Vojtko
Dime Novels: Ramble House's 10-Cent Books — *Knife in the Dark* by Robert Leslie Bellem, *Hot Lead* and *Song of Death* by Ed Earl Repp, *A Hashish House in New York* by H.H. Kane, and five more.
Blood in a Snap — The *Finnegan's Wake* of the 21st century, by Jim Weiler and Al Gorithm
Stakeout on Millennium Drive — Award-winning Indianapolis Noir — Ian Woollen.
Dope Tales #1 — Two dope-riddled classics; *Dope Runners* by Gerald Grantham and *Death Takes the Joystick* by Phillip Condé.
Dope Tales #2 — Two more narco-classics; *The Invisible Hand* by Rex Dark and *The Smokers of Hashish* by Norman Berrow.
Dope Tales #3 — Two enchanting novels of opium by the master, Sax Rohmer. *Dope* and *The Yellow Claw.*
Tenebrae — Ernest G. Henham's 1898 horror tale brought back.

The Singular Problem of the Stygian House-Boat — Two classic tales by John Kendrick Bangs about the denizens of Hades.
Tiresias — Psychotic modern horror novel by Jonathan M. Sweet.
The One After Snelling — Kickass modern noir from Richard O'Brien.
The Sign of the Scorpion — 1935 Edmund Snell tale of oriental evil.
The House of the Vampire — 1907 poetic thriller by George S. Viereck.
An Angel in the Street — Modern hardboiled noir by Peter Genovese.
The Devil's Mistress — Scottish gothic tale by J. W. Brodie-Innes.
The Lord of Terror — 1925 mystery with master-criminal, Fantômas.
The Lady of the Terraces — 1925 adventure by E. Charles Vivian.
My Deadly Angel — 1955 Cold War drama by John Chelton
Prose Bowl — Futuristic satire — Bill Pronzini & Barry N. Malzberg .
Satan's Den Exposed — True crime in Truth or Consequences New Mexico — Award-winning journalism by the *Desert Journal*.
The Amorous Intrigues & Adventures of Aaron Burr — by Anonymous — Hot historical action.
I Stole $16,000,000 — A true story by cracksman Herbert E. Wilson.
The Black Dark Murders — Vintage 50s college murder yarn by Milt Ozaki, writing as Robert O. Saber.
Sex Slave — Potboiler of lust in the days of Cleopatra — Dion Leclerq.
You'll Die Laughing — Bruce Elliott's 1945 novel of murder at a practical joker's English countryside manor.
The Private Journal & Diary of John H. Surratt — The memoirs of the man who conspired to assassinate President Lincoln.
Dead Man Talks Too Much — Hollywood boozer by Weed Dickenson
Red Light — History of legal prostitution in Shreveport Louisiana by Eric Brock. Includes wonderful photos of the houses and the ladies.
A Snark Selection — Lewis Carroll's *The Hunting of the Snark* with two Snarkian chapters by Harry Stephen Keeler — Illustrated by Gavin L. O'Keefe.
Ripped from the Headlines! — The Jack the Ripper story as told in the newspaper articles in the *New York* and *London Times.*
Geronimo — S. M. Barrett's 1905 autobiography of a noble American.
The White Peril in the Far East — Sidney Lewis Gulick's 1905 indictment of the West and assurance that Japan would never attack the U.S.
The Compleat Calhoon — All of Fender Tucker's works: Includes *The Totah Trilogy, Weed, Women and Song* and *Tales from the Tower,* plus a CD of all of his songs.

RAMBLE HOUSE
Fender Tucker, Prop.
www.ramblehouse.com fender@ramblehouse.com
318-455-6847 10329 Sheephead Drive, Vancleave MS 39565

DID3031707
L - #0324 - 250221 - C0 - 229/152/12 - PB - DID3031707